DAD
INTERRUPTED

A Novel

Van Whitfield

Harlem Moon

Broadway Books

New York

Published by Harlem Moon, an imprint of Broadway Books, a division of Random House, Inc.

PRINTED IN THE UNITED STATES OF AMERICA

HARLEM MOON, BROADWAY BOOKS, and the Harlem Moon logo, depicting a moon and a woman, are trademarks of Random House, Inc. The figure in the Harlem Moon logo is inspired by a graphic design by Aaron Douglas (1899–1979).

Visit our website at www.harlemmoon.com

First edition published June 2004.

Book design by Chris Welch

Library of Congress Cataloging-in-Publication Data
Whitfield, Van.
    Dad interrupted : a novel / Van Whitfield.—1st ed.
      p. cm.
      1. Triangles (Interpersonal relations)—Fiction. 2. African American men—Fiction. 3. Washington (D.C.)—Fiction. 4. Pregnant women—Fiction. 5. Fatherhood—Fiction. I. Title.
PS3573.H4914D33 2004
813'.54—dc22   2003067598

ISBN 0-385-50818-2

10 9 8 7 6 5 4 3 2 1

"Fatherhood is a privilege."

—SHAWN WAYNE

The Seven Different Types of Dads

1 Preach-a-Dad . . . a.k.a. "Do as I Say, Not as I Do" Dad

2 Daddy Deep Pockets . . . a.k.a. "See Ya Next Weekend!" Dad

3 Daddy Do Little . . . a.k.a. "Invis-a-Dad" a.k.a. "Deadbeat Dad"

4 Work-a-Dad . . . a.k.a. "Let Your Daddy Get Some Rest" Dad

5 Coach-a-Dad . . . a.k.a. "I Coulda Been a Contender" Dad

6 Abuse-a-Dad . . . a.k.a. "My Daddy Did It to Me" Dad

7 Daddy Dearest . . . a.k.a. "Dear Ole Dad"

1

The call should have started with "Houston, we have a problem." That would have made sense. Anytime a woman calls a guy and leaves a message that ends with the most feared, dreaded, and deflating words known to man—"I'm pregnant"— her call might as well have started with "Houston, we have a problem . . . I'm pregnant."

See it for what it is. If she were your wife or even your lady, and she knew you were up to the joy, stress, and responsibilities of fatherhood, there would have been no call. She would have taken you to the Tropicana like Lucy did Ricky, dropped some knitted booties on the table, and had the band play "Babaloo" before telling you you're about to be a dad.

Chicks you're not with, not going to be with, or *don't* want to be with make the call. They're less interested in you being a dad.

Guys are the bulls-eyes to their arrows, and those chicks come complete with a laundry list of headaches, hassles, and demands that will make you wish you couldn't even spell s-e-x.

You're about to be welcomed to a world where you'll be perceived as little more than one of "the usual suspects." And you will soon become all too familiar with the list that you've always heard about, but never thought would affect you:

"The Official Baby's Mamma Checklist"

1. A summons and the court date that comes with it.
2. Demands for Pampers and Enfamil for a baby that you're prepared to deny because "you only hit it once," *and* . . . she said she was on the pill, *and* . . . you pulled out, *and* . . . she said she never wanted kids in the first place, *and* . . . you know that the only women who get pregnant from doing it "once" are the women they warned you about in your seventh-grade health class.
3. A lawyer who swears he'll "get this thing straight."
4. A judge who swears *she'll* "get this thing straight."
5. A lecture from your lawyer on parental responsibility and on how you have to respect "the plaintiff."
6. An even worse lecture from your mother, who just got a visit from "the plaintiff" and the baby who has the same vacant stare and drool pattern that you had as a kid.
7. A piercing blood test.
8. The dreaded announcement confirming that the test proves conclusively that you are a new, not-so-proud father.
9. An examination of your pitiful financial affairs.

10. Numerous conversations identifying you as "My baby's daddy."
11. Uncomfortable explanations to any potential Ms. Rights about your baby's mamma.
12. Child support checks for a child you foolishly continue to deny.
13. Christmas, birthday, and graduation gifts for a child you will *always* deny.
14. Amazement, shock, and disappointment that the child you always denied failed to invite you to her wedding.
15. Complete dismay that the guy whom the plaintiff / baby's mamma actually married is walking your daughter—the one you always denied—down the aisle.

The Official Baby's Mamma Checklist is your worst nightmare. There's no way you could have expected all of this from a quick "hit it and quit it," but this is exactly how it worked out for your friends, your brothers, and their friends.

But, Troi wouldn't do that to me.

Or would she?

The knot in my stomach and the lump in my throat say that I'm not so sure. I've played Troi's message over and over and this is all I can come up with: My lady, Dawn, will freak because she's thinking engagement and I'm pretty sure my *baby* with Troi doesn't fit into my *engagement* with Dawn. Kelly, the best co-worker and female friend a guy could have, will say exactly what any woman would say: "You should have kept it in your pants." And my main man Donnie, who's kicked his crack habit, may kick *me* for putting myself in this position.

Troi Stevenson is pregnant *and* she's coming to D.C. Fate has dealt me a nasty blow. And this situation all but confirms what I've known for some time now.

I'm the unluckiest man in the world.

Houston, we have a problem.

2

Not much has changed for Donnie. He's "drug free," he's two months from clearing parole, and he's as happy as they come. All in all, his outlook on life is different. It's fresh and full of promise and optimism. His job at the rehab center he once called home has given him hope and a heartfelt purpose. But Donnie doesn't believe anything *really* changes. "Summer doesn't *change* to fall, it just gets tired of being summer," he once told me. "Your frail tail would get tired of being hot all the time too."

I'm sure he rationalizes not changing—or "keeping it real," as he puts it—so that he can hold on to some vestiges of his never-ending pursuit of a happening lifestyle. Donnie is committed to being as hip as he is "down" with the players, partiers, and peddlers who dominate D.C.'s notorious nightlife. And like any good middleman waiting to happen, he still knows how to get a deal and is closely tied to an enterprising network of street-corner suppliers and distributors.

His phone call all but confirms it. He claims to have a line on a brand-new, ultra-thin, Sony 42-inch flat screen plasma TV. And he says he'll help me hang it on my living room wall if I can come up with the cash before tomorrow morning.

"How much?" I asked, knowing we were only just starting to negotiate.

"My man Shawn Wayne will be watching the ball drop on a phat plasma with a universal remote!" he answered. "You'll be two steps ahead of every poot-butt fool in D.C."

"How much?" I repeated, unimpressed.

"It's not just HDTV ready, son," he insisted. "It's blingin' with high definition right now!" he exclaimed. "And check this, Shawn," he said, taking a deep breath. "This puppy is slimmer than Halle Berry on crack."

"She's not on crack," I told him.

"She was in *Jungle Fever!*" he shot back.

Donnie is stalling, which means one thing. His price is probably ten times what I'm willing to pay.

"Have you seen those bangin' commercials where the fish jumps out of the flat screen?" he asked.

"Actually a bird flies *into* the screen," I commented. "And the commercial didn't say anything about the price."

"That's because you can't put a price on top-shelf, state-of-the-art equipment like this," he insisted.

"So you're saying it's free?"

"My man wants five large," he quickly answered.

Five thousand dollars! I'm not about to part with five thousand pieces of my favorite green-colored paper for anything. And Donnie knows it.

"But my supplier is down with how we roll, so he's ready to deal," he remarked.

"How ready?"

"Two grand ready."

"You think I'm going to pay two bills to watch TV?!" I asked, alarmed.

"C'mon, Poppy," he answered. "It's going for twenty thou at Best Buy."

"I'm an accountant," I reminded him. "And I don't think you and Best Buy realize that twenty grand for a forty-two-incher comes out to four hundred seventy-six dollars an inch."

"What I realize is that you're the cheapest clown in the world," he said. "I'm trying to give you a deal on a plasma and you're talking about how much it costs an inch?" he added. "That's why Troi left you for bad and high-tailed it back to Chicago, son," he joked. "How much does a TV cost an inch?" he huffed.

"Why did you bring Troi up?" I asked, concerned.

"I can probably get it for a grand, maybe a grand and a dove if he delivers it," he said. "But I don't know if he's gonna go any lower."

"What made you bring up Troi?" I repeated.

"I'm not tripping off no Troi," he answered. "I just threw her name out there because classy chicks can spot a cheap fool like you a mile away. So you cool with a grand?" he asked.

"You think she thinks I'm cheap?" I asked, worried.

"Shawn," he answered. "I don't know, don't care, and ain't about to waste my time thinking about some fly girl who's a million miles away in Chicago."

"It's not a million miles," I told him.

"Is it another time zone?" he asked.

"Yeah."

"Do you have to put a one in front of the area code when you dial?"

"Yeah."

"Tell me what about that ain't a million miles?" he quickly answered. "And why are you still jonesing on Troi when Dawn has you locked down like one of my jailbird homies on a hunger strike?" he asked. "Dawn is here, Troi is somewhere in east-ja-blip and me and my associate have a TV to move."

"Troi is coming to D.C.," I blurted out.

"I could probably get him down to—"

His silence says it hit him like it hit me.

"What the hell are you talking about, Shawn?" he whispered, quickly.

"Troi is coming to D.C.," I whispered back.

"Oh, snap," he said, still whispering. "Does Dawn know?"

"Are you crazy?" I whispered, as if someone were in the room.

"Are *you* crazy?" he repeated. "You can't just sneak somebody as fine as Troi back into D.C. and think that Dawn won't find out."

"I'm not sneaking her back here," I whispered, even lower. "She's coming on her own."

"So where's she staying?" he asked. "And how long is she gonna be here?"

"What do you mean?"

"I mean, is she swinging at your crib or are y'all pulling a hotel move?" he asked. "'Cause if you are, I got a man who can probably hook up a suite, a couple of massages, and one of them robes."

"She's not coming for a visit. She's moving here," I whispered.

"Oh, you are crazy," he whispered back. "Dawn is gonna break your balls and have them served up like an appetizer on *Fear Factor.*"

"Not if she doesn't know," I reasoned.

"Wait a minute," he said. "You actually think that Troi is gonna just roll into D.C. and Dawn ain't gonna know?"

"Yes?" I answered, sounding completely unconvinced myself.

"Shawn," he whispered. "Take your head outta your behind. Dawn's gonna know because you don't have the heart to keep a secret from her."

"I guess that means I should tell her she's pregnant," I said.

"You should tell who that *who's* pregnant?" he quickly answered.

"I should tell Dawn that Troi is pregnant," I whispered.

"Oh shit!" he yelled, excited. "Troi is pregnant! Is it yours?"

"I don't know," I admitted.

"Did she tell *you* she was pregnant?" he asked.

"She left a message."

"And she said she's coming to D.C.?"

"Yeah."

"Your tired ass is about to have a baby, son!" he shouted. "Congratulations, fool." He laughed. "And welcome to World War III."

"What are you talking about, Donnie?" I asked, still wanting to whisper, but now talking aloud. "It's not going to be a problem. I'll tell Dawn and I'll work it out with Troi."

"*Fantasy Island* don't got nothing to do with D.C., so you can stop yapping about spilling the beans to Dawn and thinking that somebody ain't gonna take an ass-whipping," he quipped. "Look, son, don't you say a word until I get there. I mean it, Shawn . . . don't tell nobody nothing," he went on. "If Captain Kirk beams

Troi over there in the next minute and Dr. Spock beams Dawn in right behind her, act like you got lockjaw until I get there."

"Maybe you're right," I said, hearing my doorbell buzz.

"If that's either one of them, plead the Fifth until I'm on location! You know what a baby is?" he asked, not waiting for me to answer. "It's an interruption! It's not no bundle of joy or none of that *Look Who the F*ck Is Running Off at the Mouth* sh*t," he told me. "It's court dates, pinch tests, and child support. Don't fall for none of that crap, and tell whoever's blowing up your doorbell that since it's New Year's Eve, you made one of them restitutions not to talk until *next* year."

"Thanks, Donnie," I answered, laughing. "But you know its *resolutions,* not *restitutions,* right?"

"The last time I was sentenced was on New Year's Eve last year and the judge said I had to make restitution," he told me. "And after Troi hits you with child support, your size thirteens will be making restitution for the next eighteen years, so don't be trying to correct me, son."

"Okay, D," I replied, smiling. "But check this."

"Yeah."

"Are you bringing the TV with you?" I said, recalling why he called in the first place. "I'll buy it right now," I admitted. "But I won't go higher than forty bucks."

3

There's exactly one thing that could be worse than dealing with Donnie on this. And it's not Dawn.

Dawn will be fine.

She'll be pissed, she'll read me the riot act, and she probably won't want to see me for weeks. She'll take her toothbrush out of my bathroom, leave the clothes that I have at her place on the front lawn, she'll want her keys back, and will no doubt give me back mine. My number will be blocked from calling hers, she won't return the messages I leave her at work, and she'll have me barred from the set of her new TV show, which actually starts tonight.

The courtside tickets to the MCI center and the Wizards . . . they're done. The "comp" workouts at D.C.'s posh L.A. Sports Club—they're history. She'll probably cancel the DirecTV "All Sports All the Time" package she gave me for Christmas just days ago, and she may even break things off completely.

But she'll be fine.

Kelly, my coworker, won't be fine. In fact, she'll flip.

She couldn't stand the sight of Troi or the mere mention of her name. When Troi went back to Chicago, Kelly told me Troi and I were done. And when I flew to Chicago to see her, Kelly warned me that I'd get hurt and that Troi wasn't interested or even capable of sustaining a relationship. When I returned from Chicago with my heart in my hand, Kelly was there for me each and every day. The only times she didn't call were when she was already at my place. And when I went into a depression that rivaled Mike Tyson minus the medication, Kelly pulled me back from the brink.

But she'll push me over the brink or let the brink fall on me if she finds out what's going on with Troi.

And something tells me I'm about to find out just how hard a push Kelly is capable of, because she's walking through the front door right now.

"I'd wish you happy New Year, but my hands are full," she said, toting two huge bags of groceries.

"Well, you know where the kitchen is," I replied, closing the door behind her.

"That I do," she said, standing in front of me. "But somehow I confused you with one of those real gentlemen who would jump to help a lady with her bags."

"That's only when the lady's not going to stick me with the bill for some groceries I didn't want in the first place," I shot back.

"You're having a New Year's Eve party, Shawn," she said, shoving the bags toward me. "And you can't have a party without food," she said. "I even have couscous."

"You have what-what?" I asked.

"Couscous," she said, starting to unpack. "It's perfect for a New Year's meal."

"Whatever happened to lima beans and black-eyed peas?" I inquired, moving a shelf in the refrigerator.

"That's so ethnic," she quickly answered. "And do you really believe that overly salted peas and beans will bring you money or that they could possibly provide a healthy start for the New Year?" she asked.

"I have food."

"Doritos are not food."

"I have oatmeal too."

"And that's better?"

Maybe it isn't. But, it's not as bad as having to spill the beans about Troi.

"So, Kelly. What would you do if you had to tell Alan something that could blow your relationship?" I asked, as she opened the refrigerator.

"How can you live like this?" she replied, reaching for a carton of eggs. "The only thing you have in here is Kool-Aid, hot dogs, and some pudding pops."

"What if you knew he'd be pissed off and that he'd probably never speak to you again?" I said, handing her a bag of pre-mixed salad.

"I can't believe Dawn lets you live like this," she remarked. "I had to literally take over Alan's entire house," she bragged, placing a bag of French bread on a counter. "I hired a maid service, I bought him new linens, I had my nutritionist develop a menu for him—"

"Kelly," I interrupted. "I'm asking you a question."

"And I'm asking you one too," she quickly replied, placing an open box of baking soda alongside the packages of fresh bacon and sausage she'd brought in with her. "How do you expect Dawn to marry you when you're so helpless? Or are you using that to lure her in?"

"She's not a fish," I reminded her. "And that's not my problem." I handed her a bottle of champagne.

"That's an understatement," she said, opening my broom closet to find the apron she'd left there months ago. "Why don't you let my nutritionist work up something for you?"

"Look, Kelly," I said. "Donnie's on his way over here—"

"I thought he wasn't coming until eleven," she jumped in. "Or is it that he has to *leave* at eleven to check in with his parole officer?"

"What if I told you somebody was pregnant and that she's coming to D.C.?"

"It would depend," she said, walking toward the living room.

"On what?"

"On whether that pregnant somebody who is coming to D.C. is in fact from Chicago," she mused, finding a spot on my sofa.

"That would be her," I admitted.

Kelly went as silent as both Donnie and I had when we were hit with the news. But unlike me, she's clearly pissed off. She's lowering her head, shaking it no as if she'd just lost a loved one, and throwing her hands in the air in desperation.

"This can't be happening," she commented.

"That's what I said."

"You can't let her come to D.C.," she insisted. "And you can't let her be pregnant."

"How can I stop her from doing either one?" I asked, concerned.

"What if it's not yours?" she asked. "Did she actually say it was yours?"

"Well, not exactly."

"Well what exactly *did* she say?" she asked.

"She said that she's pregnant and that—"

"She's coming to D.C.," she interrupted. "That no-good heifer."

"Where did that come from?"

"I bet she didn't even talk to you," she guessed. "Knowing Troi, the tramp probably left a message."

"How did you know . . . and why are you calling her a tramp?"

"First of all, since protection clearly wasn't a priority for her, why didn't *you* think about it?" she asked, upset.

"We used it the first couple of times, but then, one night we just kind of went at it and—"

"This has set-up written all over it, Shawn," she interrupted. "She knows how nice you are, she's knows you're a decent guy, and I bet she knows about your bank account, your trust fund, *and* your stock holdings. Have you considered that Ms. Thing might not really be pregnant or that if she is, that *you're* not the father?"

"Donnie said that if she left me the message that means it's mine."

"And Donnie knows this because . . . ?"

I don't know why. But I don't know why Troi being pregnant is bothering Kelly even more than it's bothering me. I don't want kids. At least not yet, anyway. Dawn and I had discussed children many times and her take was that she absolutely had to be the mother of my "first child."

"Any child is a gift, but that first child is truly special," she said. "God kept both of us childless this long for a reason. And since we're committed and we don't have to worry about *mistakes* elsewhere, we can get our lives where we want before we start our family. I really look forward to seeing the look in your eyes when you see your first child," she went on. "And I hope we have twins! A boy and a girl would be perfect. That's always been my dream."

I guess Dawn didn't *dream* that my first child would come from another woman.

"Have you told Dawn yet?" Kelly asked, sounding worried.

"Of course not," I answered.

"You have to tell her, Shawn," she said. "And you have to tell her tonight."

"Why?"

"First, because she deserves to know and second, because after she kills you, she'll make sure that you don't admit paternity without a test or something."

"I don't think Troi is the type that would sleep around, Kelly," I said.

"She slept with you, didn't she?" she fired back.

That's true. But she liked me, just as I liked her. Before Troi came into town, I hadn't tapped any buns for ages and she said it was the same for her. Nice girls don't just sleep with anybody . . . that's what makes them nice. And though Troi had broken my heart, I'd be the first to admit that she was honest and up front.

And for some reason I have little doubt that her pregnancy is the real deal . . . and that although I'm not happy about it, I am the father.

"Look, Shawn," Kelly began. "We'll tell Dawn tonight, and then—"

"*We're* not doing anything," I interrupted. "Dawn will know well ahead of time. I just have to figure out how to tell her."

"I can already tell you that she'll be upset, but she loves you and since it happened before you guys actually hooked up, she'll forgive you," she told me. "But that's only *if* you tell her right now and *if* it turns out to be your child, and that's *if* she's really pregnant."

"That's exactly why I can't tell her," I explained. "Let's just pretend that Troi isn't pregnant or that I'm not the dad or that she becomes un-pregnant. Do I really want to risk everything I have with Dawn without really knowing exactly where everything stands?"

"Are you and Donnie smoking from the same pipe?" she answered. "If Miss Thing is actually pregnant, paternity won't be established until after the child is born. So with your reasoning, you won't have to tell Dawn until after the child is here."

"Right!" I said, enthusiastically.

"Get real, Shawn," she said, sounding like Dr. Phil. "You claim to love Dawn, so she deserves the truth on that alone."

"Well, if you believe what you said earlier, then the baby may not even be mine and she may not be pregnant at all, so what truth do I have to tell?" I asked. "At this point, all I can really tell her is that Troi called and that she left me a message, right?"

"Stop being such a man, Shawn," she begged. "You need to tell Dawn tonight. If you wait, and she ever finds out that you knew for nine months and that you hid it from her, she'll never forgive you. Tell her as soon as she gets here," she said. "And you can start the New Year off right."

Maybe Kelly's right. But what if she isn't? Dawn will forgive me . . . won't she? She has to, doesn't she? If any of this is true, whatever happened happened before Dawn. It happened before we met and before we fell head over heels with each other. It wasn't planned, I certainly didn't expect it, and knowing Troi, she absolutely didn't come to D.C. to make a baby. Dawn is as focused and as career driven as they come, but Troi could give her lessons in being a workaholic. Troi is a wonderful woman, but she's as self-absorbed and self-centered as the NFL's resident freak, Randy Moss. She's just not the mommy type.

Which makes Troi's announcement even harder to deal with.

"Just tell her the truth," Kelly insisted. "And tell her tonight, because you know the first thing she'll ask?"

"Is it mine?" I quickly replied.

"That . . . and how long have you known," she said.

"Tell her tonight," I said, trying to convince myself.

"That's the only option," she said, before standing and surveying my living room. "So where are you going to put the playpen?" she asked, laughing.

"That's not funny."

"Okay, Shawn," she replied. "I shouldn't joke about this . . . it is serious."

"Tell me about it."

"But I do have one question," she remarked. "Are you going to have the baby's playpen wrapped in that clear plastic stuff?"

"Nobody does that," I told her.

"And nobody wraps their furniture in plastic anymore, either," she remarked. "Except you . . . Daddy Dearest."

That statement alone struck fear in me and made me realize she was probably right about how Dawn would react. *Nobody wraps their furniture in plastic anymore*, I thought, flustered, as the doorbell rang. That's the same exact thing Dawn said when she saw it.

The Seven Different Types of Dads

Preach-a-Dad . . . a.k.a., "Do as I Say, Not as I Do" Dad

The original control freak, Preach-a-Dad is *never* wrong. And since he's the most important person he knows, he doesn't mind telling you. If he weren't awash in f-e-a-r, he'd have real father potential. He *fears* that his kids will do the same stupid stuff he did, or still does. It's not that Preach-a-Dad doesn't want the best for his kids, he does. He just *doesn't have a clue* how to live his own life—so what makes him think he can *control* the lives of his children? His daughter can't smoke cigarettes, but *he* smokes weed . . . and might even sell it. His son can't drink beer, but Preach-a-Dad will trample the family reunion smashed on gin and tonics. And you'd *better not* have a kid out of wedlock—like he did—because like every man with half a brain, Preach-a-Dad knows that the last thing the world needs is another loud-mouthed Preach-a-Dad . . . like him.

W aiting for Donnie is not exactly like waiting for Godot, especially since he has a TV to sell. If the Olympics were in D.C. and Donnie could sell any of the many items that he "comes across," he'd have the goods at his side and would outrace Carl Lewis *and* manage to scalp tickets to the race without missing a beat.

Which probably explains why it took him a little under ten minutes to make his way to my place.

"Poppy!" he exclaimed, reaching for a hug.

"He knows?" Kelly asked, surprised. "Is he taking bets on it already?"

"Nah, Kelly," Donnie answered smoothly. "I'm too busy gettin' odds on when your boy toy Alan is going to find out."

"Find out what?" I asked.

"That Kelly's in love with me!" he yelled, slapping me a high five.

"That's cute, Donnie," Kelly quickly shot back. "But Alan knows I'd never fall for an AC man."

"What's Donnie got to do with air conditioning?" I asked, wondering why he wasn't holding a TV.

"Not much," Kelly remarked, grabbing a bottle of water. "But he's an AC man and AC men can't do anything for me."

"What the hell are you talking about, Kelly?" Donnie asked.

"You're an AC man. As in an *after-crack* man," she said, smiling.

"Is that right?" Donnie fired back, unimpressed. "Well, at least I'm not no *in*-the-crack man like your sweet-bottomed boyfriend."

"Where did that come from?" I asked, surprised. "Why is it that every time you two are around each other for more than two minutes, you have to attack each other?"

"Actually, it only takes a minute," Kelly insisted.

"Make it thirty seconds," Donnie chimed in.

Donnie and Kelly might as well be married. Especially since they argue more than most married people. In fact, they argue so much that I once thought about hooking them up. But Donnie wasn't having it.

"Arguing doesn't mean that you like somebody," he told me.

"As much as you argue, you must like each other," I reasoned. "You're only at each other's throats because you actually care and you don't know how to process it. Look at Luke and Laura from *General Hospital,*" I went on. "They thought they hated each other, he even attacked her, and boom . . . one day they have the biggest wedding in TV history. They were attracted to each other the whole time."

"Now that's some soap opera, fantasy bullsh★t," Donnie quipped. "You want to talk about fools who argue, you can start and finish with George Jefferson and Florence. They argued like cellmates and they hated each other until the show got cancelled. And if I don't know nothing, I know that George wasn't attracted to no Florence, just like I ain't attracted to no Kelly. But I know her cute ass is attracted to me," he finished, smiling.

Maybe he's right. But it doesn't matter. Dawn loves me and even though I know *her* cute behind is attracted to me, I also know that attraction could disappear if she finds out that Troi is pregnant.

"You have to tell her," Kelly insisted, falling into a chair.

"He has to tell who what?" Donnie asked, looking toward me. "And why in the hell is your furniture still in Saran Wrap?" he went on. "Do you hear how this sh★t squeaks when you sit on it?"

"I think Kelly's talking about the Troi deal," I told him.

"How does she know?" he quickly asked. "You wasn't supposed to say nothing to nobody 'till I got on point."

"The fact is that we have a problem here," Kelly jumped in. "If I'm not mistaken, Dawn has big expectations for tonight."

"Do you mean because it's New Year's Eve and all?" I asked.

"Stop buggin', Shawn," Donnie demanded. "Dawn is expecting that after tonight, she's gonna be one step closer to her M.R.S. degree."

"What makes you think that?" I inquired.

"She said it on the commercial for her show, which debuts in about an hour," Kelly told me. "'D.C. is ringing in a New Year with the Dawn of a New Day,'" she sang, smiling. "Tell me that's not the cutest jingle around?"

"So what's that got to do with her getting her M.R.S.?" I asked.

"The topic of the show is 'Gettin' Played for the New Year'," Donnie shared. "And you're about to get played big time."

"Actually, the topic is 'Getting Hitched for the New Year,' and a little bird told me that Dawn thinks this is the night she'll be able to announce that she's getting her hardware," Kelly admitted.

"What the f*ck kind of bird was that?" Donnie said, upset.

"Are you saying that Dawn thinks I'm going to propose?" I quickly asked.

"This is her first show and she promised her audience a special surprise about her personal life," Kelly said.

"She's gonna get a special surprise, alright," Donnie added, laughing.

"No, she won't," I jumped in. "Because I'm not telling her."

"My man!" Donnie exclaimed.

"Oh, you're telling her," Kelly told me.

"Why the hell should he?" Donnie asked. "He doesn't even know if she's really pregnant or if it's even his."

"He *knows* that Ms. Thing says that she's pregnant and that she's coming to D.C., so he has to tell Dawn something," Kelly said, standing.

"Now that's some of that Oprah-in-the-afternoon, Lifetime-TV-watching, your-man-don't-know-no-better, female-type sh*t," Donnie pointed out. "Ain't no man got nothing to gain by saying to his honey that some other honey is pregnant and that the other honey is rolling into town to drop her load."

"Drop her load?" Kelly asked, alarmed. "What kind of heathen are you?"

"The same type that Poppy here is," Donnie joked. "We're the type of heathens that know when to keep our fricking yaps shut."

Donnie's right . . . almost. I'm not exactly a heathen, but I do know there's no way I can tell Dawn about Troi. And the only thing that has me even slightly concerned is a commitment we made when we first hooked up. Dawn said the worst relationship she ever had was with a guy she really cared for who had "honesty issues." She said he was deceptively deceptive and that he not only lied, but that he hid as much as he lied.

He never lied about having a degree . . . he just hid the fact that he didn't.

He didn't lie about the Benz he was driving . . . he merely hid that it was his brother's car and his brother had been called away to the military.

And he didn't lie about his wife and two kids . . . he also hid that, but Dawn never asked, so she couldn't pin him down on it.

She said that the lies didn't hurt nearly as much as his ability and tendency to keep secrets. "Lies are lies and though they're never acceptable, sometimes people lie and think they're protecting you," Dawn shared. "But when a man purposefully keeps secrets or omits the truth he's openly manipulating you and he's denying you the final say in your own destiny. It's like he's telling you that you're not intelligent enough or strong enough to process the truth."

I don't know if she could have dealt with his wife and kids, but she felt that choice should have been hers, and not his.

After that conversation, I promised that I'd *never* lie and we agreed there was no room for secrets in our relationship. And so far, I've held up my end of the deal. I don't know if I ever promised that I'd tell her about something that may not even exist. And I don't know what Troi being pregnant has to do with Dawn's destiny. Can any woman handle the truth, when the truth says that her man is about to become a father and that she might be a stepmom?

These aren't the types of thoughts anyone's supposed to deal with on New Year's Eve.

We're supposed to be celebrating the hope and promise that comes when the apple drops in New York . . . not when Troi "drops her load," as Donnie puts it. On New Year's Eve, we're supposed to make resolutions that we'll break within a week and promises to lose weight and to eat better that we'll blow off before the night is over with that couscous stuff that Kelly brought. We should be toasting at midnight, dancing like we're nuts, and watching Dawn's new show on my new TV that Donnie somehow forgot. Today's bad news will become last year's trivialities in an instant and Dawn and I will reconfirm our commitment to building and holding on to the best relationship either of us has ever had.

That's what New Year's is all about.

And if I have a say in it, that's what it will be about for Dawn and me, tonight.

5

Kelly invited Alan over to celebrate the New Year. Donnie even convinced his latest date *du jour*, Melba, to drop by to "drink in the New Year."

And though my doorbell is ringing, I don't want to answer it because my mind is light years away from anybody's happy new year.

"Could one of you get the door?" I asked, walking toward the kitchen.

"Let Miss Priss get it!" Donnie yelled.

"I'm not about to get it because it might be Alan and I wouldn't dare want him to think that I'm so excited about seeing him that I had to jump to answer the door," Kelly quickly said.

"And I'm not getting it because I don't want him thinkin' that I want to see his sorry ass, either," Donnie shot back, ignoring the doorbell.

"Get the door, Shawn!" they yelled together.

"It's open!" I yelled back.

"Hi guys," Alan said, walking in and no doubt sporting his usual "I'm on top of the world and you're not," four-foot-wide smile. "Happy, happy."

"Happy, happy my assy assy," Donnie huffed underneath his breath as he walked to join me in the kitchen. "They was made for each other," he whispered. "He's light in the pants and she's light in the head." Then Donnie laughed. "Who said there wasn't some fool for every other fool?"

Alan and Kelly are indeed perfect matches. She's a hip and happening diva of the 90s who blossomed into a well-heeled, well-shopped, well-informed woman of the new millennium. Alan is a smooth and lean M.D. with the obsessive grooming habits of a male model and a wardrobe dominated by slate grays and steel blues, like the outfit he's wearing now. His practice blew up almost overnight and he gives Kelly an incredible amount of credit for focusing him and targeting him toward success.

They met on a ski trip and have been inseparable since. Kelly's the type that isn't guy crazy . . . unless she has a guy. And Alan definitely doesn't appear to be the type who could be p-whipped, but Kelly's innocent yet sexy looks coupled with her sassy style and sophisticated self-assured air could whip any guy.

"So, Shawn!" Alan yelled from the dining room. "This must be the five-hundred-dollar tablecloth that Dawn picked up from Saks Fifth Avenue," he remarked. "She must be expecting an exciting evening."

"You ain't kiddin'!" Donnie laughed before frowning at Kelly's balanced meal selection in the refrigerator. "What's this sh★t?" he asked, passing his nose over the plate of couscous.

"Let me ask you something, Alan," Kelly said, handing him a glass of wine. "Let's just pretend, and I assure you in our case this is a huge pretend, that you got another woman pregnant, but it happened before we met. You'd tell me because you'd know that I'd understand and that I wouldn't let it interfere with our wonderful relationship, and that I'd be totally supportive of any decision you had to make and that I'd be the perfect stepmom . . . right?" she whipped out.

Alan quickly downed his drink and stared at her intently.

"Now, that's some good wine!" he exclaimed.

"Alan . . . " Kelly said.

"Of course," he answered, smiling.

"Of course what, fool?" Donnie asked.

"Donald," he quickly replied. "Happy, happy," he said, raising his now empty glass.

"It's Donnie, clown," he answered, moving to fill Alan's glass. "And what are you sayin', Doc?" he inquired. "Would you tell her or what?"

"I'd what!" Alan said, laughing.

Alan is smarter than I thought. There's no way he's looking for a fight on New Year's Eve, so he's not about to answer Kelly. And the ringing doorbell hit right on time because he needs to save face . . . for at least a moment, anyway.

"It's open!" Alan said, loudly.

It has to be one of two people. Donnie's guy with the flat screen TV that I'm hoping for, or Donnie's girl Melba, whom I would never hope for.

"Melba!" Donnie yelled, scrambling to locate a wine glass.

"Happy New Year, Boo!" she exclaimed, reaching to hug him before smacking him with a major motion-picture-style kiss.

"What are you guys doing?" I asked, looking down at my watch to time them.

"Quit hatin', fool," Donnie managed to squeeze out.

"We're almost there," Melba whispered, waving me off. "Damn, that man can kiss!" she said, coming up for air.

"You're actually supposed to wait until New Year's," I reminded them.

"That's right," Kelly said, offering Melba a glass of wine.

"I think I will," Melba said, quickly breaking away and then grabbing the glass Donnie was holding. "Yes, indeed," she said, expertly downing both. "This is some straight-up New Year's Eve cheer," she insisted.

Melba and Donnie met—where else?—at the rehab center where he works and where she calls home. Melba is a case study in medium. Her medium build is accentuated by her medium complexion and accompanying looks, which perfectly match her seemingly medium range of intelligence. Unlike Donnie, who can lose it in a minute, her temperament stays somewhere in the medium range. From a personality standpoint I don't think she'd be described as mean or nice, she just has a "medium" type of personality.

In Donnie, Melba sees success, which probably says more about her than anything else. As a recovering crack addict, not many see Donnie as a role model. Especially since he's probably breaking every rule in the book by dating a client. But Donnie's very existence is tied to breaking rules. And to Melba and many others at their rehab center, Donnie's a revelation. He's beat a problem they have yet to successfully confront. He's managed to turn his demon, crack addiction, into a story of triumph that now earns him a living at the rehab. And he's so thoroughly con-

nected that he can "hook them up" with just about anything . . .
except drugs.

"One hundred twenty-nine days," Melba said, displaying a tiny
leather key chain.

"Three hundred sixty-four and counting," Donnie chimed in.

"Impressive, Donnie," Kelly remarked. "So how are you and
your parole officer celebrating?"

"If I didn't know better I'd think that you're trying to get at my
man on the creep-creep, Kelly," Melba said, feigning a smile.

"I'm not exactly sure what the *creep-creep* is," Alan replied, sitting up. "Is that a good thing?"

"If it means your lady's tryin' to holla in this direction, ain't
nothing good about that," Donnie laughed.

"Speaking of which, I have a question for you, Melba," Kelly
said, suddenly turning toward her. "Let's say that your man . . .
and in Donnie's case that's a completely relative term . . . let's pretend that Donnie found that he was about to be a father and that
the mother was a woman that he dealt with before you. You'd understand, wouldn't you?"

"Yeah," Melba answered, downing more wine.

"You would?" Donnie asked, surprised.

"Yeah," Melba quickly replied. "I'd understand that she'd have to
take an ass-whipping," she added. "Trying to stick my man with
some baby, tying up his benefits and all that," she went on. "I know
you didn't bring me over here in front of your high-society friends
to tell me some chick is pregnant."

"Congratulations, Donnie," Alan jumped in, raising his glass,
"I guess this calls for a toast."

"You can cancel that, Doc," Donnie insisted. "Shawn's the one
who's about to be a daddy."

Those words hit hard. I'd never had it put to me like that. I'm about to be a daddy? Me? I'm not ready to be a daddy. Or maybe I am. Maybe I'm just not ready to deal with fatherhood because it would mean I have to tell Dawn. Maybe I'm not prepared because I know I'd lose Dawn. And it could be that I simply don't want to see a pregnant Troi. As far as bodies go, Troi's was far and away the best I'd ever experienced. And the fact that she's willing to ruin it in the name of motherhood would spook any guy.

But Dawn and how she'll deal with this is all that really counts. Thankfully, she's taping her show and won't be here until nearly midnight, so I have time to work on a snappy way to tell her.

"Keep it in your trousers!" Donnie yelled, responding to a loud knock at the door.

"We don't have a lot of time so let's get everybody on the same page!" a tiny man exclaimed, bolting through the door.

"Wait a minute," I said, surprised.

"I don't have a minute and neither do you," he answered, poking around my living room with a light meter.

"Who's this clown?" Donnie asked, standing in front of the meter.

"You're in my way, Darkman," the tiny man replied, pushing Donnie aside. "And the name is Legs Brunson."

"And does Mr. Brunson always make it a point to break into someone's home and inspect it with one of those things?" Kelly asked, standing behind Alan.

"It's Legs and you must be Kelly," he answered. "And let me guess? You're Shawn," he said, turning toward me.

"What the hell is going on here?" Donnie quickly asked, jumping in front of him.

"If you get outta my way, a TV show is going on here," Legs answered.

"Ooh . . . where's the camera?" Melba asked, walking toward a hallway mirror. "How's my hair?"

"I think you're in the wrong place," I told him.

"I think not," Legs answered, smiling. "How many soon not to be bachelors in Maryland are dating a woman whose name is Dawn and who has a live show that debuts tonight?"

"One?" I replied, concerned.

"And how many soon to be former bachelors actually have their bachelor pad furniture wrapped in the same plastic they were using during the civil rights era?" he asked, walking back toward the front door.

"You're in the right place!" everyone yelled together.

"Let's load in, Bugs!" Legs yelled to a waiting crew outside.

And in an instant, there was an avalanche of TV equipment. Cameras, monitors, spotlights, microphones, a director's chair, a chair with Dawn's name, and one of those black and white digital "clappers" that marks the scenes quickly found a home in my living room.

Bugs, or at least a short, fit-looking woman I assumed was Bugs, led the charge. She pulled out what appeared to be a blueprint of my living room and yelled instructions to some other woman through a walkie-talkie even though they were only five feet apart.

"Looks like we have a problem over here, Legs," Bugs alerted him. "This plastic on the sofa squeaks like hell."

"I told you!" Donnie agreed.

"Are we going to be on TV too?" Kelly asked. "Because if we

are, I actually stopped by the mall before I went to the market and I have a few alternate wardrobe choices in the car."

"I'm not up for TV," Alan admitted. "I'm supposed to be doing a charity event, if you know what I mean, so being seen on live TV doesn't actually fit into my agenda. Unless of course it's a telethon. In some strange sort of way, I think that would work."

"Is this one of these shows where I can give a shout out?" Melba asked, still preening in the mirror. "I want to give a shout out to my peeps over to the rehab in Anacostia."

"You're not in that rehab," Donnie reminded her.

"I was last year," she answered, smiling.

"Excuse me, Mr. Legs," I said, following his every step. "But can somebody just slow down and tell me what's going on here?"

"It's just Legs, boss, since you're on my cast list," he shot back. "Do you know how to act?"

"My mom always told me to act like a gentleman, and most of the time I do. There are times when—"

"Save it, buck-o," he told me. "Because if you don't know how to act, I can't tell you what's going on."

"I just told you I know how to act," I remarked. "Like I said, my mother always said—"

"I'm sure your mom is a really nice old lady," he answered.

"Actually, she's a really dead old lady," Donnie shared.

"Same thing," Legs replied. "But if Plastic Man here can't act, I can't tell him what's happening."

"So tell *me*," Donnie requested.

As they whispered, I looked around, wondering why Mr. Legs had no interest in what my mom had to say and why Donnie suddenly yelled "Now that's some crazy, get the hell out of dodge and don't look back sh*t you talkin' about!"

Donnie then motioned to Kelly and whispered into her ear before she promptly squealed, "Oh, my God! And on national TV too!"

Melba lined up for her dose of the news and exclaimed, "But can a sista get her shout out on first?"

And an unimpressed Alan said, "This can't possibly be legal."

I knew that between getting out of dodge, being on national TV, rehab shout outs, and Alan's legal analysis, I was in for trouble.

I just didn't know how much.

Hi, sweetheart," Dawn said, quickly walking through the front door. "Is everything set up, Legs?" she asked.

"Damn, Dawn," Donnie remarked. "You look like you did one of those makeover shows."

"You have such a way with those amazingly awkward compliments, Donnie," Kelly told him.

"He means well, Kelly," Dawn said, smiling. "So . . . what do you think?"

What could she think? None of us have ever seen Dawn look so good. Even though she's on TV, she's never been overly concerned about her looks. Instead of makeup, she wears pressed powder for what she calls "coverage." Her hair is usually in braids and she gives new meaning to the fashion statement known as the "sack dress."

But tonight, she's pulling out all the stops.

By way of comparison, she looks almost as done up as Troi who, besides now being pregnant, was also once the woman of my dreams . . . until I hooked up with the current woman of my dreams, the woman standing in front of me, Dawn. They are so incredibly different, but it's their differences that make things so difficult.

Troi is sexy.

And Dawn is my best friend.

Troi is easily a C cup.

And Dawn and I have conversations that actually mean something.

When my uncle met Troi he smiled and whispered, "Man, I wish I was you."

And when he met Dawn he remarked, "She's got a lot of personality."

But if he saw her now, the last thing on his mind would be personality.

"You look . . . " Kelly said, before pausing.

"Can you hook Melba up like this?!" Donnie said, excited. "'Cause this is some super amazing you oughta be dating 50 Cent or at least be in a rap video on a yacht with a bikini and thong type sh*t!" he added.

"I never been on a boat before," Melba said, grinning. "Unless you count that log ride at Six Flags."

"What's going on, Dawn?" I asked, still shocked by her incredible new look.

"There's a man in a delivery truck waiting for you outside, Donnie," Dawn said, before turning toward me. "We gave up on the getting hitched thing because Legs convinced me to do something live, kind of on the lines of a reality show," she told me. "I didn't want to tell you because we wanted our audience to see everyone in a natural, unrehearsed state," she said, adjusting her new hair. "So if the crew is ready, we're going to go live and my audience will see us ring in the New Year."

"Don't you think we should have discussed this?" I asked, as Donnie walked toward the front door.

"Spontaneity sells," she answered, applying a coat of fresh lipstick. "And it's not bad for ratings either."

"Places, everyone!" Legs demanded.

Melba, Kelly, and Alan scrambled to find places on my sofa and love seat. Kelly donned a pair of "faux" glasses—the kind that are "supposed" to make you look educated—Alan adjusted his real glasses, and Melba had two glasses of wine at her side as each of them grabbed a magazine and pretended to be deep in thought while reading.

"Two minutes!" Bugs yelled.

"I think there's something we should talk about," I said, gently grabbing her hand.

"Save it for the air," she whispered. "And I can't believe you would buy my ring from one of Donnie's hood rats. I at least hope it's nice."

"What are you talking about?" I asked, concerned.

"I just told you, sweetie . . . save it for the air."

"I think you're going to be disappointed," I told her.

"I love you, Shawn, and there's nothing that could possibly disappointment me tonight," she said. "If you think I care about how big a ring it is, I don't. I only care that it's from the man I want to be with for the rest of my life. And that it's from the man who restored my faith in men."

"But it's not what you think."

"Do you understand how much I trust you and how much faith I have in you?" she asked, applying powder to her face.

"Yes?" I answered, worried.

"One minute!" Bugs yelled, approaching us with the scene clapper.

"Do you know why my life is better and why it's so thoroughly complete? You," she quickly stated. "Tonight and what we're about to do . . . you just don't know how much I love you and how excited I am. Ask Kelly. I told her last night that I'm the luckiest woman in the world."

Oddly, *I'm* not feeling that way. Dawn pulled a boxer's move and hit me with a three-punch-combination body blow. Love. Faith. Trust. And I'm about to hit her with what? *Did I mention that Troi is pregnant? And that she's coming to D.C.? Happy New Year!* I'm done.

"I know we're about to go on the air," she reminded me. "But let's make one New Year's resolution that we'll keep and that we won't do on air," she added, looking me in the eye. "Let's renew our promise to each other that we'll never lie and that we won't keep secrets."

"But—"

"Forty-five seconds!"

"It's non-negotiable, Shawn," she interrupted. "That's what makes our relationship special. You know how I feel about secrets. There's no room for secrets between people who really love and respect each other."

"Then I think I should tell you something right now," I urged.

"Thirty seconds!" Bugs yelled. "Could you two speed this up?"

"Stop worrying about the ring, Shawn," she whispered, kissing me on the cheek. "I know my man and I know that everything he buys has the word 'bargain' attached to it. Besides, Donnie gets good deals, you've always told me that," she said, studying a huge white cue card.

"Twenty seconds!"

"Listen to what I'm saying, Dawn," I said, reaching for her hand.

"This is my first show of the year and it's so important that we get this right so please, honey, save it for the air," she begged.

"Ten seconds!" Bugs yelled.

"Look, Dawn, I think you've got this wrong," I said.

"Shawn. We talked about this at Christmas. Remember last week?" she asked.

"Five, four, three . . . " Bugs counted down.

"Dawn," I whispered, leaning toward her. "Troi is—"

"We're on the air!"

G et the hell outta the way!"

"This sh★t is heavy! Where we puttin' it at?"

"Is it cable ready?" I asked, stepping aside.

"I know you ain't paying two grand if it ain't," Donnie answered.

"I never said I was paying two large," I reminded him.

"This is Dawn Truesdale and we are broadcasting live on BET," Dawn said, interrupting us. "It's New Year's Eve, and we are ringing it in as only BET can on a special reality-TV broadcast. . . . "

"If dude ain't payin' two grand we can roll out right now," Donnie's "accomplice" insisted.

"We're live on TV and I don't believe we've met," Dawn said, walking toward the accomplice.

"Hold this," he said, motioning toward me. "We really on TV?" he asked. "Like, right now?"

Donnie and I hurried to plug the TV in and hooked it to my

cable box before we slapped two easy-stick brackets on the wall and moved to hang it on an open space in front of the sofa. As Donnie promised, it was easy to hang and within seconds, the comforting glow of ready-to-use TV told me it was working.

"So tell us your name and what you're doing to bring in the New Year?" Dawn asked.

"I'm Lester, but my dawgs call me Swipe. What's up, D.C.?!" he yelled. "Wait, wait, wait. I want to thank the man upstairs, God, for making all of this possible," he added, pointing skyward. "My peeps, O-Dog, Pookie, Tay-Tay, my dawgs in cellblock one, D.C., Jail . . . leave that swine alone! Stink, you'd better get my money, fool! And to my home detention bracelet monitor, Mr. Davis, I just moved to this house that you seeing me in, and I'ma hit you up with the number as soon as we go to commercial," he said, now breaking into the 80s dance The Cabbage Patch.

"Okay, that was Lester," Dawn said, now walking toward the sofa. "And Donnie, a lifelong friend of my boyfriend, Shawn," she added, "Tell us about your New Year's plans."

"I love that TV," Legs whispered to Bugs. "Make sure we keep camera two locked on them and we'll get them on our screen *and* on that shiny new flat screen."

"You can't tell me this ain't worth two grand," Donnie said, now admiring himself on the flat screen.

"Any resolutions this year, Donnie?" Dawn asked.

"This sh★t is really live?" Donnie asked, quickly removing his hat.

"I see you brought out your friend, Melba's her name, right?"

"H-e-e-y!" Melba purred, walking toward Donnie.

"So how are you two love birds bringing in the New Year?"

"Well, first, let me say this for the record," Donnie answered. "Mr. Quarles—"

"That's his parole officer," Melba said, priming her teeth for the camera.

"Yo, man. This definitely ain't what it looks like. I know that I was supposed to, like, check in last week, but this thing kind of came up so I couldn't, like, make it like I was thinking I was going to," he lied. "So if it's a problem, I'm sure my man Swipe here can hook you up with a little something something."

"O-kay, Donnie, and you, Melba?" Dawn asked, frustrated.

"Let me give a shout out to Gracie, LaToshia, Netoshia, Coleeta, and Lakeesha," she started. "Those are my home girls over to the Anacostia Road Rehab Center 1. Don't forget your Goldenseal!" she yelled, referring to the ultimate drug test defeater. "And to Little Wayne, Little Macaroni, Big Pimpin' Butter, Out of Sight Mike, Go-Go Rudy, Tim-Tim, Sleeves. Don't get high on your own supply!" she advised.

"Okay . . . that was Melba," Dawn said, exasperated. "I guess this is what makes live television so exciting, you never know what you're going to get."

"Is this really happening?" Legs asked, surprised. "Are these people for real?"

"Next up. My good friend Kelly," Dawn said, sitting beside her, before she literally had to tear Kelly away from the magazine she was pretending to read.

"H-h-hi, Dawn," Kelly said nervously, looking straight toward the camera.

"So your boyfriend, Alan, is here and this is your first New Year's together. Any special plans?" Dawn inquired.

"Couscous," Kelly said, grabbing Dawn's mic and staring blankly into the camera.

"What was that?" Dawn asked, reaching for her mic.

"Couscous," Kelly repeated, again taking the mic away, and looking as if she were in a trance.

"Are you saying you made couscous as part of your New Year's Eve meal?" Dawn asked, trying to bail her out.

"Couscous," she repeated, looking like she'd just stumbled in from a Prozac picnic.

"Alan," Dawn said, quickly turning toward him. "Any special plans for the New Year?"

"I, ah . . . " he started. "Excuse me," he said, reaching for his ringing cell phone. "No, I am not on TV," he explained into the phone, before spotting himself on my new flat screen.

"Actually, you are," Dawn reminded him.

"Can you tell them to get my good side?" he whispered, starting to profile.

"He don't have no good side!" Donnie yelled, laughing as the camera quickly adjusted on him.

"Is it too late to give a shout out to Russ Parr at KYS, Donnie Simpson and Chris Paul over to PGC, John Monds, T.C., Doug and Lorna at HUR, the Wild Boyz and Rain, and my main man DJ Flex?" Melba asked, waving wildly as the camera swung her way. "I got the phrase that pays and I know y'all playing eighteen in a row!"

"Somebody better get me some money for this damn TV!" Swipe demanded, the camera now focused on him.

"Couscous," Kelly muttered, with her faux glasses now sitting crookedly across her brow.

"Well, audience, I promised you something different, though I can't say I anticipated something quite this different," Dawn said. "When I was writing my column at the *Washington Post,* I shared with many of you that I'd met the man of my dreams and since it's a new year for me and my new show, I wanted to share our New Year's with you. Shawn," she said, grabbing my hand and dragging me beside her.

"Hi?" I said, managing a slight wave.

"Honey, from the moment I walked in the door tonight, you've said you wanted to say something. Now I have an idea what it is, and I don't want to let our audience down, so it's your turn . . . spring it on me!" she said, holding out the ring finger of her left hand.

"I don't think we want to do this on the air," I whispered.

"Yes we do," Legs and Bugs whispered back.

"No we f*cking don't," Donnie whispered.

"Couscous?" Kelly asked, not concerned about whispering.

"Don't embarrass me here, Shawn Wayne," Dawn said, trying to hold a smile and not move her lips all at once. "Say what you have to say . . . and please make it something juicy so that we can save this program," she begged.

"I don't think I should do this, but remember when you said you wanted us to start the New Year without any secrets?" I asked.

"Of course," she answered, looking steadily at me.

"Well, I don't know if this is what you really meant, but if you did, there's something you should probably know," I admitted.

"Yes," she said, smiling and repositioning her hand for the camera.

"I probably shouldn't do this on TV and all," I considered.

"You absolutely should," she said, smiling. "I insist."

"Well," I sighed. "Here goes. Troi is pregnant," I blurted out.

"Who's Troi?" Legs, asked searching his cast list. "I don't see any Troi here."

"Troi is what?" Dawn said, forcing an "only on TV" smile.

"Troi is Shawn's ex and she just told him she was carrying a load," Donnie whispered to Legs.

"Are you sh★ttin' me?" Legs asked, smiling. "And this clown is telling her on national TV?"

"Troi is pregnant," I confessed, embarrassingly shaking my head. "And she's coming to D.C."

"Cut!" Legs yelled, excited. "Lower the lights . . . That's a wrap! Bugs, my lady," he said, slapping her high-five, "me thinks we just won a cable Ace *and* an Emmy!"

You'se about to make history, cuz," Donnie said, slowly shaking his head. "You gonna be the first fool to be kicked up outta his own crib and then have to watch it on national TV."

"He ain't gonna watch nothin' if he don't pay me my money," Swipe reminded me.

"Can I give another shout out after the commercials?" Melba asked, carefully combing through her barely styled hair.

But I don't care about history, Swipe's TV, or Melba's shout outs *or* her hair.

My concern is Dawn and how she feels about the announcement. I know we were on national TV, but she had all but ordered a confession out of me. She didn't want any secrets between us.

We now have none.

She wanted us to start the New Year on the right note.

If being open, honest, and straightforward is *right*, then we're off on the right note.

. She didn't want her show to completely tank as a result of Alan's errant phone call during his "interview," Kelly's couscous, Donnie's and Swipe's near confessions to their respective parole officers and monitors, not to mention Melba's non-stop stream of hellos and acknowledgments.

And thanks to my announcement about Troi, the show will probably yield huge ratings, which is a plus for her and BET.

What's not to like?

I'm afraid I'm about to find out.

"Get in here right now!" Dawn yelled, storming toward my bedroom.

I quickly followed and she was just as quick with a deafening slam of the door.

"What the hell are you talking about?" she asked. "Do you re-alize what you just did? You're telling me that *Troi* is preg-nant? . . . And you had to tell me on national TV? . . . And what do you mean she's coming to D.C.? . . . Don't just stand there, say something!" she insisted.

What does she expect me to say? How do you follow up "Troi is pregnant and she's coming to D.C." with something graceful like "Have I told you how nice you look tonight?"

"Shouldn't we talk about this later?" I asked. "You only have, like, thirty seconds for a commercial, right?"

"They're doing a segment of '106 and Park' from New York, so we have more than enough time," she stated.

"You said you didn't want any secrets, right?" I asked, worried.

Her piercing stare says she's fuming.

"You told me you wanted to start the New Year off with everything out in the open, didn't you?"

It's amazing how the angriest look in the world can get even angrier within seconds.

"And now it's all out in the open," I rationalized. "I know, you know—"

"And the whole world knows," she interrupted.

"The whole world doesn't get BET," I reminded her.

"My mother gets BET and so does my father," she told me. "My pastor, my doorman, the guy who delivers my paper, and my dentist get BET. My hairdresser, my stylist, and every single woman at my salon, at the grocery store, and at the nail shop . . . they all get BET!" she exclaimed. "So don't tell me that the world doesn't get BET, because everyone in my universe gets it!"

Thankfully, her cell phone is ringing, which means one thing.

I'll get some time to come up with something really smooth to settle her down.

"Hi, Mom," Dawn said, after glancing at her caller ID. "Who's Troi? Shawn used to date her. . . . No, he's not still dating her. . . . No, Mom, I don't know why he told me on national TV. . . . Yes, Mom, we're talking about it right now. . . . She's not in D.C. yet, Mom. . . . No, Mom, I don't think that's a good idea . . . I'm not going to get myself liquored up so that I can have an excuse for ripping her hair out by the roots as soon as I see her. . . . Yes, Mom, Happy New Year to you too."

What's a guy supposed to do after a conversation like that? Dawn's not going to let me find out.

"That was my mother," she said, turning toward me.

"Why didn't you tell her I said hi?" I foolishly asked.

"Should I have told her *before* or *after* she suggested that I wait to dump you on national TV?"

"Before?" I asked, smiling.

"And after," she said, turning away.

I know I'm in for trouble.

"This can't be happening," she said, slowly shaking her head. "This was supposed to be our night. We were supposed to get engaged and the show was supposed to be a hit. I can't believe you told me on TV . . . but hey," she went on sarcastically, "it's out there now."

"And that's good, right?" I asked.

"What happened to protection? We started dating three months ago and though we just started sleeping together, we've protected ourselves every time," she reminded me.

"And I used it with her too."

"So how is she pregnant?" she jumped in.

"She just is," I answered. "At least she says she is."

"And that's good enough for you?"

"Of course not," I answered. "But what am I supposed to do?"

"I honestly don't know," she admitted. "But I do know this."

"What?" I replied, worried.

"If I had to break up with the nicest guy in the history of nice guys I'd have to come up with a monumental reason," she said. "And no matter how you slice it, this is monumental."

"You're not saying that you're dumping me?" I asked, concerned.

"What would you do?" she asked forcefully. "What would any man do? What if I told you that I'm pregnant by another guy and that since it happened before you it shouldn't be a big deal? Would you stand beside me? Would you parade pregnant old me in front of your friends and family? Would you say, 'Oh, Dawn, who cares if your first child is another man's child?' " she asked, near tears.

"It's not like you have to parade me around pregnant," I told her.

"Of course not," she said. "I'll just have to walk around and hear every woman I pass whisper 'There goes the idiot whose boyfriend told her about his pregnant girlfriend on TV . . . didn't you see it, girl?' "

"Troi's not my girlfriend," I told her.

"That's not the point and you know it," she answered. "You have a woman who is pregnant and who appears to be coming to D.C. to have her baby," she said. "Maybe she's coming to play house or maybe she wants her son or daughter to be with her baby's daddy. And you know what's missing from that picture, Shawn Wayne? Me!" she exclaimed. "And I'm missing because I don't fit. You're about to be a father, Shawn. And I'm not about to be a mother and I don't know if I want to deal with that. I don't even know if I *can* deal with it," she whispered.

The room is as silent as it is tense.

"I love you, Shawn. I always will," she said, reaching for my hand. "I know you'll be a good father—"

"They're almost done with '106 and Park.' We're back live in forty-five seconds, Dawn," Bugs said, gently tapping on the door. "You okay in there?"

"I'll be right out," she said, nodding her head. "Like I said, I know you'll be a good father," she told me, before releasing my hand and heading to the door.

She then turned toward me and a solitary tear slowly rolled down her cheek.

"But I don't think I'm up to being a good stepmother."

What just happened? Have I been dumped? And if I have, why don't I know it? Dawn said she wasn't ready to be a stepmom, but that doesn't mean she's walking away from our relationship . . . does it? Does it mean that she can't deal with Troi being pregnant? Or is she just mad because the woman who does her nails will rub it in her face?

Does it mean she's disappointed that my first child will come from another woman? Or does she just want to avoid the sneers and snickers of her staff?

Is she angry or maybe even threatened that Troi is rolling into D.C. on the Shawn Wayne Baby Tour? Or is she upset because her mother called her with a game plan before she came up with one of her own?

If people would just stop knocking at the door, I'm certain I'll figure this all out.

"You ain't tying up no sheets to hang yourself with, are you?" Donnie said, pushing the door open. "Because you did a good enough job of that already. Now, that was some f★cked up you shoulda known better, Jerry Springer–loving, I'ma tell you some freak sh★t on TV so that the whole damn audience can boo at my sorry ass type sh★t!" he said, laughing.

"This isn't funny, Donnie," I said, shaking my head, worried.

"The hell it ain't!" he answered.

"It wouldn't be funny if it was you," I told him.

"I wouldn't let it be me," he shot back. "And why you trippin' anyway? You shouldn't have told her, jack. But you did, so whoopie-damn-doo. It's not like she's gonna drop you," he told me.

"She already did."

"She didn't do a motherf★cking thing. She's on that fake female pride sh★t," he rationalized. "She's pissed because all the other broads know that some other broad got your goodies and the only problem is that the other broad has proof."

"What are you talking about?" I asked, thinking Donnie must have had a strong hit of dope.

"Let's say she thought you was screwing around but she couldn't prove it," he started. "Your problem is that Troi has proof. In fact, that sista has nine months' worth of proof."

"How about a lifetime's worth?" I added.

"Don't sweat this sh★t, Shawn," he said. "You can't let no chick, not even one like Dawn who has her own TV show, can get you tickets to damn near anything, and who all of a sudden looks like she just hit the lottery . . . you can't let none of them chicks think that you're pressed. Don't let no chicks see you sweat."

Donnie's right . . . *right?*

One of the worst things a guy can do is to let a woman know that he's overly concerned. Women generally see that as a sign of supreme weakness. It's why guys aren't big on crying in front of women, or sharing their fears, secrets, and dreams with them. In fact, it's the very reason men won't ask for directions even though they're often more lost than I am right now.

Why don't men cry?

We do. But we're not crazy enough to do it in front of a woman. And when we do, you can bet there's an ulterior motive at play. If you catch your man with another woman, and you drop him but he's not ready for it to be over—because he was just getting a piece on the side—he may turn on the tears. He'll sob, he'll tell you how much he loves and respects you, and then he'll beg like a toothless panhandler at a stoplight so that you'll give him another chance.

It's as calculated as Bush versus those weapons-of-mass-destruction wielding terrorists. But it almost always works, so tears happen.

Why won't guys share their fears and dreams?

Easy. *Fear* is synonymous with *weakness* and women are no more interested in weaknesses than they are in a man who cries . . . partially because they know a crying man is either weak, or lying, or both!

That's why you don't see a lot of brothers banging their heads to get on *Fear Factor*. Brothers aren't about to actually admit to having fears in the first place, and why should they? So that the women who prowl at clubs can throw it in their faces? Instead of recognizing a man for making the final cut and landing a spot on the show, some hood princess at a bar would ask, "Aren't you that soft-type Negro that was ascared of being in a casket with them rats?" And his shoulders would sink down past his knees because she would still find the nerve to utter, "I don't like no man who's ascared . . . but you can still buy me a drink."

And dreams? You can forget that. First off, the last brother who had the stones to go public with a dream was MLK, and who's going to top that? Second, if you can dream, you can fail and failure has never been high on any woman's wish list. Which all goes to explain why men don't, won't, and absolutely *can't* ask for directions. It's all part of the Why Men Are Lost Quotient.

Lost Man = Failure: If you're lost, you've *failed* to properly plan or navigate. And if you don't know where you're going in the online age of Map Quest and Maps.com, in your lady's mind, you're even more lost than the last loser she dated.

Lost Man = Man with No Dreams: Bill Gates has more money than Michael Jackson before the nose jobs, sleepovers, chimps, and "colorizing," because he had a dream. While his classmates were dabbling in testosterone futures, he was *dreaming* about motherboards, networks, and the Internet that Al Gore claims to have invented. The average guy is no Bill Gates, so he doesn't dream or, at a minimum, doesn't act on his dreams . . . so he's lost and of course, useless to most women.

Lost Man = Man Without Fear: The fact that a guy won't admit to fear speaks volumes about fear. What he's really saying is that he's *afraid* to admit that he's afraid. It's the greatest of the many contradictions that make men men, but when men admit to being "afraid," the women who beg to hear their fears head for the hills. Which is in line with the many contradictions that make women women.

Lost Man = Man Who Won't Cry: This is a no-brainer. A man who won't cry is completely lost. He's lost touch with his feelings. He's lost touch with his humanity. And he's lost touch with his emotions. If a guy can't tap into his own emotions, he won't be able to understand the fears, dreams, and failures of the women who enter his life. Which explains why the Why Men Are Lost Quotient always works and why men are all but lost . . . and why lost men won't ask for directions.

And all the directions in the world won't help me through this mess.

"So what would you do, Donnie?" I asked.

"What you do doesn't matter as long as Dawn doesn't see you sweat," he replied, grinning.

"So if I go out there and beg like crazy, it's cool as long as I'm not sweating?"

"Kinda, sort of," he answered. "But you ain't getting nowhere with a beg move either. You have to *tell* her what the deal is. You gotta grab her by the arm, look her dead in the eye, slap some bass up in your voice, and she has to know that you mean business. Tell shorty that *you* running things, that *you* calling the shots, and that because she's your woman she's just gonna have to deal with this sh★t."

"That might work," I said, my head nodding in agreement. "This kind of stuff happens every day and if she's going to be with me, she'll have to deal with it."

"Yeah," Donnie said, slapping me five. "Act like that Tony cat from *Taxi* and tell her 'Who's the Boss.'"

"I'm the boss!" I insisted, standing up. "This is my house!"

"Run yours, dawg!" Donnie chimed in.

Excited, liberated, and not interested in being lost, I stepped to the door with no real plan, but a ton of confidence.

"What the hell are you doing?" Donnie asked, sounding concerned.

"I'm about to handle my business," I told him.

"You don't wanna roll like that," he shot back.

"What did you just tell me?" I asked. "You nailed it, D. I'm going to grab her by her arm, look her dead in the eye, and I'm going to—"

"Get your ass kicked," he interrupted. "You just told shorty that Troi's belly is poppin' and you think you just gonna march out there and start running sh★t? You ain't that crazy, Shawn."

"Who says I'm not?"

"I don't know," he answered. "But I know that you ain't no caveman and Dawn definitely ain't no Wilma, so you can't go pullin no Flintstone-type sh★t."

Maybe he's right, but it doesn't matter. It's near criminal to pump a man up and deflate him within seconds, especially when I'm just moments away from following up the TV debut I'd made a little earlier.

I took in a big breath, eyed Dawn's reflection in the mirror as she sat on the couch holding a microphone, and headed in her direction. Donnie may have backed off, but I'm not about to.

"Look, Dawn," I said, sitting beside her. "We're not on the air, are we?"

"What are you doing, Shawn?" she asked, sitting up straight.

"You need to know what the deal is," I said, reaching for her arm.

She looked at me surprised.

"We're back!" Legs yelled.

They're back? I wondered. Where did they go?

"And what might the deal be, Shawn?" she asked, holding her mic to my face.

"First, I'm sorry. This shouldn't have happened like this and I apologize for putting our business out in the street," I told her. "You're my woman and you have to deal with this. You're not just going to up and abandon me . . . that's not what we're about. People make mistakes in relationships and the only one I made was not using protection with Troi," I admitted. "But that was before you, and all I did was be straight with you, which is what you asked for in the first place. So we're still together and we're staying together. And I'm not asking you to be a stepmom or anything like that. I'm just telling you that you're my woman, that I'm your man and that we're in this for the long haul."

"He's outta his f★cking mind," Donnie said, walking past the couch and cuddling up with Melba.

"No he's not," Dawn said, starting to smile. "I know that you're right and that this happened before me . . . before us," she said, her voice trailing off. "I still don't know how or if I'll even be able to deal with this, but maybe it's worth a try. Why you had to tell me on national TV, I'll never know. But at least you were man enough to come out and apologize on TV and I know that took a lot."

"We're on TV?" I asked, concerned.

"Yes we are, honey," she said, smiling.

"Oh, yes we are, Goofy," Legs chimed in.

"This is Dawn Truesdale live with you on BET, and we have had quite a night. We're going to have a great year. So, for those who are driving, don't drink, and for those who must drink, please don't drive."

"That would be me," Melba happily said, raising two glasses.

"To my friends who are here with me—"

"When am I gonna get my money?!" yelled Swipe.

"And to my fans and family—"

"Why would you bring couscous to a New Year's party, anyway?" Alan asked, gently straightening Kelly's crooked-sitting glasses.

"Thank you for tuning in and remember, the price of love . . . is love," she added.

"That's some of that knee deep keep your mind working while you think about it, type sh★t!" Donnie exclaimed.

"Happy New Year!" Dawn yelled. "I love you," she said, turning toward me.

"Are we still on TV?" I asked.

"Yes, we're still on TV," Legs whispered. "So don't stop now, do something else stupid."

My mind isn't 100 percent clear and my thinking isn't exactly straight. Maybe it's the hot lights, the lady crawling behind the couch pulling cords, or Swipe tapping me on my shoulder to again ask . . .

"When am I getting my loot?"

I don't know and I don't care. Midnight is here and so is a new year. Donnie is lip-locked with Melba. Alan and Kelly are kissing like newlyweds. Legs has ponied up to Bugs. The lady pulling cords just pulled Swipe behind the couch. And Dawn is kissing me like she will never stop.

"You been here all night?" Swipe asked, before she kissed him. "It's on now!" he yelled, excited.

Who cares about Troi? I thought, still kissing. *Things are going to be just fine.*

We survived "the announcement," we're going to work through this mini-fiasco and most important . . . I have a new TV!

Dawn had called it.

We're about to have a great year.

The Seven Different Types of Dads

Daddy Deep Pockets . . . a.k.a., "See Ya Next Weekend!" Dad

Back in the day, payday was an every Friday happening. Then came divorce and a new phenomenon: visitation. In little time, companies across America responded by making paydays an every *other* Friday proposition. And with that subtle move, weekend dads were born. Sometimes separated, sometimes divorced, oft times just plain excluded from the fun and frolic of fatherhood, Daddy Deep Pockets sees his kids 26 times a year, max. So, every other weekend, he's an ATM machine with legs. Why? He knows he's not around, so money, toys and gifts stand in as replacements for what his kids really need—his presence, affection and more important, his time. Daddy Deep Pockets has seen every Disney everything—Disney at the movies, Disney on Ice, Disney on stage—if Disney's done it, he's seen it, because family flicks and events dominate the weekend. And since he's not involved in day-to-day family life, he'll try to create a family existence in 26 bi-weekly intervals. Like many fathers, Daddy Deep Pockets truly cares about his children. And he'll be sure to prove it . . . next weekend.

9

Nothing beats sleeping in the arms of the woman you love.

Even if it's in a roomful of people who were supposed to be out of your place and back at their homes several hours ago.

Right after our big New Year's Eve kiss-fest, Legs and Bugs broke out an oversized bottle of pricey champagne and the toasts started.

Alan toasted Kelly and Kelly, thinking about his earning potential and the potential size of her engagement ring, toasted his practice.

Donnie and Melba toasted to a new year of sobriety . . . and then passed out drunk.

Legs and Bugs toasted an Emmy Award–winning start to Dawn's new show.

And Swipe toasted my plastic-covered furniture.

"I'd rather be down here on the floor all night than to have to sit on that sh*t!" he exclaimed. "What did you say your name was again?" he asked of his cord-pulling sweetheart.

Though I passed on the bubbly, Dawn and I toasted each other. We looked deep into each other's eyes and made a Chuck Woolery–style love connection. We're going to work things out. We're going to be better friends, better confidants, and better lovers. Nothing and no one is coming between us.

Our New Year's Eve celebration was as perfect as it gets.

But that was hours ago . . . and before the phone rang to bring us crashing back to reality.

"No this is Legs, Legs Brunson," Legs said, yawning into my cordless handset. He then handed it to Kelly, who mumbled before handing it to Alan.

"I'm not sure where he is, but I can tell you this *is* a charity event," he lied, before passing the phone to a snoring Melba. Donnie grabbed the phone from her and said, "This is three hundred sixty-five days . . . drug f*cking free," he bragged.

"The noise?" Swipe slowly asked. "Oh that . . . that's that plastic sh*t from my man's furniture," he remarked. "It's for you, dawg," he said, handing me the phone.

"Hello," I asked, gently stroking Dawn's new-found hair as she rested her head on my chest. "A collect call from who?" I asked, surprised. "Why didn't she use 1-800-Collect?" I inquired, thinking this would be an expensive call. "Well, can you ask her to call back on 1-800-Collect?" I asked, before the operator clicked off.

The phone quickly rang again, and I answered it before it could bother anyone else.

"Yeah, I'll accept," I answered. "Happy New Year to you too," I said, worried.

And I had every right in the world to be worried. But it's amazing how something as small and as insignificant as a cordless phone can shatter your nerves and get your knees shaking with just one chilling ring.

And when the voice on the other end is one you'd prefer not to hear, your options are limited. You can hang up and hope her pride kicks in and that she won't call back.

You can answer as someone else and then proclaim that you're not in, which works unless you screw it up and say, "I'm not in."

Or you can pull the tried and true, and say, "I can't talk right now," which really sucks because it implies that you'll talk later. And when you didn't want to talk in the first place, talking now or talking later are interchangeable because what you really mean is that the only time you care to talk is never.

Which is exactly how I feel. The only problem is that it's not exactly coming across that way.

"Did I catch you at a bad time?" Troi asked.

"I think its seven a.m.," I answered, looking at my watch.

"I didn't mean time, time," she said, laughing. "Can you talk?"

"Umm . . ." I answered, turning the phone away from Dawn.

"What's your take on surprises?" she asked.

"My mom gave me a surprise party when I was in the tenth grade and it was okay," I told her. "Donnie actually told me about it, so I guess it wasn't a surprise, surprise, but I really—"

"You are too cute, Shawn," she interrupted. "I'm talking about a here and now surprise."

"What's that supposed to mean?" I asked, concerned.

"A here and now surprise means that I'm here . . . right now."

"You're here?" I asked, looking around the room. "Where?"

"Are you still at the same place?" she asked. "Because I can jump into a cab and I'll be there in about twenty minutes."

"No," I quickly answered.

"You moved?" she asked.

"What I meant to say was that you're not in D.C."

"Of course I am," she answered. "My flight just landed, but I can't get in touch with my ride."

"Do you want me to try to reach him?"

"Reach who?" she asked.

"Your ride."

"First off, he's a she and second, she brought in the New Year with her latest beau, so my money says she's somewhere with him."

"So you need a ride?"

"Not at all," she replied. "I can just catch a cab to your place and maybe we can catch up over a little breakfast," she told me. "Remember how you used to bring home the bacon?" she asked, immediately taking me back to our days when she was here.

How could I forget?

Troi rolled into my life like a truck driver with road rage. She was fast, she was all over the place, and she'd done major damage quick. It's still hard to figure out exactly what we had . . . or how it ended.

She came into town for the annual Congressional Black Caucus conference, which the locals call the CBC. We met at the opening-night dance. We partied, ended up in her room, made love, and fell in love.

At least I fell in love.

Kelly couldn't stand Troi and warned me I was falling for the wrong person. I didn't see it that way. Troi is everything that every guy wants. She has model looks, a body that rivals Janet Jackson's when Janet's depressed and loses weight, her hair and especially her eyes would hypnotize a hypnotist, and she's as smart as she is funny and as innocent as she is downright naughty.

Could she cook?

I never found out, and never cared.

Did she keep a clean house?

Hardly, but it didn't matter.

Would she be a good mother?

I never gave it a thought when we were together, though maybe I should have, but as with everything with Troi, I'm not convinced it would have mattered.

Troi is every man's dream and every woman's nightmare. She's that one woman from every man's past who *if* she calls, the guy meets up with her. It doesn't matter if he's married, engaged, involved, or in a state of prolonged common-law cohabitation. Any man with a brain and a renewable prescription for Viagra is making a rendezvous with Troi happen.

When our wives and girlfriends ask about the deep, dark secrets of our past, we never admit to them, but we know they exist and they always involve a Troi. When they ask about our sexual conquests or our most salacious intimate encounters, we lie and say, "It was when you and I did this thing at this place during this time." If we thought our mates could actually handle it, we'd smile and say, "There was this woman. Troi was her name, and she blew my mind when she . . . "

And if there's a woman who could walk into any man's life and challenge his marriage, his relationships, and his very being, it's a Troi. She's that woman we can't dare acknowledge, with whom we'll never have closure, and who could still force us into terrible, life changing mistakes and lapses in judgment if she said she'd have us . . . even if she allowed us just one night.

Wives everywhere are relatively safe because even guys who cheat usually come to their senses and make their way home. It's an easy call. Though they most likely want to, husbands, boyfriends and fiancés are never cheating with their "Troi."

Why?

Because "Troi" has gone on to bigger and better. She forgot about us even before she walked out on us, which explains why she never calls, never e-mails, and never comes to town. She's our comely costar in our fantasies and exists in the depths of our memories, at the barbershop, and in locker rooms where every man feels safe discussing that one woman he shouldn't have let get away.

But I never let Troi get away. She just left.

And my biggest problem is that she's back in D.C. right now.

"Shawn?" she asked, snapping me back to a reality I wasn't ready to accept.

"Yeah?"

"What's it going to be, sailor?" she asked, her smile jumping through the phone. "Can a lonely lady interest you in a little shore leave?"

"I was never in the Navy," I answered.

"And I'm not a lonely lady," she shot back. "But I'm tired of standing at this pay phone, so I'm on the way."

"No," I said, as Dawn slowly awoke and kissed my cheek.

"No?" Dawn asked. "What, you didn't like my kiss?"

She's now hitting me with a soft, sensuous kiss that I have to like.

"Shawn," Troi slowly said, "what's going on?"

"Nothing," I mumbled, quickly trying to reel in my tongue.

"You call that nothing?" Dawn playfully whispered. "Well, try this on for size," she said, kissing me even more passionately.

"Is everything okay?" Troi asked, sounding concerned.

It's not.

I'm in the midst of one of those rare best-of-both-worlds deals. It's like going to a McDonald's drive-thru with a 5-dollar bill and wanting to supersize an Extra Value Meal. If the meal is $4.25 and you try to supersize it, you're looking at a $5.85 tab. Everyone knows that's way too much to pay for something that's supposed to be an "extra value" in the first place. But let's say that your favorite fast food server recognizes your voice.

You pull up to the window, she gives you a quick wink-wink. You tell her you really like the latest Mickey D's tee-shirt and hat combination and she gives you four ketchups, knowing that you always ask for three. She throws in napkins, salt, and a few packs of pepper and when you pull away and hit a stoplight where you can crack open your meal, you notice something that brings on a huge, satisfying smile and moves you to realize that God really exists.

She hooked you up with a supersized meal!

You look around, worried that some overblown manager with a Grill Chief certificate from Hamburger U will track you down and demand a full and complete return of your bag. And when it hits you that you're in the clear, you gobble the meal down with a sense of sheer surprise and satisfaction.

As you wash down your Big Mac with that extra large cup of Sprite, you relish the fact that you're in that rarified air known as the best of both worlds. You wanted to supersize and couldn't afford it, paid for a regular Extra Value meal, and instead received the supersized meal . . . and saved $1.60, which you didn't have in the first place.

Like me, you're in the best of both worlds.

I have the love of my life, Dawn, kissing all over me. And you have extra fries. I have the woman of any sane man's dream, Troi, trying to come to my place. And you have a bigger Sprite.

If Troi actually shows, I'll have an even bigger problem than I already have, given that she's pregnant. Though Dawn may "accept it," there's no way seeing Troi this morning will make her happy. And if you keep eating those supersized Extra Value meals, with their saturated fat, calories, and cholesterol artery blockers, you'll be even worse off than me.

We both *think* we have it good . . . but do we?

I'm sure Troi will waste no time letting me know about it.

"Well, Mr. Shawn," Troi quickly said. "It's seven ten. I'll be there by seven thirty."

"Who's that?" Dawn asked, now kissing my neck.

"Are you sure?" I asked, now worried beyond belief.

"Goodbye, handsome," Troi whispered, "I can't wait to see you."

"Seven thirty?" I replied.

"Wow," Dawn said, sitting up to see Donnie, Melba, Kelly, and Alan; Legs embracing Bugs, and Swipe huddled on the floor behind the couch with the queen of cord pullers. "We're having *more* company?" she asked, peering at her watch. "At least I have time for a shower," she remarked, locating her purse.

No you don't, I thought.

"By the way," she said, heading toward the bathroom. "Who's coming? And why is he coming so early on New Year's day?"

That's one of those *almost* good questions. She got the "why" part right, but she's way off on the "he" part. If Dawn knew exactly which "he" was on the way, she'd skip the shower, grab some popcorn, and take a first row seat to a show she'd never want to miss.

Jeez, I thought, considering my options. *I've just been supersized.*

I'm in a panic. And not just any panic, I'm in a *panic*, panic. I'm in Code Blue, DEFCON 5, and Phase 1 Alert all at once. How am I supposed to get an entire house of guests who were supposed to be gone last night out of the house and off my street in twenty minutes?

This is one of those times when you want to be the president. You want to order somebody to do something quick. You want those beefy guys with the nondescript black shades and the hidden earpieces to escort somebody someplace. You want some general in a green uniform to deliver a searing speech that will intimidate all who are listening into immediate action. You want a nerdy, scientist type who will unveil a chart detailing the imminent spread of an ungodly airborne virus that is starting right in your living room, and you want all of this done without having to answer questions at some press conference.

That's what you want at a time like this.

But I'm not about to get it.

If I make breakfast, maybe the fresh morning aroma and sizzle of breakfast meat, eggs, and coffee will wake everyone. Then they can eat and run. Maybe it won't happen in twenty minutes, but there's a chance Troi will get one of those scheming, scenic route cabbies who will take her all over D.C. before actually delivering her to my spread in Lanham, Maryland.

Unwrapping bacon, cracking eggs, and measuring coffee are near impossible when you're in stress mode. My mother was an ace at it. She could read the morning paper, drink a cup of coffee, flip pancakes, fry up sausage, clip coupons, discipline me *and* my father, plan her dinner meal, and still apply makeup and wash dishes without a blink. But I'm not my mom.

In fact, I haven't actually cooked in my house in over a year. I usually eat out or at Dawn's place when she's not working, so cooking is never really an issue. It also never much matters because like many guys, I can't cook. Unless you count microwave popcorn as a "cookable" item.

"What are we doing for breakfast, hon?!" Dawn yelled from the shower.

"I'm jumping on it right now!" I answered, juggling a slab of bacon and a bowl of eggs.

"That's a joke!" She laughed. "What are we really doing? We should pile up in your SUV and head over to the Waffle Shop," she suggested.

"Are you talking about that hole-in-wall across from Ford's Theatre?" I asked, now breaking the eggs and plopping them alongside the bacon that had already started an early morning sizzle.

"Are you kidding me, Shawn?!" she yelled. "They have the best food in the city!"

"But they can't get these clowns out of here before Troi shows up," I muttered, throwing bread into the toaster.

"What was that?"

"I didn't say Troi," I foolishly spat out.

"You didn't say what?!"

"I didn't say *Joy*?" I said.

"What are you talking about?" she inquired, turning the water down.

"Joy," I said, searching for an answer that made sense. "I wouldn't want to miss the *joy* of a home cooked meal to start the new year off right."

"You're going to have to come up with a better one than that, Shawn Wayne," she said, now out of the shower. "The only joy you get out of cooking is not doing it. I'll be out in just a second, so don't do anything rash," she added.

She's too late.

"Shawn . . . " she said, sounding worried. "What's that?"

"What's what?" I asked, my nose buried in the refrigerator in search of some butter that I didn't have.

"Are you cooking?" she asked. "Or are you really trying to bring the new year in with a bang?"

"I'm making breakfast!" I answered.

That's what I told her. But it's not what the smoke detector is telling me. The screeching yelp of the smoke detector confirmed my worst fears and substantiated Dawn's precise nose for de-tails . . . and smoke.

That age-old adage of where's there's smoke, there's fire is proving to be more than an overused cliché. And my beautifully polished, rarely used, stainless-steel stovetop is bearing more than enough proof.

It's bad enough that Troi is on her way and my houseguests are nowhere near gone. It's a near tragedy that Troi will meet Dawn and will become reacquainted with Kelly before I have a chance to feel her out about this whole pregnancy thing. And it's a shame that Donnie and his parole-straddling, TV-selling partner Swipe will hit me up for an orange juice chaser before demanding a cool two grand for their hot flat screen that is hanging so proudly in my living room.

Though all of this should mean a great deal to me, right now it doesn't. But, then again, it can't. Especially since my kitchen appears to be on fire.

"Shawn!" Dawn yelled, panicked. "What are you doing?"

"Cooking?" I asked, desperately searching for water.

I instinctively tossed the closest liquid I could find onto the flames, a glass of pulp-filled orange juice, which is perhaps the worst thing you can do for a grease fire.

"Where's your fire extinguisher?!" Dawn yelled, fighting her way through the smoke.

"Why do I need a fire extinguisher?" I asked, adding fuel to the fire with another glass of orange juice. "I'm making breakfast."

"If this is breakfast, I'd hate to see lunch," Donnie joked, reaching for a box of baking soda that Kelly had planted in the refrigerator. He then rushed to the stove, tossed the baking soda toward the middle of the flames, and covered it with the tablecloth he'd snatched from the dining room table.

"Do you know how much that cost?" I asked, remembering that Dawn had picked it up from Saks.

"It was actually on sale," Dawn whispered. "And if it puts out the fire, I'll take the loss."

She was about to take it.

"What the f*ck is all the noise?" Swipe said, still entrenched behind the couch.

"This is one hell of a way to start the new year," Legs commented.

"Is this going to be on TV too?" Melba asked, grabbing Donnie by his waist.

"Well, now that Shawn has given each of you a wake-up call as only he can, I'm suggesting that he take us to breakfast, and that he treats," Dawn, said, fanning smoke away from her face.

"If he's treating, I'll pass," Donnie remarked.

"And if Donnie's passing, I think we'll pass," Alan agreed.

"Hold up," Swipe interrupted. "Y'all are passing on a free bref-fas?"

"If he's paying, it probably will be free," Melba chimed in.

"Yeah." Kelly laughed. "Free of food!"

Everyone laughed along as they moved to straighten out clothes that were ruffled, rumpled, or partially removed last night.

"Why don't we meet up at the Waffle Shop over on tenth?" Dawn suggested.

"My parole officer *and* my home detention monitor both eat over there," Swipe admitted.

"So do mine," Donnie said, slapping him five.

"It's a date," Kelly said, still fanning smoke out of the room.

"I'm going to stop by my place and get some clothes that don't have this smoke flavoring," Dawn joked, reaching for her purse. "Are you riding with me?" she asked. "Or do you want to meet there?"

"Why don't I meet you there?" I replied, opening some windows to air out the kitchen. "I need to get rid of this smoke."

"You need to give me my money too!" Swipe insisted. "But we can straighten it out down to the waffle joint," he added, as the cable-pulling woman lured him back behind the couch.

"You've been a real decent-like host," Legs said, clutching onto Bugs. "We'll remember you in our Emmy speech."

"Happy-happy," Alan said, escorting Kelly toward the front door.

"Call me on my cell," Kelly whispered, holding up her hand like she was holding a phone.

"See you, hon," Dawn said, kissing me on the cheek. "And don't think you're off the hook. At least not all the way off the hook." She giggled.

"We'll catch you at the spot, money," Donnie said, walking alongside Melba.

Or will they? This is perfect. My house had been cleared out in record time and I'm now ready to meet Troi head on. Well . . . I'm almost ready.

"Hey, Swipe," I said, peering behind the couch. "I think they're waiting for you guys outside."

"My bad, cuz. Let's roll, sweet-tart," he said, carefully helping his cable-pulling mistress to her feet and directing her toward the door. "I *think* I asked you this earlier, but, what did you say your name was?" he asked her, as he pulled the door shut.

D-day is slapping me in the face and I'm as ready as I'm going to get.

Between the slowly rotating ceiling fans, the humming exhaust on the range hood, and the wide open windows that have ushered in the cold, the smoke is steadily clearing. I never thought Donnie would actually be my hero, but he saved the day like a

New York fireman. I don't know what I'll say to Troi and can't imagine what she'll say to me, but the ringing doorbell is telling me that it's time to face the music.

Troi Stevenson is back in town and it's about to get live. Which would probably bother me more if I weren't confronted with a bigger, even more distressing dilemma for any guy. With the bread in the toaster and the eggs and the bacon in the frying pan all burned to a crisp, what are Troi and I going to do for breakfast?

This is one of those times when you truly don't want to answer the door. It has nothing to do with the smoke, which has all but dissipated. And the lack of breakfast food after a long night and a hectic morning means little.

The problem is one of fate. It's one of those immediate fate deals that you'd rather stall on or forget altogether. You'd rather ignore the problem that's right in your face because you know that regardless of the hand that's dealt, you have no shot of winning.

It's like attempting to convince Michael Jackson that trying to get the LaToya look, who was trying to get the Janet look, who was trying to get the Michael look herself, just isn't cutting it. Like being an overly hyped white rapper *without* a hulking posse at the Source Awards. And like engaging in an argument with your wife or your girlfriend when her mother makes a weekend visit.

You can't win.

And neither can I.

The buzzing doorbell is a sobering reminder of everything I've tried to duck since Troi called and left the message announcing her pregnancy.

Do I want a child with Troi? Nope. Do I want a child at all? Nope . . . at least not yet anyway. The bottom line is that I don't want a child. Not here. Not now. And definitely not out of wedlock.

So I'll have to hold my ground, despite what hers might be. And I'm sure I'll find out just where she stands when I open the door so we can have at it.

"I love you—"

And that's all that got out. My lips are engaged in a kiss that's on the A-list for passion and purpose. This is one of those "come hither" kisses that makes you want to do exactly one thing . . . come hither (wherever that is). This is the type of kiss that says I'm here to stay and you're here to stay with me. It's the kind you read about in cheap, dime store romance novels and that you see in the movies when somebody is trying to make a statement. As we embraced and then slowly pulled apart, the statement was made as clearly as it always was.

A pregnant woman can't kiss like that, I reasoned.

"I love you, Shawn . . . I just want you to know that."

What do I do? This isn't how things are supposed to work out.

Troi was supposed to show up, look a mess, and argue with me about how she doesn't need, want, or expect anything from me . . . as long as she gets her child support. She's supposed to have the kid's life all planned out and kick me *beneath* the curb . . .

as long as she gets her child support. She's supposed to tell me off, curse me out, and then threaten to move herself and her child far from me and cut off any chance of visitation . . . as long as she gets her child support.

That's how it's supposed to happen. But it didn't. Which leads me to believe that someone somewhere forgot to inform *Dawn* of exactly how the scenario was supposed to work.

"What are you doing here, Dawn?" I asked, still flushed from the warmth of her kiss. "You're supposed to be at the waffle place."

"Well, I didn't want my man to be all alone on New Year's Day, so I decided to wait it out right here with you."

"You did?"

I'm as done as Clarence Thomas at a Black Panther rally.

"But I remembered that I was treating, so I'd better get going," she realized.

Yes! I thought, relieved.

"Hey," she said, turning toward the door. "You know that guy down the block, the one with more boyfriends than J-Lo? He may have changed his stripes," she shared. "This beautiful woman in a tight, little black leather mini skirt just walked up to his door."

"Maybe she's a hooker," I remarked, trying to hurry Dawn to her car.

"Hookers don't show up with flowers," she said, starting to close the door. "I have to stop by the studio after breakfast, so I might be gone when you get there, but I'll call before dinner."

"I'll be waiting," I said, thankful that Troi still hadn't showed.

I'm running to the kitchen, shutting the windows and watching to make certain that Dawn makes her way toward a breakfast I'm happy to miss. I don't see her car, which doesn't surprise me.

The doorbell is ringing again, but this time I'm prepared.

"I'm starting to think you're interested in a booty call," I said, opening the front door.

"I guess the flowers gave it away . . . Hi, handsome."

It's not a booty call. And it isn't Dawn.

"Troi?" I said, surprised, noticing her slender, sexy legs. "You're the hooker?"

"I'm the what?"

"The gay guy . . . down the street . . . you were just there."

"Oh, that," she answered, smiling. "I went to 1424 instead of 1442. And that guy looked at me like I was—"

"A dirty old woman," I interrupted.

"Exactly," she answered. "But that didn't stop him from asking me where I got my skirt." She laughed.

"So," I said, showing her to the living room. "Welcome to D.C."

"Any big plans for New Year's Day?" she asked, clearly making small talk.

"Football," I quickly answered. "There's nothing that can keep me from football on the first day of the year."

"Why does it smell like I just missed Smokey the Bear?" she asked, waving her hand.

"I was doing a little breakfast thing and the stove kind of lost it," I told her.

"That's so sweet, Shawn, but you didn't have to."

"I didn't."

"You didn't . . . do what?" she asked.

"What I meant to say is that I didn't mean to almost burn the house down," I confessed. "I was just trying to make breakfast."

"Well, I am a little hungry," she shared. "They didn't exactly serve up a meal on the flight."

"I thought we were supposed to talk," I reminded her.

"About what?" she asked. "Truth be told, I'm starving, and since you burned breakfast, I'd imagine you're hungry, so let's eat."

"I don't have anything here," I admitted.

"Of course you do," she answered, walking toward the refrigerator and then opening it. "You have . . . couscous?"

"I thought it was Cream of Wheat," I replied.

"I can't imagine you with couscous," she said, smiling. "So tell me."

"Tell you what?"

"This has woman written all over it. Just like this blanket," she said, referring to Dawn's tablecloth, which was still covering the stove. "So Shawn Wayne has gotten himself hooked up, I see." She laughed. "Did you tell her I'm the jealous type?"

"No?"

"So who is she, then?"

"Who's who?" I quickly asked.

"The woman whom you didn't tell how easily jealous I get," she shot back.

"I didn't say there was any woman," I answered. "And I never knew you did the jealous thing."

"Of course I do," she said, smiling. "And if there is another woman, she should probably know about my jealous streak."

"What makes you think there's a woman?" I replied, dumbly.

There is. And she knows it. And the only thing that makes it worse is that she knows that I know that she knows. But why should it matter? Dawn is my woman and Troi is . . . the woman

who claims to be pregnant. I should have told Troi about Dawn
the moment she called. I should have shared with her that when
she bolted back to Chicago and dragged my heart along with her,
that I regrouped, refocused, and found my one true soul mate.
Troi needs to know that Dawn is the love of my life and that I'm
not about to let her or any other woman come between us.

And as soon as we finish breakfast, I'll be sure to tell her.

"I'm glad there's not another woman because I wouldn't want
anyone to get in the way of our plans," Troi admitted.

"We have plans?" I asked, beginning to worry.

"Of course," she said, again smiling. "How do I look?"

You don't look pregnant, I thought, looking her over.

And she doesn't. I've done the math on this a million times over
in my head and the numbers add up. She rolled back to Chicago
in October and called me in December, which means she could
be two to three months pregnant. So it makes perfect sense that
she wouldn't be showing.

When Sarah Jessica Parker was pregnant, she never looked like
she was expecting on *Sex and the City.* I saw Whitney Houston
give a full-blown concert in D.C. *and then* watched her bail Bobby
Brown out of jail two days later on CNN and no one would have
guessed that she was pregnant. And when Toni Braxton was
sporting skin-tight mini dresses with bare-belly, midriff tops,
who could have possibly known that she was due to have a child?

If I ask Troi about her pregnancy, it's a no-win situation. If I'm
not the dad, she'll think I'm prying. If I am the dad, she may want
to know "my real intentions."

Either way, she'll most likely be insulted because she'll think that
what I'm really questioning is her honesty. Am I saying she's not

pregnant? Am I saying that she's not pregnant by *me?* Or am I saying that if she answers "yes" to either, that there's no way I'm ready
to deal with a baby (with Dawn as my not-so-happy girlfriend).

Maybe it doesn't matter because Troi appears to be as *un*pregnant as any woman I know. She looks as slim and trim as she was
when I last saw her in Chicago. Her tight, black leather miniskirt
appears to be airbrushed to her shapely hips. Her legs, which were
always the centerpiece of one of the most beautiful women God
ever assembled, are as sleek and sexy as they were when we met
just four months ago in September. And I'm willing to bet that her
stomach still more closely resembles a Depression-era washboard
than it does one of those blouse-popping, midwife-needing, rub-
my-tummy-and-bring-me-some-pickles-and-peanut-butter bel-
lies that you usually see when you're stuffing your cart at the
grocery store.

All told, Troi is the female equivalent of Denzel Washington.
He's all male all the time and she's all woman all the time. And if
Troi's pregnant, every woman should be pregnant because she
looks awesome. But I'm not about to tell her that.

"How do you look?" I asked, searching for an answer. "You
look . . . exactly like you did the last time I saw you."

"So you didn't notice?" she asked.

". . . That you did something to your hair?" I guessed.

"I lost weight!"

"But—"

"I tried the Atkins diet, cut back on my carbs, slowed down on
the red meat, and I've lost four pounds."

I always thought gaining weight was a part of the whole pregnancy deal. Especially since Donnie revealed to me that when
women complain about pregnancy, it's a total smokescreen.

"Chicks whine about morning sickness, pain, and some more sh★t." But if it was all that bad, they wouldn't keep getting their asses pregnant," he reasoned, conveniently ignoring the role that men play in the process. "The way I see it, being knocked up ain't nothing but an excuse to stress the next man out. And for real, Shawn," he finished, "all pregnancy is, is a license to get fat."

On the surface, it made sense. Many a man has shared horror stories about girlfriends, wives, and chicks on the side who blew up ten dress sizes in nine months. We've joked about women who looked like they were busy eating twins instead of having them. And we've laughed at women who gained all the weight their frames could possibly handle, only to gain even more weight than their frames could possibly handle in the name of childbirth and motherhood.

Which really wouldn't be a problem if the women could or even would just lose the weight. Donnie's statement didn't seem so half-baked when we went to our five-year high school class re-union and later, our ten-year extravaganza. After figuring out where half the guys had been locked up—in either a local jail or in some federal penitentiary—we guessed at how many children each woman had by their increased "tonnage."

Trish Goodman, the editor of the school paper, looked like she was a size ten as opposed to the size eight she was at graduation, so we correctly pegged her for one child.

Linda Flowers was a sexy, svelte size six who wore a bikini beneath her prom dress and swam laps in the hotel fountain after she'd downed her third Long Island Iced Tea before the prom was even over. But at the five-year reunion, it was clear that she had a sizable charge account at Lane Bryant . . . and at least two kids.

Adrian Madyun maintained her size. She could have worn the

same sleek pantsuit that she wore when she was inducted into the National Honor Society. Adrian was smart, appropriately sassy, and as career-driven as any high school senior on the planet. We weren't too surprised that she didn't have any kids.

Donnie may have been right. But in Troi's case, he couldn't have been any more wrong.

"You lost three pounds in four months," I remarked. "I guess that's impressive."

"And I plan to keep it off," she said proudly. "But we'll talk about that after we eat."

"I'd order in but I don't know what's open considering it's New Year's Day," I told her. "What did you have in mind?" I headed to the closet to locate my coat.

"Remember that little dive you took me to?"

"Which one?" I asked, walking to the door.

"It was totally retro," she said, quickly walking toward my truck to beat the morning cold.

"Do you mean retro as in retro or retro as in old?" I asked, reaching to open her door.

"A little of both," she answered as I headed toward the driver's side door. "But the food was fab and I thought it was so quaint."

"And you went there with me?" I inquired, starting the engine and then backing out.

"Of course. You're the only man I've been with since we've met."

"Are you sure?" I asked, wanting to slap the words back in my mouth.

"What are you trying to say, Shawn?" she asked, sounding angry.

"Do you remember the name of the place?"

"Don't ignore me. What are you trying to say?" she repeated.

"You remember when you made that joke about being jealous about another woman?" I asked.

"Who said I was joking?"

"Well, I might be jealous too . . . except I'm not," I told her. "You're a beautiful woman and I'm pretty sure you've been around some beautiful men."

"Beautiful men?" she commented.

"You know what I mean," I said, hanging a right onto Central Avenue. "Nice guys. The responsible types who are good earners and who pay their child support," I stupidly said.

"O-h-h, those guys," she remarked. "The kind that don't call back when a woman leaves a message and says she has good news."

"Who said being pregnant is good news?" I said flatly.

"So that's what this is about," she stated. "Pull over, Shawn." She pointed, directing me toward a McDonald's parking lot.

Something's telling me we're about to have our first fight, and that there's no way I'm going to win.

"Shawn, I'm pregnant and it's 5000 percent certain that you're the father," she told me.

Five thousand? I thought, worried.

"You're the only man that I've been with. And you need to know that I didn't come here to tie you down or to get child support or any of that," she told me. "I just landed a great position with Spencer, Armstrong, Posey, Brown, and Colbert, the top PR firm in D.C. They brought me in as a VP, practically *gave* me their top political accounts, and I'll make partner in about eighteen months if everything works out. And so that we're on the same page, I don't want anything from you, don't need anything from you, and won't be bothering you. In fact, if my ride had bothered to show up, you would have never heard from me," she finished. "At least not yet, anyway."

The ball's now in my court. But what am I supposed to do with it? She gave me the classic "I don't need anything from you" speech, which works until she actually has the baby and then slaps you with a paternity suit. But Troi might not be that type. According to her, I'm 5000 percent the father of her child. But she's 5000 percent a straight-up independent woman who doesn't seem to rely on anyone for anything.

When she came to D.C. in October, she wasn't pressing me for more time. I was pressing her. And she wasn't concerned about how to reach me and where I'd been when she couldn't. I was the one who had to track her down when she went back to Chicago and "forgot" to give me her number.

And even now, she's not playing, acting, or even looking the role of a soon-to-be drama-loaded baby's mama. She's as sexy as she ever was. But can I take her at her word?

"I never said I thought you were trying to tie me down," I began.

"You didn't have to," she interrupted, with an edge in her voice.

"So you're really here for a job?" I asked. "You're not even interested in how I feel about this?"

"I have to admit that I thought you were different," she answered. "But when I really considered it all, I knew you were a man and I know what that means."

"What does it mean?"

"As far as choices go, you'll *choose* not to be involved. You'll pretend that this is all my fault and that I wanted to trap you or take something from you. If you asked if I'm happy about this, I'd honestly tell you that I'm not," she admitted. "But this is the hand I've been dealt and I don't believe in abortion, so guess what, Shawn? I'm having a baby and even though I didn't get pregnant by myself, I'm prepared to go it totally alone."

"I didn't say I wanted you to do it by yourself."

"So what are you saying, Shawn?"

What am I saying? I don't want a kid! Just because she's playing the hand she's been dealt, why am I going to have to play it for the next 18 years? She doesn't believe in abortion, so I'm going to be dragged into court, pay child support, and go to dozens of bad plays, nauseating school programs and pageants, cheesy fundraisers, and stressful conferences with teachers I'd probably rather be dating? And I'm going to get stuck with this because of her beliefs? What about my beliefs?

I didn't use birth control and that's *my* fault. But is it a mistake that should net an 18-year sentence? What if I don't believe in children out of wedlock, but don't see her as wife material? What if I think that adoption is an option? What if I simply don't want a baby with a woman I know only through some of the best sexual encounters any man has ever had?

Troi is as beautiful as it gets. But she's not wife material. And I bet she's not mother material either. And that's not a putdown. Some women, like many men, are so career driven that children truly just don't fit into the overall equation of their lives. They'd rather be hovering over spreadsheets and flow charts than boiling bottles and changing diapers. They're much happier engaging in deal-making conference calls than listening for cries, yelps, and mishaps through a baby monitor.

They've given new livelihood to an ever-expanding network of au-pairs, nannies, and caretakers who care for and ultimately

raise their kids so they can stay connected to their careers and focused on what really matters . . . the bottom line.

Many women, like men, know that children—as great as they
can be—are an interruption. If I'm reading this right, Troi is
about to hit me with a kid. And both of our lives, along with
Dawn's, will be forever interrupted.

12

A re you going to tell me what you're thinking?" Troi asked, turning toward me and placing her purse on top of the dashboard.

"What if I'm not ready for a kid right now?"

"Are you suggesting that I should delay the pregnancy until you get ready?" she asked.

"What if I never wanted kids?"

"Well it's not like *you're* having one," she reminded me. "Why do men always think that every woman who's about to have a baby wants to ruin their lives? What ever happened to women just wanting to be moms?"

"Court orders and child support happened," I quickly answered. "You say you don't want anything from me now, but after a couple of years of formula, diapers, and sleepless nights, you'll be like, 'Why doesn't *he* have to deal with this?'"

"And?" she said, unimpressed.

"And you'll talk to some lawyer and some girlfriend who'll tell you that child support isn't about you and me. It's about the kid. And then we'll be in court."

"But it is about the child," she remarked.

"No doubt," I agreed. "But when I don't have a say in this child being here, doesn't it strike you as odd that I'll have to deal with it for the rest of my life?"

"You had your say when we slept together," she said, forcefully.

"But I didn't sleep with you to make a baby," I told her. "You even said that you didn't want kids, so I just figured—"

"You figured you could just walk away from your responsibilities."

"So you're saying that because we had sex, I should have expected that you'd hit me with a kid?"

"Oh," she said, excited. "So now you're going the real man route."

"What's that supposed to mean?" I asked.

"It was just sex to you," she quickly said.

"I didn't say that."

"I don't even know why I let my guard down with you, Shawn," she told me. "Did I expect to get pregnant? Absolutely not," she admitted. "But I just expected better from you. I felt you might be the one man who would accept this or even embrace it and that you would be a real dad. I remember when you told me about your father and how you looked up to him," she went on. "And when I found out, I thought, hey, at least you were smart enough to get pregnant by a decent guy," she said, slowly shaking her head. "But you're just like everybody else."

Besides "I just want to be friends," "We have to talk," "That's it?" "Did you sleep with her?" And "Not tonight, I'm on," those are the worst words a woman can say to a man. "You're just like everybody else."

Guys spend a ton of time trying to convince women that they're different. And sadly, as time passes, it becomes clear that we're no different from the last guy she "let her guard down" for. We're as non-committal as the last guy who dumped her. We think that we're slick, when she knows that we're trifling. And, when she announces she's pregnant, we're like every other no-good guy. We think our lives are doomed. We blame it on her. And we're out faster than a Seinfeld sidekick sitcom.

I never expected any of this. And I know my mother is probably turning over in her grave because she has to be as disappointed as I am pissed. She demanded that I accept responsibility for my actions and that I understand the consequences associated with everything I do. Her warnings kept me clear of drugs, gangs, and violence. In my world, trouble wasn't even part of my vocabulary and drama was a class in school as opposed to a lifestyle. She didn't just have me walking the straight and narrow. Thanks to my mom, I was running it!

But where the heck was she when Troi popped her bra off and dangled her C cups in my face that night? Where was my mother when Troi did like the Staple Singers and said, "Let's Do It Again!"? And what holier-than-thou advice would she have when Troi drags me into court for a kid I didn't want in the first place?

"So now I'm like everybody else," I said, searching for a snappy comeback.

"I'm glad you agree."

"Check this, Troi," I said, quickly. "I'm not like every other guy, I just feel like you're keeping me out of a decision that's going to affect the rest of my life. You're right. We made love and it was great. But I didn't know I'd be reminded of it for eighteen years."

"So first you say we just had sex and now you're saying you were ready to forget about it," she pushed.

"I didn't say those things either," I stressed. "And if I did, I didn't say them like that. When this happens to other guys, you just say, 'I feel you, bro,' but you never think it's going to happen to you."

"I can't believe I'm hearing this!" she exclaimed. "What would you propose that I do, Shawn?"

"What about adoption?"

"Are you smoking crack?" she asked. "You think that I'm going to carry my baby for nine months and then sign it over so that some fiend like O.J. can adopt him?"

"So you're saying O.J. did it?" I quickly asked.

"Of course he did," she answered. "You think he didn't?"

"The jury didn't," I fired back.

"Well, let's just hope that we don't get the same jury when we have an insanity hearing," she said.

"For who?" I asked.

"For you, Shawn! Adoption," she huffed. "What would have happened to you if your mother put you up for adoption?"

"I wouldn't be sitting here on New Year's Day wondering why I'm about to become a father when I don't want to be a father," I replied.

"What do you have against kids?" she asked, upset.

"It's less a kid and more the situation."

"What's the problem?" she asked. "I'm not trying to tie you down. I'm a working girl, so I don't need your money. And we're both single, so it's not like anyone's in the way to cause any problems."

If we didn't already have a problem, we've got one now. Troi might not have anyone around, but I don't think Dawn exactly considers herself a nobody.

"It's not about people," I replied. "This is our problem."

"Mistake!" she exclaimed, flashing me "the hand," and then waving her forefinger. "My baby is not a problem."

"It's a problem right now," I told her. "But you know what? This is not worth arguing about."

"So now you're saying your son or daughter has no worth?"

"Why do you keep putting words in my mouth?"

"Because you clearly don't know what to say," she remarked.

She's right. I'm in the proverbial no-win zone. If Regis had led me to an unknown million-dollar question, I'd be without an answer and out of lifelines. *The Weakest Link*? I am the weakest link, and that mean British babe's saying, "Good-bye," so I can take a much deserved walk of shame. And if I was on *The Price Is Right* and Bob Barker invited me to "Come on down!" to play Plunk-It, I'd be plunked.

When I said it wasn't worth arguing about, what I really should have said was "Touché, you win." She has me by the balls and she knows it. No answer is the right one. Everything I say sounds stupider than the last stupid thing I said. And the reality I'm facing at this very moment is one that every man fears. I have absolutely no say. And I absolutely hate it.

The Troi I'm seeing now isn't even close to the Troi I saw just a few months back. She actually seems happy about being pregnant and I just don't get it. I can't figure out what her real angle is. Is it money? Is this her way of showing that she's in charge and that her word is what really counts? Or is she just trying to mess with my mind to see where I really stand?

"You're right, Shawn," she told me. "We shouldn't be arguing."

"Tell me about it," I said, restarting the engine. "Why don't we grab a bite and give this a rest?"

"We should celebrate," she suggested.

"Do you mean the New Year?" I asked, pulling away from McDonald's and back onto Central Avenue.

"No, silly," she answered, smiling. "We're about to be parents!"

"Whoopee," I sighed.

"Come on, Shawn," she said, reaching for my hand. "We're going to be D.C.'s newest power couple."

"I don't think the power couple thing is in the making," I told her.

"It was in the making when I was here in September. And after we eat, we'll have to head back to your place to seal the deal," she said, now stroking my hand. "In fact, we can actually skip breakfast and head back right now as far as I'm concerned."

"That's not a good idea," I said, crossing Benning Road and passing the flower and newspaper hackers who dominate the grassy median strip.

"Maybe you're right," she agreed. "We're both hungry, so we'll eat first and then head back."

This is one of those "by the mile" problems, because it seems to grow with every stoplight and with every mile we drive.

"I think I need to tell you something," I told her, thinking of Dawn.

"You're pregnant too?" she joked.

Which isn't funny. And I don't think *any* jokes about pregnancy and women carrying kids that men have no say in will ever make me laugh again, especially when the joke's on me. But my ringing phone and Dawn's cell number flashing on the caller ID is telling me that I really don't have anything to laugh about.

"Hello," I said, answering and immediately looking over at Troi.

"Is this formality bit something for the New Year?" Dawn asked.

"Pardon me?" I replied, concerned.

"Pardon who?" she asked, surprised. "I didn't even know you were familiar with the term." She laughed. "Did I just pass you?"

"What?!" I replied, instinctively stepping on the gas and hoping she was nowhere near me.

"Shawn!" Troi exclaimed, surprised.

"Who was that?" Dawn asked.

"Who was what?" I answered, hurrying to turn up the radio.

"I thought I heard a woman," Dawn told me.

"Oh that," I said, looking over at Troi, whose eyes were locked on me. "You mean the radio?"

"And someone just happened to say your name?"

"And you're calling me because?" I asked, hoping to quickly change the topic.

"Oh, yeah," she said, helping me to save face. "I'm headed over to the studio. BET wants to re-air last night's show, so we're going to look it over, repackage it, and maybe they'll run it tonight."

"So what you're really saying is that . . ."

"You got me," she admitted. "I'll be late."

"Again!" we both exclaimed.

"But I promise not to be too late and I'll make it worth the wait. See you tonight, sweetie," she said before hanging up.

"Well," Troi asked, her arms now crossed.

"What do you have a taste for?" I feebly asked.

"Who was that?" she asked, staring me down like I was in a line-up.

There's only one way to go with this. And though it's probably not going to work, it may buy me just a little time. Or it may bury me even more than I'm already buried.

Troi asked me who was on the line and I don't have an answer that will cut it. Like I said, the only thing that's going to work to-day is "Touché, you win." And when you're about to lose because the woman you're riding with is asking about the woman who just called there's only one answer that will work, and I'm about to use it.

I've replayed the question over in my head several times over and it only gets worse.

"Who was that?" she asked, obviously upset.

My answer might be as weak as an old man on Enfamil, but it's my answer and like any man who's been jammed, I'm sticking to it.

"Who was that?" I replied, worried. "You mean the radio?"

13

The only thing that's working about this morning is that Dawn is on her way to work, which means I can take Troi almost anywhere without getting caught. It's not like I'm sneaking around, but this is one of those delicate situations that women always jam men up on and it's one of the reasons—albeit one of the truly lamer reasons—why men cheat like they do.

You can be out with another woman on legitimate business, and if your lady's friend spots you, the speed-dial on her cell phone will be fast at work. Your lady, who most likely called you or two-wayed you hours ago, is waiting by the phone, hoping you'll call. Thinking it's you, she's excited when the phone rings and a smile jumps to her face. But that smile quickly fades to a frown and then a scowl because it's her friend with news of you and "some other woman."

The only problem is that nobody bothered to check who you were actually out with and why. Before the drinks arrive, your two-way goes off. When the salads hit the table, your cell is ringing like it's in Bat-phone crisis mode. And when the entrees arrive, your lady is showing up right along with them. She's demanding to know who the hoochie is and why you thought for one minute that you could cheat behind her back.

You waste time trying to explain and trying to introduce the hoochie as a business associate, but it doesn't fly. Your lady and her girlfriend have already determined that you're a no good two-timing man and they've nabbed you and tagged you as just another pathetic cheater. They don't know or even care that they've embarrassed themselves as much as they've embarrassed you, and that the contract you were hoping to deliver to your boss is all but blown. There's no "Way to go!" from the boss, no big, surprise bonus, and you won't even get dessert because both your girl *and* the business associate will stomp out in disgust.

Like any man, you reason that if you're going to catch all this grief, you might as well be cheating. At least that will make it worthy of the drama. So you vow that if you're ever out, you'll just be slicker and craftier and that you won't get caught. And you wisely steer clear of any store, club, or restaurant that may be frequented by your girl or her girls.

But unlike you, I'm a mope. And since I'm not cheating, we're pulling into a spot dead smack in front of the Waffle Shop. I guess it helps that I already know that Dawn is long gone and on her way to BET. But it doesn't help that thanks to last night's show, people recognize me . . . and they seem to know Troi.

"Hey, you're that guy," a man said, handing me a crumpled napkin. "You mind signing this? It's for my kid."

"Is this the one who's pregnant? You don't look pregnant, darling," his escort commented. "Must be on drugs," she whispered to her date.

"Did I miss something?" Troi asked, understandably confused.

"We'll get to that," I said, hurrying toward the front door of the Waffle Shop.

The Waffle Shop is a D.C. original, a 'round the clock, come-as-you-are-and-eat-what-you-can diner that serves up some of the best fare in the city. It's not your average greasy spoon . . . it's more like a greasy ladle. With its dusty chrome trim and smoked mirrored décor, which I'm sure was all the rage in the 1950s, you'd think you'd walked into the land that time forgot. But the unmistakable aroma of sugary, malted waffles and fresh country-style sausage and bacon quickly affirm that you're in one of those rare places that puts tasty food over contrived ambiance every day of the week.

What Troi and other tourists quite possibly see as a trendy and retro eatery, we in D.C. see as just plain old. And old isn't helping me now, because I need something new, as in a "new" excuse to get out of here. Because like the guy who just asked me for my autograph out on the sidewalk, I've been recognized again.

"Hey, look, it's Shawn! We're over here!"

I can't play it off because she's waving like she was a flag girl in the final battle of the bands scene in *Drum Line*. And since we're no longer in the car, the tried and true "You mean on the radio?" line probably won't work either. It also is not helping that Troi has an incredible memory . . . but then again, when it comes to other women, women always do.

"Isn't that your friend Kelly?" Troi asked, now waving back.

"You mean on the radio?" I instinctively answered.

This couldn't be worse.

I figured that when Dawn left, everyone left with her, especially since she was treating! But I couldn't have been more off base. Legs and Bugs are gone, which actually works in my favor. But Donnie and Melba are still here. Swipe and the cable-pulling lady are still coupled up. Alan still appears to be lost in space. And Kelly, who has never said anything even remotely decent about Troi, is looking like she's ready to pounce on her the way Lionel Richie's wife jumped on his mistress.

"Did you know they were here?" Troi asked, as we headed in their direction.

Do you think we'd be here if I did? I thought.

"So you must be Troi," Melba said, looking her over. "That skirt is off the hook, girlfriend," she said, slapping her five. "And you'd better not be looking, Donnie."

"Have you lost your f*cking mind?" Donnie asked, pulling me aside. "This is some of that you'se about to get your ass kicked, her ass kicked and our asses kicked for just being up in here with you type sh*t," he remarked.

"Damn, she's fine!" Swipe observed, reaching to shake Troi's hand.

"Are you sure you're pregnant?" Alan asked, also checking her out.

"Hello, Troi," Kelly muttered, unimpressed.

"So I guess you guys are about to leave," I said, hoping they'd get the hint.

"Uh, yeah," Donnie remarked.

"We were just about to do that," Melba answered, reaching for her coat.

"I think I might have to do my rounds," Alan said, pulling out his Palm Pilot.

"I ain't going no motherf*cking where!" Swipe insisted. "With your fine ass up in here," he added, nodding his head and winking at Troi.

With that, the cable-pulling lady quickly left.

"What?" Swipe asked, hurrying to catch up. "I was just bull-sh*ting!" He turned back to Troi. "She ain't as fine as you. She is one fine piece of black ass, playa!" he said to me, following his date out the door. "If sh*t don't work out with him, give me a holla! Sh*t, you can just holla for the sake of hollering!" he yelled back.

Donnie and Melba rolled.

Alan is putting on his coat.

But Kelly . . . she's not moving.

"I think our friends would like a little time alone," Alan whispered, gently grabbing Kelly's arm.

"'Friends' is plural and that presupposes that there is more than one friend here," Kelly said, slowly wrapping a beautiful brown scarf around her neck.

"What do you have a taste for?" I asked Troi, showing her a menu.

"Since she's *supposedly* eating for two, I'm sure this will help foot the bill," Kelly said, handing me a credit card. "This is D-a-w-n-'s card. She just treated us to breakfast. Dawn," she said pointedly, "is my friend."

Allen cut in before Kelly could continue. "Well, Shawn, Troi, the hash browns are great. We'll be going now, so enjoy your meal and tell Dawn next time, breakfast is on us."

This is worse than being whacked on *The Sopranos* and then being buried on *Six Feet Under.*

"I'll make sure to pass that along, big Al," I answered, frustrated.

He and Kelly turned to leave, but not before Kelly took another long look, which more closely resembled a Mike Tyson stare down.

"This should be an interesting breakfast," Troi commented, scanning the menu. "Last time we were here, I had eggs and the driest dry toast I've ever had in my life. I think I'll try a waffle this time. And didn't he say the hash browns were good too?"

What is she up to? I thought, worried. *Kelly practically just blew her out of the water and she's asking about hash browns?*

"Have you ever had their corned beef hash?" she asked, flipping the menu over.

"Are you okay?" I asked, ready to deal with the fallout from Kelly's obvious swipes.

"I can't decide," she answered.

"If you're okay or not?"

"No, silly. Bacon, sausage, or both?" she asked, pointing at the "Specials" section.

"I'd try the sausage," I suggested. "The patties are better than the links."

"Who's Dawn?" she asked, quickly turning toward me.

"Kelly's friend?" I uneasily replied.

"I'm thinking she must be your friend too," she said. "Especially since Ms. Thing left her credit card with you."

"That's . . . a good point," I told her.

"Is she the couscous lady?" she playfully asked.

"That's Kelly," I answered. "Dawn is the tablecloth lady."

"She has good taste."

"That's what she told me."

"So let me guess," Troi said. "You had a little New Year's Eve get together and Kelly and her good friend D-a-w-n stopped through."

"That's a good guess," I remarked.

"Kelly brought couscous, D-a-w-n showed-up with a festive tablecloth, and since the after-party clearly was here, D-a-w-n and her date left early."

"I don't think it worked exactly like that," I said, waving down a waitress.

"So how did it work?"

"You remember when you asked who called when we were riding over?" I asked.

"You mean the lady on the radio?" she replied.

"Right," I answered, handing our menus to the waitress. "She was the lady on the radio."

"She was the lady on the TV too!" the waitress said, deliberately crossing her arms. "Don't even waste your time on him, honey," she warned Troi. "He already messed over Dawn and if that ain't enough, he has the nerve to have some floozy pregnant. What do you want to eat anyway, Mr. no good can't be trusted—she shoulda dropped you before the commercial—but she's too nice?"

"I'll have eggs over easy."

"And you?" she asked, turning toward Troi.

"Do you have anything in the "special" section that's fit for a floozy?" Troi asked.

"Oh my God!" the waitress squealed, surprised. "You're the . . . "

"floozy," I finished for her.

"But . . . she doesn't look . . . " the waitress started.

"Pregnant?" Troi jumped in. "Most of us don't. It's a floozy thing," she whispered.

The waitress looked at Troi, surprised, and now she's looking at me. What am I supposed to do? She may see me as a jerk and Troi as a floozy, but *she's* the one who went on record with it. And then she'll still expect a tip.

"Why don't you be a good girl and bring the floozy a nice waffle, some sausages, and a side of corned beef hash," Troi requested. "And when we're done eating, make sure I get to see the manager," she added, smiling. "Got that sweetheart?"

The waitress walked toward the long, sizzling grill like she was marching away from a marine drill sergeant, so I gathered that "sweetheart" got it. But something tells me she didn't get it nearly as bad as I'm about to.

"So let's get down to business here, Shawn," Troi said, refocusing her energies on me. "Who the hell is D-a-w-n?"

"Kelly's friend?" I answered.

"Kelly's *friend* wouldn't just leave a three-hundred-plus-dollar tablecloth at your place if there weren't a connection. And Kelly wouldn't have given you her *friend's* credit card if she didn't know you'd be seeing her soon. So I ask again, Shawn Wayne, exactly who is Dawn?"

"Kelly's friend" isn't working any more than "the lady on the radio." But why is this a problem? D-a-w-n, as Troi calls her, is my woman and I'm as happy as I am proud of her and our relationship. I have absolutely nothing to lose by telling Troi that I've met my soul mate and that she'll see me through raising a kid that even I don't want to have. I don't know if Troi really meant what she said about being the jealous type, but it doesn't matter. If she's jealous, that's *her* problem and she'll have to deal with it. Though Troi and I "made love"—again, *her* interpretation—we didn't have, never had, and never will have a relationship.

I love Dawn and Troi needs to know that, before the food gets here in case it pisses her off and she wants to throw something.

"Dawn is my girlfriend," I blurted out.

"How quaint," Troi said, smiling. "Shawn has a girlfriend. And his other girlfriend is pregnant."

"What other girlfriend?"

"Me," she answered, carefully sipping her coffee. "The floozy."

"One eggs over easy and one waffle platter," said the waitress, sliding our plates in front of us.

"Thanks," I said, looking up. "You're not our waitress, are you?" I asked.

"She's on, and she left," our new waitress said, providing much more information than we really needed. "So let's get things straight before I do a whole lot of walking. You look like one of those cheap-style Value City–buying type negroes," she remarked, pointing at me. "And I don't play that cheap crap, so if you're not tipping *at least* fifteen percent, you can just give them plates back and you can fantasize about those pictures on the menus."

"I'm thinking there's a manager here," I shot back.

"This ain't IHOP so we don't do the manager thing," the waitress spat out. "So if I show up with some extra napkins or some syrup or something, remember, twenty percent."

"You just said fifteen," I reminded her.

"That was before you asked for a manager."

"I didn't come here to be anybody's floozy, so you need to straighten things out," Troi remarked, refocusing us on our real dilemma.

"I think things are pretty straight," I told her. "Dawn already knows—"

"I think not," she interrupted. "Here's how it works, Shawn."

"Look, if you're not feeling the twenty-five percent tip, I'm betting you won't be feeling the free refills on the coffee this morning," the new waitress commented.

"Is D-a-w-n pregnant?" Troi asked.

"No," I quickly answered.

"Well, I am, so guess who you're going to be with?" she inquired.

"Well?" the waitress added.

"You?" I asked, worried.

"You damn right!" Troi and the waitress exclaimed, slapping each other five.

"Now that deserves a free refill *and* some toast," the waitress told Troi. "How do you like your liver pudding, honey? Because what you just did definitely deserves some liver pudding. Take that fool for everything you can get. Score one for the sistahs!"

I'm not scoring anything for anybody. But I knew this was coming. Troi didn't need anything from me, except me. She doesn't want my money, may not be interested in child support, and probably isn't concerned with visitation. If I'm reading this right, she wants me. And not just *me* me. She's expecting a relationship.

"I will not be a single mom," she insisted.

"But I'm in a relationship," I reminded her. "I have her credit card. Her tablecloth is at my house."

"That's really cute, Shawn," she said, cutting into her waffle. "But while her tablecloth is covering your stove, you have a baby in the oven right here," she added, patting her flat tummy. "I'm sure your little Dawn is a wonderful woman, but I don't think another woman really fits into this equation."

"We don't have an equation," I countered.

"But we do have a baby on the way," she reminded me.

"And you have some scrapple too," the waitress chimed in. "You just keep doing your thing. And I'll put it on *his* tab."

"Look, Troi," I said. "I'm not about to leave Dawn."

"I'm not asking you to leave your little D-a-w-n or whatever her name is," she told me. "But I know you're a decent guy. It's not like I want you, God knows I don't want you, Shawn. We had a *fling*," she asserted. "But I'm not going to have a baby with a man that's attached to some other woman and her fricking tablecloth." She prepared to stand.

"If you don't want me, why did you just call yourself my girlfriend?"

"I was kidding, Shawn," she told me. "Am I surprised that you've already moved on? Yes. But please don't confuse things. This isn't about you, me, or D-a-w-n. It's about *our* child!"

"Why do I know there's another part to this?" I asked.

"Like I said," she went on, putting on her coat. "At heart, I know you're decent. And I know you'll do the right thing."

"He better do the right thing," the waitress blurted out. "Because I'm thinking he's already in the thirty-percent tip zone."

"Why don't you tell D-a-w-n that if things don't change soon, you'll be a father without a baby?" Troi calmly stated.

"What?" I asked, concerned.

"Tell your little girlfriend that you'll never see your baby or be a part of your son's or daughter's life if she doesn't get out of the way," she warned.

"First of all, Dawn isn't in the way of anything," I said. "And second, if you want to threaten me you can do better than that. You're going to keep me from a kid I never asked for in the first place? Can I get that in writing?"

"You can get this *check* in writing," the waitress interrupted, sliding me a grease-stained sheet of yellow paper.

"As they say, the ball is in your court, Shawn," Troi said, walking away. "You know how to reach me."

"I don't want to reach you," I muttered, staring at the check.

"Well you can *reach* into your pocket for my tip," the waitress quickly stated. "Thirty-five percent, no less."

She's going to keep me from a baby that I don't even want? I thought, handing the waitress my check card. Is this a good thing? Or am I missing something?

The Seven Different Types of Dads

Daddy Do Little . . . a.k.a., "Invis-a-Dad" a.k.a., "Deadbeat Dad"

Children aren't children to Daddy Do Little, they're "situations." So, Daddy Do Little doesn't pay child support, doesn't call or visit, and basically doesn't care about the kids he helped to create. In his mixed-up universe, Daddy Do Little doesn't owe his kids anything. Why? 1. All he did was have sex with his kid's "no-good" momma. 2. Everybody knows that sex is about pleasure. 3. There's absolutely *nothing* pleasurable about kids who do little but take up time and money. Why should Daddy Do Little pay child support and thereby help purchase his baby's momma's new house when he's still stuck in *his* momma's house? Why should he call and have to put up with "that tramp who tried to trap him?" And why would that same woman expect him to take care of *her* kids, when she *knew* he wasn't involved in the lives of the children he'd fathered long before hers? Daddy Do Little will have the audacity to show up at graduations and weddings where he'll falsely take credit for being a concerned, involved, and supportive parent. And sadly, Daddy Do Little's kids often fall for it, hook, line, and sinker. Ultimately, though, reality sets in and his kids see Daddy Do Little for what he really is—a *Daddy Do Nothing . . .* who *is* nothing.

If you're a guy, New Year's Day is really about one thing . . . football!

It's not about examining the mistakes of the past year or about preparing and planning the coming year, and it certainly isn't about figuring out how to deal with a girlfriend who wants kids or a non-girlfriend who claims to have one on the way. It's not about being a dad, not wanting to be a dad, or considering the joys and pain of potential fatherhood.

Women don't like hearing it, but to guys, New Year's Day has never been and will never be about bonding with family or eating nauseating foods like collard greens and black-eyed peas that are supposed to guarantee prosperity, good times, and cold, hard cash but actually do little more than send you to the bathroom. New Year's Day 3000, 4000, and 5000 won't be about any of that.

The goal is as simple now as it always will be and there's exactly one way to get there—a full-function remote with antenna switching capabilities for both digital cable and DirecTV.

The New Year's Day formula is straightforward. It's about kicking back, talking crap with your boys, and watching every stinking bowl game that TV executives can cram down your throat.

Despite the fact that the day started somewhere between the toilet and the sewer, this particular New Year's Day will be no different for me. And I'm certain Donnie, who just arrived, feels the same exact way.

"You got some drama with you, son," Donnie remarked. "What were you thinking when you paraded Troi up in the waffle joint?"

"I was thinking that she was hungry and that I could use a coupon I downloaded from their website," I answered.

"No, you didn't?!" he said, surprised. "You tried to use a coupon with Miss Troi? You don't use no coupons with somebody as fine as her."

"First of all, it's New Year's," I reminded him. "So why are we talking about her anyway?"

"Because this time next year your sorry ass is gonna be on daddy status," he said, laughing.

"Try Daddy Dearest," I mumbled.

"So what did she hit you with?" he asked, sounding almost excited.

"She's pregnant, I'm the father, and she's keeping it," I confessed.

"You hit the trifecta, dawg!" he exclaimed.

"Did you bring any chips?" I asked, wanting to change the topic.

"Why I gotta bring chips up in your place?" he asked. "If we was at my spot, I wouldn't be asking you about no chips."

"Your place is a rehab," I reminded him.

"So?" he said, not missing a beat. "We got TVs and snacks just like you."

"And don't forget the blood test kits and urine cups," I said, laughing. "Which, by the way, leads me to the question of the year."

"How you gonna have a question of the year when the year just started?" he asked, searching the refrigerator. "You shoulda been hitting *Troi* with some question of the year sh★t."

"Are you trying to get with her?" I asked, scanning channels to find some sports.

"With who?" he asked, placing bowls on the kitchen counter.

"With Troi," I answered. "Because you keep bringing her up, and I'm not trying to hear about her on New Year's Day when we're supposed to be watching football."

"So what's a brother trying to talk about?" he asked, dumping a bag of Doritos into a shiny, silver bowl.

"Tell me the deal," I quickly stated.

"You tell me the deal," he shot back. "You been talking in riddles since I got here kid," he observed. "What the f★ck is up with you?"

"That's exactly what I'm talking about," I quickly said.

"There's something wrong with you, son."

"I guess you would say that," I replied, still changing channels. "But what's the deal with you and Melba? I'm trying to figure out what's up with the happy little couple."

"We're just doing our thing," he answered, plopping down on the couch. "She loves a brother natural style and a brother definitely digs her."

"But how did it get like this?" I asked, reaching in his bowl of Doritos. "I remember when you met her and you said she was alright, but I didn't think you'd be doing a love thing. I mean, what do you see in her, anyway?"

"She's my queen," he asserted.

"And let me guess," I interrupted. "You're her king."

"Think about how we met," he said, removing his shoes. "She had just got to the rehab and they assigned her to my caseload. I saw something in a sister and told her that the only thing holding her back was that she had no ambition."

"So you're saying she should have showed up at the rehab with a resume and some business cards?" I asked, laughing.

"Sister girl had been so strung out for so long that she basically had stopped doing the real living thing."

"Is that different from the *fake* living thing?"

"Any time you chasing that rock or priming your veins, it's fake," he warned. "And she was so bad off, queen had gave up on life."

"So you're saying she was suicidal?"

"Ain't nothing more suicidal than drugs," he said, looking me in the eye. "Except a hottie that says she's on the pregnant side. But sister girl wasn't doing nothing but scoring dope, sleeping, and getting high some more."

"So knowing that she was living the autobiography of *you*, Mr. Donnie Black, why did you want to get with her?" I asked.

"Because she chose me."

"So that's all it takes? 'I want you, Donnie,' " I said, mocking Melba. "Regardless of where your head is, all a sister has to do is say she's interested?"

"I don't have TV star chicks like Dawn and model freak types like Troi knocking down my door," he remarked.

"Oh," I quickly stated. "You're settling because you don't think you can do any better."

"Maybe I don't want to do no better," he admitted. "What you don't understand is that for a brother like me, chicks add up to one thing."

"I'm listening."

"Stress," he fired back. "If I'm swinging with a high-class mommie, she's gonna expect me to carry it like them Joe Poindexter college types."

"I'm still listening," I told him.

"And then she's gonna want me to have some serious-type sh*t to talk about and she's gonna try to sweat me to have a *wardrobe* instead of some clothes," he added. "And because all I'm really trying to do is pop the strings, I'm out here trying to be some sh*t that I ain't and the next thing I know, I'm on a Ike Turner stress tip."

"So you're saying that when you date nice women you beat them?"

"What I'm saying is that I lose it and when I get stressed, I get high. And I ain't met no woman *yet* that's worth getting high," he told me.

"There's a level somewhere where this makes sense," I admitted. "But that still doesn't explain Melba."

"First of all, my queen don't need no explaining," he asserted. "The bottom line is that she's into me because I bring her life balance. We've walked that mile in the same shoes–type sh*t and she respects me and looks up to me. She told me I was her king and that all she wanted was to make me happy, because that would keep her happy and that she don't do no drugs when she's happy, so we're hitched."

"So the basis for your relationship is that you keep each other from getting high," I commented. "Except for last night, which was a celebration, so I guess that doesn't count," I added dryly.

"That and the fact that she's into threesomes!" he exclaimed.

She's into threesomes? No wonder he's so into her. I don't know a guy who doesn't fantasize about being with his woman and another woman. The topic comes up in almost every relationship, but because guys are essentially wimps with duct tape–bound testicles, we pretend that we were merely trying to gauge where our mate stands on the subject.

If your lady asks you if you are interested in a ménage-à-trois, you kick on the afterburners to lie and would sheepishly say no. But if you ask *her* about a threesome and she says yes,—and actually means it—you'd be putting together the pieces that night. You wouldn't wait until the next day so that she could change her mind, you'd jump on it before her thong got cold.

But it almost never happens that way. If you were on *Family Feud* and Richard Kern said, "What's the number one thing a woman won't accept in a sexual relationship?" the survey would say, "Threesomes!"

At some point almost every guy has tried to introduce the topic, but we always seem to fail. Your girlfriend tells you a threesome is the one thing she can't and won't deal with, which you understand, until she tells you she can't and won't deal with your next sexual request or fantasy. Our only mistake is that we buy it.

Instead of saying, "I've always wanted to try this and it's not going away," we say, "You're the only woman I *ever* want to be with. I just wanted to see how you felt about it."

And we do this because? Because woman absolutely freak when guys mention threesomes. When guys say, "I'm interested in a threesome," what women hear is, "I'm not even slightly satisfied with you, your body, or our ridiculously boring sex life, so to spice things up, I'd like to sleep with a woman with implants and a jaw like a Hoover vacuum cleaner and oh, yeah, why don't you join in?"

They're not hearing that we want to explore a long-forbidden taboo or that we want to see what Caligula and his Roman cronies saw when they first defined "smorgasbord" as it relates to sex. They don't understand that we want to act out what we've seen in cheap porno flicks for years. And they can't seem to grasp that we're not looking for a relationship outside of the relationship we're already in.

We don't want a threesome so that we can introduce another woman and her problems into our already overly complicated love lives. We don't want some other woman that we have to call, pretend to listen to, and hang out with, when we already don't halfway want to hang out with the woman we're with.

Women take the notion of threesomes as the ultimate insult. If you told your lady that she's a disgusting, nauseating pig whose only real value to humankind is that her waste can be used as sub-urban garden compost, she'd be pissed. But if you added to that statement "We should try a threesome," she'd totally lose it. She'd throw something at you, she'd dig her nails into your forearm, and she'd probably put a vice grip on your love wand to remind you that it's hers and hers alone.

But she wouldn't take as much offense with the nauseating

pig part of the statement because that has nothing to do with an-other woman. On the surface, it doesn't challenge her sexuality and doesn't put her at odds with her own sense of security and monogamy. If she's a pig, she already knows it anyway, so that doesn't actually threaten her. But the fact that you're fantasizing about or even thinking about another woman scares her to death.

Some women don't take it as such an insult and hit you with the proverbial "I'll allow another woman into our bed if you do the same with another man first." This is the ultimate bluff and a virtual impossibility because the only thing a woman fears even more than her man in bed with another woman is her man in bed with another man. If guys called that bluff, they'd possibly luck into a threesome and the fun that comes with it.

But how did Donnie pull it off?

"Check this, Shawn," he said, smiling broadly. "For my birthday, she told me she was going to give me what every man wanted."

"She had courtside season tickets to see Maryland play in their new arena?" I quickly asked.

"No, you poot-butt fool," he answered. "Shorty booked a room over to the Red Roof Inn around the corner and rolled through with some hottie that had a tongue as quick as a snake's."

"So she didn't have the tickets?"

"Are you f*cking nuts?" he asked. "All the tickets in the world wouldn't have been better than that night. Man, we was doing stuff that I didn't think happened in real life. And then she was like, this is how she rolls and I'd better get used to it."

"What's to get used to?" I asked, surprised.

"You know how hard it is to make one woman reach a cli-max?" he asked.

I just gave him a sympathetic look.

"Well, imagine how crazy it is when you're trying to make it happen with two!"

I couldn't help but laugh.

"I know you're not trying to hear this, son," Donnie said, turning serious. "But you got some sh★t to deal with."

"That's the first time I've heard a baby described like that," I answered.

"I'm talking about the situation," he replied. "Troi looks even better while she's carrying a load than she did when she wasn't. And I ain't buying what Dawn's selling."

"What are you talking about?" I asked.

"She might think she can deal with it, but once she sees how fine Troi is, she's gonna blow her stack."

"Why?" I asked. "Dawn is comfortable with who she is, plus she's around beautiful women all the time, so she won't be threatened by Troi."

"Her being around fine-ass chicks ain't got squat to do with you having a bambino with a hot body who should be doing cover shots for Victoria's Secret," he remarked. "But I'm gonna let you do the fantasy thing. I just want to know how this sh★t's hitting you."

"Hard," I confessed. "Real hard."

"How hard?"

"You remember how my father used to give us those manhood lessons?"

"Pops would sit us down like we was being interrogated over to the precinct," Donnie joked.

"He was interviewing us," I reminded him.

"Same thing," he shot back.

"That meant something to me," I told him. "It made me want

to be like him and to accept responsibility. But I didn't count on anything like this. It's like it's happening at the worst possible time. I've played it out a million times and I hate to say it, but I don't want a kid."

"So tell her and then tell her to roll her ass back to Chi-town," he said.

"She's not going for that," I replied, worried. "Plus, I keep thinking about my parents and how much they meant to me. And even though I don't want a kid, how can I just abandon it?"

"You ain't abandoning nothing," he told me. "The kid will have the finest mother in D.C., so some fool is gonna jump up and play daddy just to get to her. And then, bam!" he yelled. "Your frail ass is off the hook."

"But how is that fair to the kid?" I asked, nervously changing channels. "It's not like he asked to come here."

"It's a boy?" he asked, excited.

"How should I know?"

"Well if it's a little knucklehead, you can at least take him to the gym and to some strip joints," he replied.

"Now who's nuts?" I inquired. "You don't take a kid to a strip club."

"The hell you don't!" he fired back. "If I had a youngin, I'd have his little ass in a booty house with the quickness."

"What are you talking about?" I asked, not really wanting to know.

"Think about it, Shawn," he said. "When Troi pops out a kid, what's the first thing the little crumb snatcher's gonna try to do?"

"Cry?"

"And why will his sorry little behind be wailing like he just had a ass whipping?"

"Because he just had one?" I asked. "You know how the doctor slaps them—"

"Can that," he interrupted. "He's blowing his lungs up because the only thing he can think about is getting at Troi's boobs. And if you think about it, he's gonna spend the rest of his life trying to get with every poked-out rack of boobs he can get a hold of."

"Do you realize you just made a case for at-birth adoption?" I asked, smiling.

"You do your thing and I'ma do mine," he told me. "But you better find out what your thing is."

"I saw this show on TV the other night and it was talking about how bad black fathers were," I said, almost nodding my head in agreement.

"So?" he huffed.

"So?" I asked, surprised. "So, what about black fatherhood and the fact that so many of our kids are growing up without fathers or male role models?"

"What about it?" he asked, casually downing some chips.

"Do I want to be a statistic?" I asked. "Shouldn't I want more than that for my own child?"

"Why should you?" he inquired, reaching for a soda. "You didn't ask for no kids."

"And she did?"

"Who's the one who's pregnant and who had to sprint to D.C. to tell it?" he reasoned. "Let *her* ass have *her* kid. Why should you suffer because she's trying to be one of those supermoms?"

"Why should the kid suffer?" I asked, looking him in the eye.

His silence says that he's as uncomfortable with the answer as I am. But if I know Donnie, it won't last long.

"So now you're ready to have a kid because of some sh*t you

saw on TV?" he asked. "Why didn't your stupid ass just change the channel?"

"I did," I said, embarrassed. "But I can't change the channel on this, D. This is real," I reminded him, before pausing. "You remember the first rule of those manhood lessons?"

"Yeah," he said, laughing. "Get the hell up out the room before your old man could get too serious!"

"I'm serious," I told him.

"So was he," he joked.

"The day that you'll know you're a man . . . " I began.

"Is the day you'll meet your responsibilities head f*cking on," Donnie finished for me.

"He didn't say it like that," I said, slowly shaking my head.

"He would have if he knew you was going through this sh*t," he observed.

Maybe he's right. But does it matter? Like Troi, and my father in his own heaven-sent way, Donnie had done his part to ruin my day.

On the first day of the year, when life is supposed to be about marching bands, cheerleaders, and touchdowns, I've been blitzed, blind-sided, and sacked. And on a day where my concerns should be targeted on making this year even bigger and better than the last, my mind is locked on one question . . . and it scares me even more than the thought of manhood lesson number one.

I asked it of myself earlier and like many guys who either don't deal with the situation or don't know how to deal with it, the real dilemma rests not in the answer, but rather, with the question. Why should the kid suffer?

Why?

W omen.
I don't know that God created anything better. When
I think that the greatest, strongest, and most complete person I
ever knew was a woman—my mother—it says to me that women
are everything that men aren't.

Where men are closed and deceptive, women are open, honest, and revealing. While guys are "wham, bam, thank you,
ma'am," women are playful, sexy, and romantic. And when men
are lost, befuddled, and downright confused like I am at this moment, women are bright, focused, and resourceful.

God definitely created women because he had the wisdom to
know that men needed a smarter, kinder, and much gentler better
half. He knew that men would make a mess of things and that
women would clean it all up. He knew that men would be stub-
born, while our counterparts would be understanding. And he ab-

solutely knew that children needed mothers because no-account fathers would feel that kids represent the ultimate interruption.

We need women more than we'll ever understand, acknowledge, or admit to. Which begs the question . . . If women are so great, how can they so easily screw everything up?

You give them a New Year, and they can make you wish it was the year you left behind. You give them a gift out of the blue and they'll swear you were cheating. You give them the remote and they'll have you watching some tear-jerking chick flick or something that even the executives at Lifetime would pass on. We can't live with them and wouldn't *dare* live without them.

And something tells me that attached to the other end of my doorbell is a set of slender, feminine fingers that will have a hand in further ruining my day and my new year.

"Who the heck is that?" I asked, looking down at my watch to see it was almost noon and time for today's first kickoff.

"Don't answer that sh*t, son," Donnie warned.

"Did you invite somebody?" I asked, still ignoring the ringing bell. "I hope you didn't tell Melba it was okay to drop through."

"I know the deal, kid," he answered. "No chicks, female types, and no damn women who can screw sh*t up because they don't know jack about football."

"So who do you think it is?" I asked, not concerning myself with the loud knock that replaced the doorbell.

"I hope it's not my parole officer," Donnie said, worried. "You'd better answer that sh*t, 'cause I don't need him to think I'm ducking him."

"Will you ever be off parole?" I asked, standing to walk to the door.

"I hope the hell not," he quickly stated, now commandeering

the remote. "Because if I'm off parole that means that they gave my sorry ass some time and sent me to the pen."

That's a heck of a way to look at it, but he's right.

Though I'm expecting the worst, I'm answering the door. Maybe it's Ed McMahon with my Publisher's Clearinghouse sweepstakes prize. With my luck, I'll win a subscription to *No-Good Parents* magazine. Or it could be Pizza Hut, telling me I'm their millionth customer and that I'm getting free breadsticks for life. But with the way things are going for me, I'll get stuck with the cost of marinara sauce and delivery charges for life.

Or maybe it's Troi, Dawn, or worse, both of them. Troi will demand that I make a choice, as will Dawn. They'll have their arms crossed, and their heads will be bobbing and weaving more than Suge Knight on the stand.

Troi will probably turn on the tears and Dawn will be wearing her "I didn't sign-up for this crap" look and things will go from bad to worse to ridiculously worse in a flash. In a matter of moments I'll go from good boyfriend to bad boyfriend to ex-boyfriend to father-in-the-making to father-on-the-fringes to father-on-the-run. And the worst part is that regardless of what I do or say, it will be wrong. I'm in a completely no-win, can't-win, and as Donnie would say, "Ain't gonna win type of sh*t situation."

I feel like I'm on another planet, where women run everything. What am I talking about? That's earth. But this feels different.

Maybe I'm in space or in another world where things are truly as bad and as desperate as they appear. I may not want the kid to suffer, but that doesn't mean I want to be a dad. And is that so wrong? Shouldn't fatherhood be a choice as much as motherhood is? Shouldn't I and every guy who's been stuck in this situation have a say in any, if not all, of this? And why can't I make sense of it?

I wish that I could wish all of this away. I wish it were a nightmare that I could wake up from in a cold sweat. I'd even take a Wizard of Oz move right about now. I'd just close my eyes, tap the heels of my Nikes, and repeat that famous line, "There's no place like home . . . there's no place like home."

"You are home."

"I . . . what?" I said, in a daze.

"Are you going to invite me in, or would you prefer to daydream a little longer?" she asked.

"What are you doing here?" I asked, surprised.

"Now that's the nicest greeting I've had this year," she said, brushing me aside and forcing her way in. "Are you always so gracious on New Year's? Or is this part of the Troi effect?"

"What the hell is she doing here?" Donnie asked.

"Your parole officer couldn't make it, so I volunteered," she shot back.

We may as well accept it. When Donnie's around and Kelly attacks, she's officially "in the house."

"Do you know what today is?" I asked, hurrying to stand in front of her.

"It's the day that you're going to get out of my way so that we can talk," she insisted.

"Y'all ain't talking about sh★t," Donnie told her.

"Y'all?" she said, looking upset. "Can it really be that hard to say, 'you all'?"

"You f★cking all ain't talking about a motherf★cking thing," he said, sitting up. "This is New Year's."

"And the only thing we're talking about is football," I told her. "And women and football don't mix."

"That's so cute," she countered. "So how do you explain those people with the *Extreme Makeover* silicone chests and the mini skirts?" she asked, eyeing the remote.

"You don't have no skirt and no pom-pom," Donnie told her.

"And you don't have a helmet and those shoulder thingies," she answered, grabbing the remote and quickly turning to The Learning Channel. "They're having a *Trading Spaces* marathon."

"I wish we was trading f★cking spaces," Donnie grumbled.

"We're not watching any interior design shows," I insisted.

"Am I staying?" she asked.

"Hell, no!" Donnie exclaimed.

"Look at those drapes," she replied, ignoring him and staring at the TV. "They're hideous."

"I don't think they're so bad," I told her.

"They look okay to me," Donnie joined in. "If I was doing my own spot, I'd roll with those."

"You would," Kelly answered.

"What's wrong with them?" I asked. "What would fit better in that room?"

"You could probably slap some of them Next Day Blind joints up in there," Donnie suggested.

"I don't think that would work," I said. "You can go a little more dressy with the drapes."

"But you don't necessarily want to do that dressy sh★t," Donnie told me. "It's better to dress *down*, so you can dress up on the accessory tip."

"You're bugging," I told him. "Why would you dress up with

accessories when you can just as easily rely on your primary pieces?"

"Both of you are crazy," Kelly interrupted. "I definitely didn't expect this." She changed the channel.

"What are you doing?" I quickly asked.

"Yeah," Donnie said, jumping in. "This is the part when the other couple's supposed to come back and be pissed off 'cause they f'd-up their spot."

"Whatever happened to cheerleaders and football?" Kelly asked.

"We watch that sh*t every year," Donnie remarked.

"Plus, we just want to see what happens," I admitted. "Then we can catch the games."

"What do you suppose *Troi* is watching?" Kelly asked, smiling.

"Her two-way, to see what her next step is," Donnie said, again slumping back into his chair.

"What next step?" I asked, concerned.

"The one where her lawyer says to take you for everything you're worth," Kelly reasoned.

"Or the one where the real father checks to see if she reeled you in," Donnie joked.

"What is it about Troi that makes you give her such a bad rap?" I asked Kelly.

"Besides the fact that she doesn't care about you, *and* that her pregnancy is even more planned than a mob hit, *and* that she'll try to ruin you and Dawn?" she asked sarcastically. "Nothing."

"None of that's true," I told her.

"The hell it ain't," Donnie said, laughing. "And now you're ready to pony up and play daddy-o," he added.

"Did I miss something?" Kelly asked.

"Prince Charmington here was looking at some TV crap, so now he wants to keep the world safe for fatherless kids."

"That's a good thing, Shawn," Kelly said. "Especially since there exists this ugly reality that black children are suffering from a lack of fathers or even positive males in their lives, for that matter."

"Now that's some media conspiracy, propaganda that George W. and the Republicans put out there type of sh*t," Donnie quickly replied.

"I think not," Kelly countered. "Just look at the facts. Four out of six black kids are living without day-to-day, week-to-week, and even year-to-year contact with their fathers. And the worst part of it is that many of them are living in abject poverty. They wake up each day not knowing where their next meal will come from or how they'll even make it through the morning," she went on. "It's not propaganda to say that black children need their fathers and that black fathers owe it to their kids to step up to the plate."

"How in the hell are we supposed to step up to some motherf*cking plate when we don't have no choice in what's being served up at the table?" Donnie remarked. "Troi went and got her ass knocked up and now the rest of his life is supposed to be f*cked up and he don't have no say in it?" he asked, angrily pointing at me.

"He *did* have a say and he made the wrong say," Kelly answered. "I'm happy that Shawn *at least* is going to meet his responsibilities because there's not a black man anywhere who can afford to let another child go astray."

"You can cancel that," Donnie charged. "She's gonna hit his ass up for some bullsh*t-ass child support and then she's gonna tell his sorry ass that he don't have a motherf*cking say in a motherf*cking thing. All the stepping up that you bullsh*ting-ass women want is a motherf*cker to step up with a godamned checkbook and some cheddar in the bank to back that sh*t."

"It's not about money, it's about responsibility," she told him. "It's about doing the right thing and about sharing the load for parenting."

"If I serve a woman up right and I leave the spot knowing that I rocked her world, I ain't trying to see no damn baby nine months later and I definitely ain't trying to get on no responsibility roll when all I was trying to do was tap that ass in the first place."

"Thank God that Shawn's not *you*," she huffed.

"Troi's fine ass ain't got nothing to do with God," he said. "'Cause if she did, she wouldn't be doing like every other female and try to trap my dawg. Would she, Shawn?"

"She's right, D," I lamented. "At least she's halfway right."

"Excuse me," Kelly said, jumping in. "Halfway. Me?"

"Yeah," I sighed. "You're right about the responsibility thing, but it's bigger than that. It's about the kid, it's about doing right by the kid and about making his life better and his place in the world more secure."

"It's a boy?" Kelly asked, surprised.

"I already told him, I'm the first one that's rolling him through a strip joint," Donnie bragged.

"You'll be the only one," I said, starting to grin.

"I won't even ask what that's about," Kelly remarked. "But I do have to ask one thing, Mr. Mom. How's Dawn taking this?"

"She loves me, so she'll stand by me," I told her.

"Is that before or after the kid comes and your time gets sucked up like a hooker that accepts food stamps?" Donnie asked.

"Prostitutes may do many things, but accepting food stamps is not one of them," Kelly said.

"You obviously ain't been selling no ass in a minute," Donnie observed.

"I can't say that I have," Kelly remarked. "But he's right, Shawn. I love Alan dearly. But if some hoochie popped up with his child, it would be lights out."

"So you're the clearinghouse for women?" I asked. "Dawn and I have something different and if she says she'll deal with it, I'm taking her at her word."

"You ain't got no choice!" Donnie exclaimed.

"How did he manage to be right twice on the same day?" Kelly asked. "I hope this isn't a trend for the new year."

"It's not," I assured her. "He's not right about anything."

"I beg to differ," Kelly quickly said. "If Dawn says she'll see it through, you can bet she means it, because she's a woman of her word."

"That's what I'm saying," I replied.

"But what you *ain't* saying is that there ain't no way that's she's gonna see some sh★t like this through," Donnie remarked. "If she was popping out a kid and some other fool was the father *and* he was hanging around trying to change diapers, buy up Pampers, and some more sh★t," he added, "would your ass hang around?"

"I guess," I answered.

"I guess not," Kelly said. "It's just not natural. You might see it as right because you love Dawn, but trust me. It would get old real quick."

"So I'm supposed to just forget that I have a kid in the world?" I asked.

"What she's saying is that your ass is gonna have to forget about Dawn," Donnie said.

"Do you realize he's said three correct things in one day?" Kelly asked. "Is he on some new medication?"

"That's not an option," I replied.

"Troi won't make it an option," Kelly insisted.

"She's gonna make it a f*cking *non* option." Donnie laughed. "You and Dawn are gonna have to get with *her* program."

"What happened to *Trading Spaces*?" I asked, annoyed.

"Changing channels won't get you out of this, Shawn," Kelly reasoned.

"All I got to say is that if you and Dawn break sh*t off, make sure you hit it first," Donnie advised.

"What are you talking about?" Kelly asked, surprised.

Donnie's talking about break up rule #2.

Break up rule #1 is that as a guy, you never break up with a woman. You either drift off, drift away, or just plain get lost. Especially when you know that if you play your cards right, she'll break up with you first, which means that she can't lay any guilt trips on you about how you wasted her time or how she gave you the best two minutes of her life. She can't say that you used her up or that her friends told her that you sucked all along. If she dumps you, you're off the hook and it's difficult if not impossible for her to justify major drama like slashed tires, broken windows, or phone calls to your new lady warning her that you're a serial heartbreaker.

But when you know you're either about to violate rule #1 and actually be stupid enough to break up with a woman, or you're about to get dropped, dumped, or otherwise relieved of the actual hassle of dealing with your girlfriend, lady, wife, or mistress, rule #2 takes immediate effect.

You have to get one last roll in the hay.

You want her to see what's she's going to miss, even though you'll miss it ten times more than she will. You want to experience her love, her affection, and the special way that she does that special thing, but she'll be completely detached and over you before you even finish climbing back into your clothes.

The simple truth is that you want, deserve, and desperately need at least one more solid chance to shoot your wad, because you don't know when you'll be able to either convince or hoodwink another woman into sleeping with you. Meanwhile, your lady will have no problem getting off because the vibrator that she bought to replace you has fresh AAs and a sensorizing rotation clip.

When it came to Dawn, I never imagined that I'd have to deal with break up rule #2. And I'm hoping it doesn't come to that.

"You think that women want to sleep with men that they're going to break up with?" Kelly asked, concerned.

"Some women will definitely give you a sympathy piece," I told her. "They know you're going to go without, and since they did like you at some point, they'll give in."

"Do you know how ridiculous that sounds?" she asked. "If I've reached the point where I don't want to be with a guy, the last thing I want is to sleep with him."

"That's 'cause you ain't been with nobody who knows how to work that thing," Donnie told her. "I always gets my last piece," he bragged. "I'm usually plotting that last action before I even get it the first time because the last action is always the best."

"At least now I know you're not going to be right for the entire year," Kelly remarked.

"He is right," I told her. "When it's a last shot, you're both putting out your best because you want it to be known that your best is the best they'll ever get. It's like a pride thing."

"Yeah," Donnie chimed in. "What do you think Vanessa Williams was yapping about when she said, 'You always save the best for last?' That was a fricking tribute to all the men she gave a last shot to."

"I think I'm going to throw up," Kelly said, sounding upset.

"While we're on the topic of throwing up—" Donnie began.

"What would you do if Alan told you he wanted a three-way?" I interrupted.

"I *am* going to throw up," she insisted.

"Does that mean you would get with it?" Donnie asked.

"Are you speaking of my murder trial or the sentencing phase?" Kelly asked, quickly regaining her composure.

"So you're saying you wouldn't?" I asked.

"I'm an open woman, and I love my man, so if he wanted a three-way, I'd give it to him," she said, shocking both of us.

"That's some bullsh*t," Donnie remarked.

"I would," she said, turning the TV back to *Trading Spaces*. "But he'd have to give me a three-way with another man first," she laughed.

Women, I thought, exasperated.

Women.

Kelly has a way of getting under your skin. It's not like she tries, because she's actually a wonderful sister, who is as smart and as sassy as they come. Her claim to fame is that she's seen it all and survived it all and is a better, stronger, and more determined woman for it. She generally dates men for six-month clips and then pulls a black widow move to kill the relationship off. She says she does it to keep her life fresh and the guys honest.

But I know different. She sends guys packing because ultimately, she'd rather dish the pain than receive it. Simply put, Kelly doesn't want to get hurt.

"Since mouth-almighty's still here and our football deal is blown, I'm outtie," Donnie said, starting to stand.

"Great. Can you leave a urine sample in case your parole officer stops by?" Kelly said, unfazed.

"Where are you going?" I asked, surprised.

"I'm going to meet a man about a dog," he answered, reaching for his coat.

"Can you get his sample too?" Kelly teased, flipping channels and reaching for her ringing cell phone. "Happy New Year," she answered.

"She needs a good stiff d . . .," Donnie whispered.

"I guess I should be relieved that you probably can't get it up," Kelly quickly said, catching Donnie off guard. "Not you," she said to the person on the phone.

"You damn right not me," Donnie shot back.

"Great!" Kelly exclaimed. "I'll be right over."

"Let me get my ass outta here before I say some sh*t that *you're* gonna regret," Donnie warned.

"Call me, hon," she said, kissing me on the cheek and then rushing toward the door. "And Donnie," she began, staring him down.

The pause and the silence say that something's coming.

"There's hope. Perhaps not for you," she added, grinning. "But there is hope."

"Whatever, you toy diva," he muttered, before leaving out behind her and closing the door.

This is one of those moments where my circumstances are supposed to hit me like a ton of bricks. I've always relished times like this because I can deal with my problems and sort through my issues at my own pace in my own space. I don't have to deal with a woman who will tell me to turn the TV down or, worse yet, demand that I change the channel to some mushy, chicky station like Kelly had just done. I don't have to answer the phone, or check my E-mail to learn the secret powers of the latest replacement for Viagra. And I absolutely don't have to contend with a kid, his leaking bottle, or his crusty diapers.

This is precisely why I like my life. If I'm going to be hassled, I'm not about to invite it into my home. I don't want to be forced to share my tranquility or to trade it in for overblown weekend visits, all-night sleepovers, and strings of adolescent lies that start with "What had happened was" and end with "I'm *never* gonna treat my kids like you treat me."

Unlike Donnie, I know what's right. Kelly's and my dad's manhood lessons are unnerving reminders that I and Spike Lee's pigeon-toed, pizza-hauling Mookie share a cautionary commonality. He wasn't big on fatherhood either, but like him, I have to do the right thing.

And the right thing right now is to answer my door, so that the doorbell can get a well deserved break.

"Hey, honey muffin," Dawn said, leaning up to kiss my cheek.

"Honey muffin?"

"We're going to do a segment on pet nicknames, so I'm trying to expand my universe," she told me. "What do you think of sugar pudding?"

"Doesn't Bill Cosby do commercials for that?" I quickly replied.

"Ha-ha, Mr. Funny-man," she answered, before suddenly turning serious. "Did you like our sex last night?"

"As opposed to our sex the night before?" I asked.

"I'm serious, Shawn," she remarked. "Did you like it?"

"Are you crazy? I'm a man, I always like it," I admitted. "Don't you?"

"All I could think about last night was you," she said softly, "and Troi."

This is one of those times when no answer is the best answer because the best answer is to have no answer.

"I looked in your eyes and saw you looking at her, except you were looking at me, which was like you looking at her since all I could see was you looking at her."

The answer that just eluded me is probably even better than the answer I don't have right now.

"I know that's she's probably gorgeous, beautiful, sexy, and all those things and I know she's coming to town and that you're going to have to see her and I guess I just want to know that you're not going to get sucked in like you told me you did when you first met her," she said, sounding worried. "It's always just been us. And I'd be lying if I said this isn't making me just a tad bit insecure."

"She is pregnant, you know," I said, hugging her.

"So if she wasn't, do you think she could—"

"Not a chance in the world," I reassured her. "Nobody's coming between us."

"Are you sure?" she asked, grabbing my hand and leading me to the living room.

"Since we're doing the whole New Year's honesty deal, I think there's something you should know."

"I already know she's pregnant, so nothing could top that," Dawn said, smiling sadly.

"Troi's here and I saw her," I confessed.

She quickly grabbed a nearby bottle of champagne left over from last night's celebration and hurried to down a huge gulp.

"Well," she said, "at least you didn't tell me on the air."

"She gave me an ultimatum," I went on.

Dawn took another swig.

"She told me that if I wanted to see my son, I had to break things off with you."

"It's a boy?" she nervously asked.

"She didn't say that . . . but I guess if it has to be something, I'd rather it be a boy."

"So you're saying you want a boy?" she asked. "You would be happy if she was having your son?"

"It's not like I'm happy," I admitted. "I don't even want a kid. But if she's going to have a kid and I'm going to be the father, I'd rather see her have a son."

"And where does that leave me?" she asked. "You'll be off with your family, your son and *her*. And where do I fit in?"

"You don't," I whispered.

"I don't?" she asked, surprised.

"No," I confessed, holding her hand. "And neither do I."

"So what are we going to do?" she asked.

"We're staying together," I promised her.

"But what about your son?"

"I'll deal with it," I said. "This is my problem."

"You're calling your child a problem?" she asked, surprised. "How can you do that?"

"Why are we even talking about this? I'll get everything under control and we won't even have to deal with it."

"And how do you propose to do that?"

"I'll . . ."

"You'll . . . ?"

"I know what's right, but I didn't want a kid in the first place," I said.

"You just said that you wanted a son," she reminded me.

"I didn't say I wanted a son. I said that if she was going to have a kid, I'd rather it be a boy."

"That's the same thing," she told me.

"No, it's not," I answered. "I don't want a boy, I don't want a girl, I don't want any kids period."

"So now you're saying that you don't want us to have kids?" she asked.

"I didn't say that!" I exclaimed.

But it doesn't matter. Kelly and Donnie were right. Dawn won't be able to handle this. She's already freaking out about a kid that's not even here yet. And if she saw me making love to Troi when I was making love to her, we're really in trouble. This is hitting us hard, but for entirely different reasons. Like Donnie predicted, Dawn is worried about Troi's looks. And as Kelly said, she's concerned about where she stands in all of this. I'm shocked Dawn doesn't know that she has nothing to worry about. My heart is with her, my mind is on her, and she's my one true soul mate.

As far as I'm concerned, there's nothing that could ever come between us.

And I can only hope that she feels the same.

"I appreciate your honesty," she said, kissing me. "Where did you run into her?"

"Here." I answered.

"She was here . . . in our space?"

"It's not exactly our space," I reminded her.

"Oh, so now that Mommy Dearest is in town, this no longer qualifies as *our* space," she said, an edge in her voice.

"I didn't say that, Dawn."

"And how did she feel about *your* space?" she asked.

"She liked the tablecloth," I offered.

"She saw my tablecloth?" she asked, incensed. "Did you let her put her hands on my tablecloth?"

"I thought it was my tablecloth."

"Well since you're about to be a family man, maybe you'll need it," she huffed.

"Why is this happening?" I asked. "Why are we arguing?"

"Because *you* brought her in here behind my back," she said, pointing at me.

"No, I didn't," I answered. "You saw her before you left."

"Before I left when?"

"This morning," I reminded her. "You remember the woman who was at the door down the street?"

"The hooker?" she asked. "The hooker with the fricking flowers?!" she said, rushing to the kitchen. "She brought you flowers and you put them in *my* vase?!" she screamed.

"Your vase?!" I yelled back. "You gave me that vase when you gave me the tablecloth!"

"Why are you doing this to me?"

"You were the one who didn't want any secrets," I told her. "And it's not like it meant anything. I don't care about those stupid flowers. I'm a guy!" I exclaimed. "I don't even like flowers."

"Okay," she fired back. "So now you're saying you didn't like my flowers."

"I didn't say that, Troi."

"My name is Dawn!" she screamed. "D – A – W – N, Dawn!"

"I didn't mean to say that."

"This is exactly what I saw when we were making love," she told me. "Your mind is on her. She just got here and you're already calling me *her name*. You let her touch my tablecloth and you put her flowers in my vase. You allowed her to invade *our* space, Shawn," she observed. "This is even worse than I anticipated."

"Look, Troi," I quickly said.

"I am Dawn, dammit!" she reminded me. "Look at me Shawn. I'm not Troi . . . I'm not pregnant and I'm not having your son! And when I leave, I'm taking back my tablecloth, I'm taking back my vase, and I'm taking back . . . this!" She grabbed a heart-shaped refrigerator magnet with a picture of us in the middle.

"That's mine," I insisted.

"It *was* yours," she said, stomping out of the kitchen.

"Well, since you're taking back everything, would you mind taking back these beets?" I asked, opening the refrigerator.

"So now you don't like my beets?" she asked.

"I don't like beets at all."

"First you don't like my flowers, now you don't like my beets?" she said, upset.

"I'm not a beet man," I admitted.

"Well, you were a beet man the night I brought them over here," she told me. "You were eating them like they were Chee-tos."

"I'm not a Chee-tos man, either."

"Great," she said, marching back into the kitchen and opening the pantry. "Had I known, I wouldn't have bought these for you either," she said, removing a huge, red bag of Chee-tos. "Apparently, you don't like anything I buy."

"That's not true and you know it," I replied.

"Name one thing," she demanded.

"What about the Wizard's tickets?"

"I didn't buy those, they're comps."

"Wait a minute," I said. "You gave me free tickets?"

"I gave you free *courtside* tickets."

"Yeah, I guess I shouldn't complain about that," I reasoned.

"You sure shouldn't."

"But they're not really gifts if you didn't pay for them. So they don't go on the screw-up list," I added, smiling and reaching to hug her.

"We shouldn't be arguing," she whispered. "I can't even believe I was acting so crazy."

"Try jealous."

"You think that I'm jealous?" she asked.

"Crazy *and* jealous," I joked.

"I'm sorry, Shawn. This is just so beyond anything I ever expected," she admitted. "I told you that I'd deal with it and that was my intention, but I just don't know," she said, heading back to the living room.

"What is it that you don't know?" I asked, worried now.

"She's beautiful," Dawn said. "She's like Halle Berry, but with a cuter face and a better body. And she calls herself pregnant? *And* she brought you flowers?" she asked. "How can I compete with her?"

"You can't," I remarked, smiling. "Because there's no competition. First of all, it's all about you and me, and second, Troi's not into me, we just had a fling."

"Did she say that?"

"She sure did."

"Then make me a promise," Dawn requested.

"Shoot."

"If she ever comes to her senses and changes her mind, I want you to promise to tell me."

"I have to tell you if Troi decides she likes me?" I asked, surprised.

"Promise me, Shawn," she demanded. "There's already enough

to deal with, and I deserve to know if Miss Troi has designs on my man."

"I can deal with that," I said, knowing it would never be a problem. "Especially since Troi's not thinking about me. The only thing on her mind is child support."

"Why don't we just get rid of these," she said, walking back into the kitchen and dumping Troi's flowers into the trashcan. "I don't want any reminders lurking around when I'm gone."

"What do you mean, when you're gone?"

"I think this is one of those 'you need to be seated' moments," she said, again returning to the living room.

She's about to dump me! Just like she just trashed Troi's flowers. What am I supposed to do? Kelly and Donnie called it and I can't believe it. The mere sight of Troi has Dawn shaking in her boots and instead of standing by me, she's about to roll. Doesn't the hard work we put into this mean anything? Shouldn't our commitment count for something? And most important, will she at least be honorable enough to invoke break up rule #2 and allow me one last roll in the hay?

"You're a lucky man, Shawn Wayne," Dawn said, reaching for my hand. "You have a woman who adores you, that would be me, D-a-w-n, Dawn," she remarked, smiling. "And you have this vision of a woman that I totally have no words for because I've never seen anything like her in my life, carrying your child," she spat out. "She's telling you that if I'm in the picture, you're not going to see your child who may very well be the son that you want—"

"I didn't say I wanted a son, Dawn," I reminded her. "You're putting words in my mouth."

"Okay," she answered. "But either way, you have a huge responsibility . . . an awesome responsibility. You're about to be a dad and I can't stand in the way of that. It doesn't mean that I don't love you, you know that I do. But I know you, Shawn. And I know you're the type of man that would do right by your child," she said, slowly releasing my hand.

"Does this mean I'm not getting a last piece?" I blurted out.

"Excuse me?" she asked, shocked.

"I . . . I was just thinking," I started. "You're about to break up with me and we should at least—"

"What?" she interrupted. "You don't think you can get rid of me this easily, do you? I am leaving," she told me. "But I'm not leaving you."

"So who are you leaving, then?" I asked, confused.

"I got some of the best news in my life this morning."

"You're not pregnant, right?" I asked, concerned.

"If I am, I hope I look as good as Troi," she confessed. "Damn, she's beautiful. Are you sure she's not a model or a—"

"Your news," I said, refocusing her and distracting her from Troi.

"Guess who saw the show last night?" she asked.

"Do you mean besides your mother?"

"I'm really going to miss you," she said, retrieving my hand. "Oprah saw the show, she called this morning, and while she's on vacation, instead of airing reruns, guess who's sitting in?" she gushed.

"Are you kidding me?!" I said, hugging her.

"We're actually going to tape my show at Harpo's studios for a while, so I can learn at the feet of the master."

"So you're going to be the new Oprah!" I said, excited.

"I'm going to be the new *Dawn*," she asserted. "You remember how you said there will never be another Jordan? Well, I can guarantee you that there will never be another Oprah."

"So when is this happening?" I asked, excited. "After the February ratings sweeps?"

"I leave tomorrow morning," she said, softly.

"As in tomorrow in the morning?" I asked, worried.

She looked me in the eye and slowly nodded her head.

"You can't leave later?"

She shook her head no and then slowly laid her head on my chest.

Neither of us is saying a word.

I'm certain she doesn't want to leave with so much in the air. She'll be as concerned about Troi as I am, but our reasons will be way different. She'll wonder how I can keep myself and my eyes away from a woman who has even *her* head spinning. And I'll wonder what Troi's next stunt will be. Dawn will worry herself about my role as the father to Troi's child. While I'll consider holding Troi to her promise to keep me out of the kid's life. Dawn will be concerned that Troi will prove to be too seductive, too appealing, and too irresistible for me to refuse. And so will I!

"We may have only been dating three months this time around, but we do have a history, Shawn, and if you just came to your senses in college, we'd probably be married right now," Dawn said, smiling. "You've always been honest even when I didn't exactly like what you were telling me. But this is really going to test us. I can trust you, can't I?" she whispered.

"One hundred fifty percent and then some," I answered.

"You won't cheat on me and you won't let Troi back into your space?" she asked.

"*Our* space," I reassured her.

"You're a good pooh bear," she told me.

Pooh bear?

"Maybe that's what Oprah calls Stedman," Dawn said, grinning. She then pulled back and looked me dead in the eye. "You really thought I was going to break up with you?"

"Kind of," I admitted.

"And you were just going to let it happen?" she inquired.

"If you were going to roll, how could I stop you?"

"You could beg, whine, plead, and then beg a little more," she said, laughing. "But you're probably right . . . it wouldn't have mattered."

"That's my point."

"You could have at least tried," she whispered.

"Tried what?" I asked.

"To see if I was interested in break up rule number two," she answered.

"You know about break up rule number two?" I asked, surprised.

"Every woman does," she said, reaching to turn out the lights. "Who do you think invented it?"

M aking love to Dawn is like magic. And I could tell that this time, she had no thoughts of Troi. She was on fire and I could barely keep up.

Which all but confirms that she's fully acquainted with break up rule #2. Though she's leaving D.C., and not us or our relationship, she wanted me to know that the best sex I could ever hope to have is with her.

And when she woke me up for a second round, her point was all but made.

I know this isn't the best time to talk," she said afterward, lying across me. "But, how are you feeling about everything that's happening?"

"I already told you, I'm a guy, so I'm cool *anytime* we make love."

"I wasn't talking about that," she answered. "I'm wondering how you're dealing with becoming a dad."

"I'm not."

"That's borderline impossible," she insisted. "You have to have some feelings about it."

"As in I'm not ready to be a father and it's screwed up that I don't have a say in it, and don't give me that 'I had a say in it when I slept with her' crap, because I wasn't exactly thinking that I'd be looking at being a dad because I had sex with her."

"At least you didn't say you made love to her," observed Dawn.

"I feel like my whole life has come down to a moment that was nothing more than that . . . just a moment."

"Something tells me you didn't see it as just a moment when you two were together."

"It wasn't a moment that was supposed to end up with me dealing with a million more moments of a kid I didn't ask for," I acknowledged.

"Now I get it," she replied, slowly sitting up. "In your mind, this is all about you."

"How's that?" I asked.

"You're worried only about how this will affect you and how your life will be changed. You don't care about her and you certainly don't appear to care about your child and though I'm not happy with the situation, I'm actually a little disappointed in you."

"I don't understand it," I answered. "How does a woman have all the say in this? Just because she decides she wants to have a kid, I should have to deal with it for the next eighteen years?"

"My parents tell me that parenting is like having a lifetime job that you never really apply for," she said.

"That's what I'm saying."

"You applied, all right." Dawn laughed. "And she's making sure you serve a nine-month probation period to prove it."

"How would you handle it?" I asked, gently stroking her hair.

"I'd probably be upset just like you," she shared. "And like you, I'd meet my responsibilities head on."

"That's a woman's line," I told her. "Do you know what Donnie told me about women getting pregnant?"

"I hate to ask," she said.

"He said that when a chick gets pregnant, that she's giving you a license to leave," I told her.

"Do either you *or* him know how incredibly stupid that sounds?"

"In this day and age, when a woman gets pregnant, she knows what she's doing," I contended. "And she knows that part of the deal is that the guy will probably break camp."

"That's because so many men are prepared to shirk their responsibilities and to deny their own children," she told me.

"And that's because men are completely eliminated from the decision part of it," I stressed. "It's almost like work."

"*Work?*" she asked, surprised.

"How do you feel when your boss tells you that you should do a show that you *know* won't work and you tell him that you have a better idea, but he says he's not interested in what you have to say and that it's his way or the highway?" I asked.

"My boss is a woman," she informed me.

"That's my point," I said, excited. "When a woman gets pregnant, it's like she's the boss and the guy's a low-level employee who has no say at all in how the job gets done. And then, instead of getting paid, the guy ends up paying the boss for having to work for her."

"You could not have come up with a more senseless analogy,

pooh bear," she joked. "You're not paying because you worked, you're paying because you played."

"I'm getting *played*," I told her.

"The only one who would get played in your equation is the child," she said soberly. "And if you're staying in my life, that's not an option."

"Do you know how crazy that sounds?" I asked.

"Tell me."

"Troi says that if you're in the picture, I'm screwed," I explained. "And *you're* telling me if you're in the picture, I'm screwed."

"You're not exactly screwed, Shawn Wayne," she offered. "And all I'm saying is that I have no intention or desire to see you become either an absentee father or a deadbeat dad. You're not the victim here," she reminded me.

"It's not about being a victim—"

"It is if you're talking about being anything but an involved and supportive parent," she cut in. "My father was always there for me. You remember when I didn't have a date for our high school prom because you had to play in some all star game in Pittsburgh?" she asked.

"How can I forget?" I grumbled. "You reminded me every day until you left for college."

"My father actually tried to convince me to go with that Delonte Brown guy," she admitted.

"The guy with the calculator watch?" I asked, surprised.

"My father thought that was a good thing," she said. "But when prom night rolled around, and I was without a date, he walked into my room, tapped me on my shoulder, and said, "Let's go, princess.""

"That was better than Delonte Brown," I said, and laughed.

"We had such a good time that I stopped being mad at you," she said. "At least until I saw you and the anger came right back. When I think about him, I think about you," she told me. "My father was everything fathers are supposed to be about. He cared, he was supportive, we communicated, and to this day, I know that if I'm ever in need, my father will be there for me. I see the same qualities in you," she admitted. "And to be honest, it's why I'm so attracted to you, Shawn."

"I see what you're saying, Dawn," I replied. "But, what if a guy really didn't want a kid . . . didn't even want children in the first place? You're saying he should have to deal with something as critical as a kid when he's not ready and when he has absolutely no say in the matter?"

"That man had a choice. He could have used protection, or hey," she said, smiling. "He could have just as easily abstained from sex altogether."

That's a rich one. Abstinence? I don't even think it comes up when Democrats are in office. And I guarantee it wasn't an accepted theory when Clinton was on the prowl.

Abstinence is a Republican concept along the lines of Willie Horton, "Just Say No," and the war on drugs. Only the first one worked, when Lee Atwater used Willie Horton as the boogie man to scare voters away from bleeding heart liberals who favored probation and parole over prison and hard time.

Many men believe that sex is a natural extension of a relationship. When that line doesn't work, it's a natural extension of what's supposed to happen if he and a prospect make it to three dates and he's paid for each of them. While women are thinking they should practice either abstinence, celibacy, or just plain holding out for marriage, guys are evaluating them on two levels.

Level one is the classic answer to an easily answerable question. Is the woman sitting across from you cute enough, attractive enough, or downright *fine* enough to run the "I'm celibate, I'm not sleeping with anyone or cohabiting at this time" line on you? If her initials aren't H.B. and her husband's not pulling the grandest stunts in history—"I'm not having affairs, I'm just doing the sex addiction thing, my bad"—and if she hasn't won an Oscar or an Olympic gold, or hasn't landed a Victoria's Secret, *Maxim, King,* or *Playboy* cover, you're not buying the celibacy rap.

The other level's different.

When a guy is "courting" a woman, it would help everyone involved if he fessed up that from day one and *date one,* the meter's running. The first date is a veritable freebie. She might not like you, you might not like her, and you may be as compatible as a vegan and a beef tenderloin. But if you decide to take her on a second date, she's thinking, "Okay . . . he's nice," and he's thinking, "One more date and BAM! It's on!"

By the third date, the woman is on high bliss alert and doesn't want to look too eager, too anxious, or overly affectionate, while the guy is thinking he's hit the jackpot because he's footed the bill(s) and therefore has paid his dues.

In his mind, sex is the reward for having been a nice, compassionate gentleman, who listened to her blather on about her screwed up job, her passionless past, and her no-account baby's daddy. He's emptied his pockets, played his role, and the payoff is that perennially awkward first foray into the bedroom, which always works because you always get a second shot just to see if the first shot was really as great or as terrible as both of you guessed it would be.

The only thing guys conveniently forget is that there's always a chance that the lady whom you properly courted may actually wind up pregnant, and then *you'll* be that no-account baby's daddy who will be the object of her wrath.

Had you gone Republican style and "just said no," you wouldn't be dealing with what I'm dealing with right now. You can practice abstinence, you can say no and you can have a choice in your fate.

It sounds crazy, and probably as loony as Dennis Rodman in a wedding dress *without* heels, but it's no more ridiculous than having a child you're not prepared for, dealing with a baby's momma (and not a wife), and spending your entire life telling your child to do as you say and not as you *did* when he or she was conceived.

Abstinence is much more than a concept. It's a reality, it's an option, and more important . . . it's a choice. Right now, even though I just finished making it with Dawn in a major way, I wish that I would have chosen abstinence instead of a life of uncertainty and getting played by Troi.

"This is going to be quite a situation," observed Dawn. "And I'm sorry I won't be here to help you through it. At least I won't be here at the beginning, but I'll be back in time for your big day."

"You'll be here for the child support hearing?" I asked.

"No, pooh bear," she said, smiling. "I'll be here when she has your son."

"I don't even plan on being here," I answered. "I mean, I'll be here, but I won't be there."

"Oh, you'll be there," she said with certainty. "This is your first child and you're going to be a good father if it kills both of us."

"Why would you even care?" I asked, surprised. "It's not like it's your kid."

"I'm selfish," she said, reaching for her blouse. "First, I need to see if you have what it takes to be a dad. And second," she said, grabbing her skirt and imitating Donnie, "Miss Troi needs to know that Ms. Dawn ain't going nowhere."

"So you're saying you're in for the long haul?" I asked.

"We're both in," she replied, slipping on her shoes. "I'll pick up a book on stepparenting at the airport and the next time you see me, I'll be stepmommy deluxe."

"I don't know if that's a good idea."

"It's better than sitting on the outside and wondering what's going on behind my back."

She has a point. But then again, she always does.

"I have a ton of packing to do, but I'll be back tonight," she said, picking up her purse.

"Thanks a lot," I answered. "I'm glad you'll be able to fit me in before you leave."

"I'm fitting you in because I need a ride to the airport," she said, laughing. "See you about eight, pooh bear," she added, kissing me on the cheek and heading for the door. "And answer the phone."

"It would help if it were ringing."

"It will," she answered.

"What are you talking about?" I asked, surprised.

"Whenever the woman leaves, the phone starts ringing off the hook the moment she's out the door," she remarked. "You know that."

"That's crazy," I told her.

"I could stand here for another ten minutes and the phone wouldn't ring," she answered. "But when that door closes, you know and I know that this place will turn into a hotline."

"Who calls me?"

"If I had more time I'd find out," she told me, opening the door. "But as long as I'm here, the phone won't ring, so what's the use?"

"I love you," I said, before the door closed behind her.

"Then answer the phone," she said, making her way down the sidewalk.

And amazingly, just as she predicted, the phone rang.

"Hello," I answered, surprised.

"Couldn't wait, could you?" she asked.

"Dawn?"

"I left my earrings on the counter," she said, laughing. "I'll pick them up when I get back."

"Not a problem. See you then," I replied, noticing I had another call. "I, uh . . ."

"Have a call coming? Works every time, pooh bear," she teased. "See you at nine."

"I thought you said eight?"

"And I thought *you* weren't paying attention," she told me. "See you at eight. Go get your call, honey muffin."

"Honey muffin?" I said, accidentally clicking over.

"That's cute, Shawn . . . it's much better than our last conversation."

"Troi?"

"What happened to honey muffin?" she asked.

"It's a pet name thing . . . for a new show . . . forget it," I said, already getting frustrated.

"We need to talk," she quickly said. "I think I came across wrong and I'd like to clear the air. Can I stop by?"

"Why don't we meet somewhere else?" I asked, remembering not to invite her to what I'd described to Dawn as *our space.*

"It's New Year's Day and I doubt that anything's open until later on," she reasoned. "And since I'm less than a block away, I should be there in about five minutes."

"I'm not here," I said, panicking.

"You're not?"

"What I meant to say is that I'm not going to be here."

"Well, good. Since I'm about to pull up, I'll go with you," she responded.

"Maybe we should just stay here," I reasoned.

This is happening way too fast. I'm not ready or even interested in talking to Troi about anything . . . at least not yet anyway. But the doorbell is already ringing, and as is always the case with Troi, it doesn't seem that I have a choice.

"Aren't you happy to see me?" she asked, catching me completely off guard.

No, I thought, methodically looking both ways before closing the door behind her.

"I know I should have called sooner, but this couldn't wait," she said, pushing past me to walk into the living room. "This thing is getting totally out of hand, but before you make any decisions, there's something you should know."

"Do you want some orange juice?" I asked.

"Orange juice?" she replied, sounding surprised.

"I have apple juice too," I told her. "There's also some Chee-tos, if you're hungry."

"Chee-tos?" she asked. "I come over here to bare my soul and you want me to eat Chee-tos?"

"I don't like them either," I answered. "You want some beets?"

"Listen, Shawn," she said, grabbing me. "I shouldn't have called you on the phone and left you a message about being pregnant . . . that was wrong. I apologize and I just want to clear the air. We have a serious situation to deal with, a life-changing situation. I shouldn't have acted like I did at the Waffle Shop, especially when there's something you should know."

"Something like what?" I asked, worried.

"I have a confession."

Yes! I said to myself, excited. She has a confession. Either she's not pregnant, which wouldn't surprise me, because the guys I shoot hoops with look more pregnant than she does, Or, if she is . . . she's pregnant by someone else. Either way, I win. And so does Dawn.

I can't wait to tell Dawn! It will be just what she needs to hear before she leaves.

The Seven Different Types of Dads

Work-a-Dad . . . a.k.a., "Let Your Daddy Get Some Rest" Dad

Work-a-Dad is a throwback to the days when men were the sole source of income in their households. They work, their wives stay at home, and their kids stay out of the way. Work-a-Dad is an outstanding provider and as such, their families always know that the water will be warm, the lights will be on, and that overall, they will have a comfortable existence. He may not have a degree, so he believes that work is his way toward a better future and a sense of security for his kids. But Work-a-Dad often tolerates unappreciative bosses and supervisors at work in the name of making a better way for his family, and his kids sometimes suffer because of it. He may scream at home to compensate for the yelling he endures at work. He might shut down and avoid communication with his kids because he can't properly reduce the stress and frustration he experiences on the job. And worse, Work-a-Dad may turn home into an alternative workplace where he is the boss and can run things. He can order his kids around or create fanciful tasks—like "landscaping" as opposed to mowing the lawn, or "home improving" instead of fixing the lamp—that keep him emotionally detached from his family. Work-a-Dad cares, and will do right by his family, especially if they leave him alone and allow him to rest so he can do what he does best for his kids . . . work.

I've hit the jackpot! I knew all along that Troi's not pregnant. It's a slam dunk. And if she is, she's not pregnant by me.

Troi pegged it when we were having breakfast at the diner. She came into town. We jumped into the sack. And we had a first-rate fling. She was beautiful, we had fun, and the sex was great. For a minute, I thought she was the one, but she never bought into it. She was no more interested in a relationship than a married man is with either his wife *or* his mistress. They both fill needs in his lackluster life, just like I filled a void for Troi.

Troi and I weren't friends, we didn't have a relationship, and we weren't in love. Which makes the fact that she's about to spill the beans all the more satisfying. The way I see it, she doesn't even need to confess what I knew all along. She may have had me guessing and I was definitely stressed, but in my heart, I knew the real deal.

This whole pregnancy thing is a farce. And since she's not pregnant, it doesn't even matter why she went through such a production number and nearly put a chokehold on my life.

You remember when we were at breakfast this morning?" she asked, standing in the middle of the living room.

"How could I forget?" I answered. "The waiter wanted a thirty-five-percent tip, plus the orange juice was two dollars."

"Is that what you remember?" she asked, sounding surprised.

"Well, the eggs were three ninety-five. They were good and all, but I was thinking, four bucks for some eggs? I should be raising chickens."

"Okay, you're a cheap accountant, so that makes sense on some level," she said. "But I was going in a different direction."

"What . . . you didn't like the eggs?"

"I could care *less* about eggs," she confirmed. "I told you I have a confession, so I hope you'll hear me out."

"I already know what you're going to say and it's okay," I told her, confidently nodding my head.

"It is?" she said, smiling.

"I may not be a woman, but I know a thing or two about what you ladies go through when it comes to guys."

"You do?"

"You're alone in Chicago, you get your new job here in D.C., and you're thinking, 'Hey, I already have a connection there.'"

"I'm listening," she remarked.

"And who is your connection?" I asked. "Me."

"So far so good."

"And you don't want to be alone in a brand new city, so you call, leave me a message, and now, you're here," I told her.

"That I am."

"But you didn't have to do what you did," I said, slowly shaking my head. "I'm here and even with my situation, I don't think I would have just kicked you to the curb. In fact, as far as your confession goes, let's just keep it on the hush. You have nothing to prove to me and knowing what you must have been going through, I understand," I said, reaching for a line that would make me look cool. "I, uh . . . I feel you."

"You do?" she said, excited.

"I sure do," I said, smiling.

"I was so worried," she said, sounding relieved. "I wasn't counting on feeling like this, but only a man like you could take the pressure off me and sum it up so well at the same time."

"A real man doesn't need to drag things out," I told her. "I knew where you were taking it. And like I said, I feel you."

"You really do know women, don't you?" she asked. "I'm so glad you 'feel me' as you put it."

"That I do," I proudly answered.

"So when did you know?" she asked, excited.

"I think I figured it out when I saw you first thing this morning," I confessed. "I looked at you and said, hey, this isn't what a pregnant woman looks like. You still had that perfect waistline, your feet weren't big and fat, and—"

"Excuse me?" Troi interrupted.

"Your feet," I said, pointing down. "I was saying that they're not fat."

"I got that part," she said testily. "But what's this 'a pregnant woman doesn't look like me' nonsense?"

"You don't," I answered. "And that's when I knew."

"What is it that you know?" she asked, no longer smiling.

"The same thing you know," I explained. "That you're not pregnant."

"I'm not *what?*"

"You're not about to drop a load . . . you don't have a cake in the bakery . . . there's not going to be one of those crumb things," I replied.

"Crumb *snatchers?*" she asked.

"Them," I answered proudly.

"Let's sit down," she said, reaching for my hand. "Touch my stomach," she said, slowly guiding my hand beneath her blouse. "What do you feel?"

"A six pack," I said. "You must do like a hundred sit-ups a day."

"Try a thousand," she bragged. "But what you're *really* feeling is your child."

"He has a six pack?"

"You are too cute," she whispered, kissing me on the cheek. "I said I have a confession, so here goes."

"Hold up," I interrupted. "We've already been over your confession and as far as I'm concerned, it's cool. Why drag it out?"

"Because you're way off," she remarked, again smiling. "At breakfast, I told you I didn't want you and that I had no feelings for you. But that was a lie," she said, slowly shaking her head. "You're the nicest, most decent man I've ever met. I'm honored that you're the father of my child. And though I was stunned to learn that you had a girlfriend, I remember the fire that we had, and I can't let it go. I know I'm babbling, but what I'm really try-ing to say," she said, raising her head to look me in the eye, "is that I love you, Shawn Wayne. I really do love you. And I'm glad you feel the same way."

"I do?"

"You said you were feeling me, didn't you?" she asked.

"That's when you were confessing . . ."

"And I just confessed."

"But you confessed to the wrong thing!" I said, worried.

"So you're saying that you don't love me?" she asked, her eyes starting to water.

This is one of those times when a man just doesn't want to be a man. Guys are smart enough to know that when they're not actually in love, the only time you invoke the "love" word is when you're trying to accomplish something.

My mother always told me that I'd one day tell a woman I love her in pursuit of something I probably didn't need or wasn't ready to have. When Donnie told his first girlfriend Rose that he loved her, what he was really saying was that he wanted a Popsicle. He didn't have a quarter, she did, and when he dropped the "love bomb," he was eating Popsicles for a week, until she told him to prove it.

But my mother was more on target. "Men will use love or the concept of love to get sex. But women?" she warned. "We'll use sex to get love."

I don't love Troi. And I doubt that she really loves me. Which leaves us with exactly one problem . . . she's really pregnant!

"What's love got to do with it?" I asked, thinking that as a line, it worked for Tina Turner and it might work for me.

"I love you and I know I haven't handled things right, but we're going to be parents, and love, parenting, and children go together," she told me.

"That makes sense," I answered. "But I already have a girl—"

"Ouch," she said, grabbing her stomach. "I think I'll take you up on that juice."

"Do you want some Chee-tos too?" I asked, hurrying to the kitchen.

"I think I need to lie down," she said, slowly standing and heading toward my bedroom.

"Don't go in there," I warned.

"I need to lie down."

"But not in there," I said, worried. "It's a mess. Why don't you just . . ." I paused, not knowing what to say. "Just lay down on the floor."

"I have a bad back and I don't think it would be best for the baby," she answered, pushing the door aside and walking into my bedroom.

"Neither would Chee-tos," I mumbled.

"Are you bringing the juice?" she asked from the bedroom.

Boy, am I.

I'm not about to let her get a minute in my room. A guy's bedroom is his safe haven. It's a combination sleeping area, romance headquarters, and security vault. Everything that a guy doesn't want a woman to see is hidden somewhere in his bedroom. The old love letters, poems, and cards are probably nestled beneath the mattress or on the top shelf of the closet. The pictures, gifts, and extra condoms are either stuffed in the TV stand or are stashed within reach behind it. And the girlie magazines and the nude pictures you have of your former flames are tucked, where else? Right behind the headboard!

And why the bedroom? Because it's the only room in the house where any guy can claim complete control. With all the prep work and makeup that goes on in the bathroom, men have no control there. The same goes for the kitchen, the den, and the makeshift office. If you have a basement, it's probably because you have some pimple-faced kid who's already taken it over, so you don't stand a chance on that front.

But in the bedroom, you can run everything. You can keep the lights lit or turn them off. You have a real say in the pace, style, and result of any actions and encounters you have with women. And most important of all, you can keep a firm grip on the remote control.

But to keep the upper hand, you can never leave a woman alone in your bedroom. Women are better snoops, P.I.'s, and spies than 007 himself.

And every guy knows that giving a woman free reign in his bedroom is like sentencing himself to the death penalty.

"Are you okay?" I said, noticing that Troi was clutching her stomach while lying on her side.

"Cramps," she blurted out. "Terrible, terrible cramps."

"Do you think it's the sit-ups?" I asked, concerned.

"This is no time to joke," she warned. "Take off my shoes, my jacket, and my earrings."

I hurried to help her.

"Did you bring the juice?"

"Oh, yeah," I said, quickly standing. "The juice."

I rushed back to the kitchen, dropped her earrings on the counter, quickly poured some orange juice into a tiny glass tumbler and then raced back to the bedroom. Even though she appeared to be sick, she was still in my domain and the sooner I could get back, the better.

"Do you need anything else?" I asked, propping her up on a pillow.

"I could use a hug," she quickly replied.

A hug? I thought, surprised. *Is it okay for us to hug? And is hugging cheating when you're dedicated to your soul mate and you have no feelings for the person you're hugging, who claims to actually need a hug?*

If she's sick, why does she need a hug? But maybe that's why she needs a hug . . . because she's sick. And if she isn't sick, why is she pretending to be sick? It doesn't make any sense.

But if she's sick *and* she's pregnant *and* I don't give her a hug, I could be looking at a crisis on the lines of an international incident. Like I said, it's my bedroom and I'm the master of my domain. I'm in complete control. If an innocent little hug will help her out and get her out of my bedroom, it'll be worth it.

"One hug on the way," I said, opening my arms.

But with the way my lips are feeling, I would have been better off saying, "One *kiss* on the way."

"What are you doing?" I asked, pulling away.

"What does it feel like?" she asked, pulling me down to her. "You're kissing me."

"You're kissing *me!*" I shot back. "*Who's kissing who?* I wondered, as our tongues collided.

This is bad. But it's not medicine bad. Even when medicine is bad, it's actually doing you some good. But this is doing me no good at all. Especially since it feels so good and . . . because her lacy bra is in my hand!

"Whoa!" I exclaimed, instinctively throwing it to the floor. "This isn't happening."

"It's already happened," she said, smiling.

"I have a girlfriend," I reminded her.

"If your girlfriend was a *real* concern, I wouldn't be here," she commented.

"You're here because you had a confession and because you got sick and because you needed some orange juice," I pointed out.

"What's my bra got to do with orange juice?"

Nothing. Not a daggone thing. Why did I let her in my bedroom? I didn't . . . she just barged in. Why didn't I insist that she *not* go into my bedroom? I did, but she was sick and she needed to lie down. Why did I kiss her? I didn't, she kissed me.

Or did she?

If she did, why was I so excited? How did my tongue get involved? And worse, how did her beautiful, lacy, and extremely sexy bra end up in my hands?

"You're still hot for me, Shawn," she whispered.

"I have a girlfriend."

"You should probably tell him that you have a girlfriend," she said, seductively grabbing my crotch.

"He has a girlfriend too."

"You know you want me," she said, slowly sitting up. "But you still have some things to work through, so we'll just wait."

"It's not like we were going to do anything," I remarked, quickly downing the juice that I'd brought in for her to cool myself off.

"Were we going to kiss?" she asked.

"No."

"Did we?"

"Yes?" I answered, worried.

"There you go," she said, now standing. "This was just a taste. And when you straighten out your little situation, there's more where that came from," she told me as she headed for the door.

"My situation *is* straight," I insisted.

"If it were, you wouldn't be so worried," she said, slowly opening the front door and blowing me a kiss. "I meant what I said. I do love you, Shawn. And now I know for certain that you love me too."

She then closed the door behind her and I was quickly reminded of Dawn's earlier words of warning. *That door must be attached to a radar,* I thought, concerned.

Because a woman just left and the phone is ringing off the hook. Again!

19

"M eet my sorry ass over at Jerry's."

"Jerry's in Lanham?" I inquired, fluffing my pillows and straightening out my comforter. "Is it open?"

"Oh, it's open, fool," he answered. "And you ain't gonna believe who's here."

"Who?" I quickly asked, feeling even lower than an identity-hiding online gossip hound.

"Somebody that ain't gonna be here if you don't hurry up and get here."

Though I hate to admit it, I could stand a dose of Donnie's streetwise logic.

And Jerry's is the best place to get it.

J erry's is far and away the premiere seafood eatery in Prince George's county, Maryland. "PG," as it's affectionately called, is the richest primarily black county in America. Top jocks, lawyers, doctors, and the nouveau rich folk stake claims in Woodmore's exclusive gated community and country club, which dots the center of the county. Farther north, in Laurel and College Park, professors, educators, and other professional types are shaping careers and futures at the University of Maryland. And the southern tip of the county houses PG's "old" black money by way of homes facing the Potomac River in Oxon Hill and Fort Washington.

Jerry's is in Lanham, which besides having perhaps the best seafood restaurant in the state, has little else other than a Red Roof Inn and a Toys 'R' Us, which made national news when its roof caved in during a blizzard.

Donnie has his own table at Jerry's. It borders the kitchen. Actually it's a booth on the back wall, which allows him to see literally everyone who walks through while they can't see him. He knows that Jerry's is a hot spot for the politicians, movers and shakers, and cash-carrying bargain hunters who, like everyone else, appreciate Donnie's street-sweetened deals. And he sometimes holds court two or three times a week.

But today, according to Donnie, somebody else is holding court.

"So you remember that scene in *Mommie Dearest* when Joan Crawford is sporting a dancing gown and mowing down her rose garden?" Donnie asked, arranging packets of Equal into a straight line on the table.

"What were you doing watching *Mommie Dearest?*" I asked, surprised. "And what does Joan Crawford and her rose garden got to do with who's here?" I went on, looking around.

"No fricking wire hangers!" he yelled, attempting to quote a line from the movie. "Ever!" he added. "Who the hell wouldn't want to watch that?"

"So who's here?" I inquired.

"You know why she was cutting down the rose bushes?" Donnie said, still arranging the Equal packets.

"I don't care why."

"Check this," he said, leaning over. "Joan had just begged her manager to hang around after she'd insulted him 'cause he was hitting that thing."

"And?" I asked, unimpressed.

"And she was pouncing on the roses 'cause she knew that a high-class hottie like her shouldn't have been begging no man for nothing," he reasoned.

"I'm not seeing what this has to do with who's here."

"When a chick is reduced to begging, she's gonna eventually strike out. But back then, they had dignity, so she went home and did her damage," he explained, seemingly finished with the Equal.

"What's dignified about that?" I quickly asked.

"The f*ck ing gown, fool!" he quipped. "Do you think some chick today would slice your tires or spray paint your ride in a gown?"

"I wouldn't give a woman a reason to mess with me like that in the first place," I answered.

"But he would," he slyly replied.

"Who?" I shot back.

"Follow the Equal," he said, pointing toward the table.

Donnie had neatly arranged the Equal into an arrow that was pointing toward a table that sat catercorner from ours. As is often the case with Donnie's table, we could see the occupants, but they had no idea we were in full gaze with them. We could see them holding hands. We watched as they played footsie beneath the table. And when they crossed the line and reached across the table to kiss, we were both shocked that he was bold enough to pull off a New Year's Day lip lock . . . with a white woman.

I wonder how he'll explain it.

But I can't imagine how Kelly will take it.

She'll be pissed from the jump because Alan is out with another woman. And if you add in that he's out with another woman in a restaurant that they regularly frequent, Kelly may boil over to full frenzy mode. Kelly's one and only love is committing the ultimate act of betrayal. And my money says she'll whack his tires, smash his windows, and slice his medical jackets with incredible precision. Like Joan Crawford, she'll perhaps even save her dignity and do him in while wearing an evening gown.

But that will only be a start.

The whole white girl thing will really get her going.

Sisters would rather you cheat with a guy than catch you with a white woman. If you're caught with a white woman, it's the one time a woman will numbly recite the line "I'm no longer responsible for my actions." In fact, the very first legal plea of "temporary insanity" can probably be traced to a sister back in the day who wiped out her old man after she caught him bedding down a white woman.

Sisters can deal with almost anything. You can steal their money. Wreck their cars. And even commit unspeakable indiscretions with their best friends. You can cause them to lose jobs because you act like a nut at their workplaces. You can not pay the mortgage and have them evicted. And you can curse their parents, family, and friends and ruin relationships they've held long before you and that they'll rekindle long after you.

You can commit all levels of malaise, mischief, and mayhem.

And the average sister will find it in her heart to eventually forgive you.

But if you cheat with a white woman, you're done. White women represent the point of no return. They are the apple in the Garden of Eden . . . the original sin. Simply put, when it comes to white women, "Sisters ain't having it!"

Why?

Some would argue that white women are everything that black women can't be. But brothers and sisters alike know that's a joke. Sisters don't want to be like white women. They're having too much fun being themselves.

Others would have you believe that white women have an unnerving affect on the overall psyches of black women. With their easy-to-style hair, naturally light eyes, and carefree, eager-to-please personalities, any white woman is a threat.

Those myths stopped the day that brothers and sisters started to move up the corporate ladder and had to compete with or outright work for white women. The white woman who demanded that you stay late to crank out a report that you should have turned in two weeks earlier wasn't the Sweet Polly Purebread that you thought all white women were. She's not the social worker who instantly changes the lives of inner city kids with her innovative work plans. And she isn't the white woman who represents the overblown "virtues" of European white style and beauty.

The white woman at work is the *white chick* who is as tough and as smart and as condescending as the white men that everybody's pissed at.

Sisters can't tolerate their men cheating with white women for one simple reason. Sheer numbers. Black women make up the largest group of single people on the planet. There are more single black women than single black anything. A sister past age 30 will win Powerball before she finds a committed relationship. And if she hits 35 without a serious commitment, she might as well set up an exploratory committee and run for president, because she'll have a much better chance at running the free world than she does at walking down the aisle.

Sisters know the numbers aren't in their favor. Sadly, there are more brothers wasting time with the criminal justice system than there are pursuing degrees, careers and futures in colleges and universities. There are brothers to be had, but far too many make sisters feel like they've been had.

And for sisters insisting on "quality brothers" who can juggle jobs, love lives, and conversations that don't end in "you know what I'm saying?" the pickings are slim. They're not about to share those pickings with anyone. They especially won't share them with white women. This doesn't fully explain how Kelly might react, however. Especially since Alan is white.

"Whatever happened to once a fool goes black, he don't go back?" Donnie asked, laughing.

"Alan's not a fool," I answered.

"He is if he thinks he can pull this off on Kelly. A white boy cheating on a sistah with a white chick," he observed. "That's like double identity."

"I think you mean double indemnity."

"I know what I mean, son," he shot back. "That fool's gonna wish he had another identity when Kelly gets to his sorry ass."

"It's not like she's gonna walk in here and catch him," I observed.

"The hell she won't. I was going to save this for later," he said, reaching for his pocket. "But the situation calls for it. Here."

"What's this?" I asked, now holding a tiny gift-wrapped box.

"I missed the whole Christmas thing with that little situation over to the rehab," he explained. "So I had to go all out for a brother," he added, smiling.

"So they really locked the whole place down because they caught a couple having sex?"

"That's how it works," he answered.

"But they were married!" I reminded him.

"It's a rehab thing," he muttered, shaking his head. "You wouldn't understand."

"So what is this anyway?" I asked. "And exactly how hot is it?"

"It's one of them cell phone, two-way pieces with the Internet slapped up in it," he said. "T-Mobile makes it and it's called a Sidekick, but I call it 'how to save Shawn Wayne from hanging hisself,'" he reasoned.

"I'm afraid to ask," I admitted.

"Before you hang yourself out to dry, you can hit me up on a two-way," he said, pulling out a gold-toned Sidekick of his own, "and we can set your ass straight."

"So if I'm out on a date and things are getting a little sticky, I'm supposed to pull out this *machine,* type in some words, send you a message, wait for your response, and nobody's going to notice that any of this is going on?" I said sarcastically.

"You don't know how to mack," Donnie remarked.

"I don't want to know how to mack," I protested.

"As soon as you pick Troi up, you need to act like 'I'm one of them important motherf*ckers that's got to be in touch with some other important motherf*ckers because we working on some big-ass, chedda'-making-deal, business-type sh*t,'" he told me. "And while your ass is poking keys, she's gonna be getting her thong up in a bunch because she's gonna think, *I'm out here styling with a two-way-slinging, important-type motherf*cker.* And then," he finished, "you'll be macked out."

"Do you know how stupid that sounds?"

"I already programmed in my number and I put Kelly on your speed dial," he said, pushing #2. "So you can holla at her right now and tell her she can get over here and play emergency room on her little doctor boy."

"Hello," said Kelly, quickly answering the phone.

"Wrong number," I said, wasting no time in hanging up.

"What you scared of?" Donnie asked, surprised. "You ain't the one down here with no white chick."

"Tell me about it," I replied. "I'm the one who's here with a certifiable nut. I'm not about to see Kelly hurt because I don't know what's really going on."

"Is that right?" he asked, again pointing toward Alan. "My three-year-old cousin would know what's going on with that," he said, watching Alan and his companion kiss.

"You mean the one with the braids?" I asked, referring to his cousin.

"Hell, yeah," he answered.

"He's three years old, he can barely walk, he's still wearing diapers, and he sucks on a pacifier," I reminded him.

"So you trying to talk about my cousin?" he asked, sitting erect.

"I'm saying that he's a little on the s-l-o-w side, so he wouldn't know anything," I insisted.

"I'm saying that if he saw his momma with her lips slapping against some poot-butt clown's soup coolers, he'd know he was two steps away from another little brother or sister," Donnie explained.

"And what would that make, four kids in their happy household?"

"Seven," he answered, poking buttons on his Sidekick. "Unless you count the two that's locked up," he casually stated. "And then that makes nine."

A buzzing from my new "phone" is telling me I have a call and is stopping me from almost laughing out loud at Donnie's logic.

"Pick it up," Donnie ordered. "I put it on vibe so nobody would know you getting called."

"Hello," I answered.

"Did you just call me?"

"It was a mistake."

It's Kelly.

"What are you up to?" she asked. "And who's number are you calling from?"

"Donnie got me a new cell phone," I told her.

"Great. So we'll all go to jail for using yet another of Donnie's illegal contraptions," she said. "Where are you, anyway? Let me guess. You're either at some rehab or some halfway house."

"We're at Jerry's," I blurted out.

"I'm right around the corner."

"We're about to leave," I quickly answered.

"Well, I'll leave with you," she said. "Pretend that you're going to leave a tip. That should keep you there at least another *hour*," she joked.

"We're walking out the door," I lied.

"So I'll be walking in," she said.

If she does, she'll be shocked. Because at this moment, her heartthrob is walking out of the door hand-in-hand with a real babe whose breath probably smells like a jumbo shrimp cocktail.

Knowing that Kelly's pulling up, Donnie and I are doing what any good P.I.s would do. We're scampering to the front door to see how a doofus like Alan will handle getting pummeled by Kelly.

We can actually see Kelly pulling up, so this is actually cool, kind of. We're saved from bursting Kelly's bubble and we're right on the spot to help her deal with the situation. She'll be pissed, we'll tell her that maybe she was mistaken, she'll tell us how men universally suck, and we'll pretend to agree. She'll order a drink, we'll order an appetizer, and we'll tell her that she's better off without him. Then, reality will kick in and she'll whine about how he was so perfect and that we were right about her overreacting. And she'll want to call him, but we won't let her. We'll confirm that he indeed sucks and point out that he even dared to bring his little vamp to one of our hangouts.

And if all that fails, we'll hit her with the white girl card, and that will seal the deal.

But by the look of things, none of this is going to happen. Kelly is walking in the door like she just won a Fendi bag stuffed with free MAC makeup. She's smiling, she's giving Jerry, everybody's favorite restaurateur, a generous New Year's Day hug, and she has a sassy strut in her step.

And we're falling over each other to get back to our table.

"Maybe she's into three-ways," Donnie reasoned.

"The only three-ways she's into are when she calls me and then calls Macy's so I can pay off her card when she overcharges," I replied.

"Why are you paying off her credit cards?" he asked, surprised.

"Because she pays back," I told him. "With interest."

"So what the heck is going on here?" she asked, approaching our table.

"Nothing." I answered.

"How long have you been here?" she asked, her hands now squarely on her hips.

"Not long enough," Donnie volunteered. "We didn't see nobody doing nothing."

"And if we did," I jumped in, "we can't even be sure that we saw what we saw."

"Why am I lying for this fool?" Donnie exclaimed. "That's some bullsh*t! I know what the hell I seen."

"It probably wasn't what it looked like," I chimed in. "Hey, is this the coolest thing, or what?" I asked, changing the subject and proudly displaying my new Sidekick.

"What in the world are you talking about?" Kelly asked, staring us down.

"This is some try to catch us in a lie so she can trip off of how men ain't about sh*t type of sh*t," Donnie grumbled.

"I think not," Kelly replied. "This is some why is Shawn sitting on Donnie's side of the booth when we all know that our favorite parolee absolutely refuses to sit anywhere with his back to the door so that he doesn't miss anything type of thing. If I didn't know any better, I'd think you're up to no good," she went on, sitting beside me. "In fact, I do know better so I'm *certain* you're up to no good."

"Speaking of no good," I said, quickly.

"Was there any haps in the parking lot?" Donnie added.

"Has it occurred to you that English is actually a language of words?" Kelly asked. "'Haps'?" she huffed, looking at a menu.

"Yeah," Donnie countered. "As in did you see any *happening* ladies climbing up in anybody's rides?"

"How did this happen?" Kelly asked, sounding upset.

"It just happens sometimes," I told her. "You've told me a million times yourself. Men will be boys."

"That I did," she admitted. "But even *boys* can talk like they've at least attended an English class. We went to the same high school, Shawn, so I ask again," she said, pointing toward Donnie. "How did *he* happen?"

"I happened just like that blonde that your man was just sucking up to happened," Donnie fired back.

"Does he mean Rachel?" Kelly asked.

"You know her?" I inquired.

"She's one of Alan's interns," she said casually. "He's helping her prepare for her residency at Hopkins."

"That ain't all he's helping her with," Donnie shared.

"Alan was doing his rounds at Doctor's hospital and Rachel was there. He wanted a bowl of chowder and she came with him," she said, smiling. "Knowing Alan, he was probably boring her with his theories on nuclear medicine research."

"That and some autonomy bullsh*t," Donnie let out.

"Do you mean 'anatomy'?" I asked, kicking him under the table.

"Same thing," he calmly replied.

"According to Alan, Rachel is going to be quite the M.D.," Kelly remarked.

"He should fricking know," Donnie sarcastically remarked.

"And you're cool with this?" I asked, surprised. "None of this bothers you?"

"Why should it?" Kelly asked. "My mother always told me, 'If you're going to date a doctor, you have to trust that doctor.' At this point, I would trust Alan with my life."

"So would homegirl," Donnie observed.

"Speaking of trust," Kelly said, clearly prepared to change the topic, "Does *Dawn* know about your little breakfast soiree with Miss Thing?"

"As a matter of fact she does," I replied.

"I hope y'all got some waffles," Donnie put in.

"So what does Miss Entrapment Deluxe have to say for herself?" Kelly asked.

"Did y'all have the waiter with the buck teeth and the big ass?" Donnie asked, ignoring the conversation.

"Besides that she's pregnant, she's having it, and that she expects me to drop Dawn, not much of anything," I told her.

"You take a woman with ass and teeth like that, and it's on," Donnie insisted.

"You've got to be kidding," Kelly replied.

"Hell, no I ain't," Donnie answered. "When's the last time you seen ass and teeth together like that?"

"She told me that we're going to be together and that she loves me," I admitted.

"The one with the ass and the teeth?" Donnie asked. "You ain't trying to be with her. You just want to hit it a couple of times."

"Hitting it is what got him into this mess," Kelly interjected.

"You hit that already, son?" Donnie asked, reaching to slap me high-five.

"She's not exactly my type," I replied, laughing.

"That's what you should have said to Troi," Kelly remarked.

"That's some female player hating from the sideline type of sh★t," Donnie observed. "Ain't no man alive gonna tell Troi that she ain't his type. Them two gay dudes on *Six Feet Down* would straighten up for her."

"First off, it's *Six Feet* Under," Kelly corrected him.

"And second," I added, "They don't need to 'straighten up' for anybody," I told him. "They're who they are and they're happy with it. Isn't that what really counts?"

"Not if somebody like Troi is flapping her bazookas up in your grill," he shot back.

"So that's all it takes for men?" Kelly asked. "A nice set of breasts and you're no longer responsible for your actions."

"That, some buck teeth and a big ass," Donnie said, reaching up to again slap me an enthusiastic high-five.

"I'm through with this," Kelly insisted. "What are you going to do, Shawn? If you let Troi get in between you and Dawn, I'll take it as a personal affront and I'll never forgive you."

"I'm not about to dump Dawn," I answered. "But she is going to Chicago, so that will at least buy me some time."

"Dawn is rolling out?" Donnie asked, surprised. "It's about to be on up in this camp!"

"Has she lost her mind?" Kelly asked, worried. "She can't leave you here with *her*."

"It's not like Troi and I are going to hook up," I said, motioning to our waiter. "It'll just give us a minute to address the problem and set ourselves straight without having to involve Dawn."

"This has 'bad' written all over it," Kelly mused, ruefully shaking her head. "It's like a wolf having its way with the sheep."

"That's what I'm talking about!" Donnie said, excited. "Hey," he whispered, looking toward Kelly. "Which one of 'em is the wolf?"

"If you have to ask, you need not know," she fired back, now standing.

Then she looked down at the table and took a thoughtful

glance at the packets of Equal that were still arranged into Donnie's arrow.

"What's this?" Kelly asked, smiling. "Somebody getting in touch with their inner child?"

"What's this?" I repeated. "It's a . . ."

"It's one of them . . ." Donnie said, trying to save face.

"It's an arrow," Kelly commented. "But why?"

Though Donnie and I are looking at each other, it's clear neither of us is about to let on. If Kelly thinks that Rachel is just another resident, it stands to reason that Hillary thought Monica was just another intern. It took a federal probe from Ken Starr, several million dollars, and some of America's funniest illegal telephone tapes to expose Monica as an executive-level vamp. And since Ken Starr is now somewhere teaching bad law to a future generation of bad lawyers and Linda Tripp is now somewhere whining about her bad plastic surgery, Rachel's and Alan's secret is safe with us. Kelly's shrewd, so she'll find out before he ever tells. I can only hope to be somewhere in the room when it happens. Which takes us right back to square one.

"So is someone going to explain?" she asked, pulling out her cell phone and most likely preparing to call Alan. "Hello," she remarked, smiling. "Rachel?" she said, surprised. "Where's Alan?"

"Ain't this some sh*t?" Donnie commented. "This clown's not just a clown. He's a stupid clown."

"Great," Kelly answered. "Just tell him I called."

"What was that about?" I asked, knowing she was getting closer to Alan's ugly little truth.

"They're back at the hospital and Alan's seeing a patient in intensive care," Kelly told us.

Donnie and I are again looking at each other, and the only thing that's keeping us from blowing the lid on Alan and Rachel is the waiter, who just slid the check squarely between us.

"So does this arrow symbolize something?" Kelly again inquired.

"Does this arrow mean something?" I repeated to Donnie.

"Hell yeah," Donnie jumped in, obviously ready to blow the doors off of Alan and Rachel.

"But like you said to Donnie just a second ago," I told Kelly, "If you have to ask—"

"Your ass don't need to know," Donnie finished.

"Cute comeback, fellas," she said, wrapping a tan scarf tightly around her neck. "You're almost as slick as Alan," she added, walking away.

Not quite, I thought, concerned.

Not quite.

The Seven Different Types of Dads

Coach-a-Dad . . . a.k.a., "I Coulda Been a Contender" Dad

He pushes, prods, badgers and begs. He expects perfection and demands results. Coach-a-Dad's kid will be the jock he never was, especially since he spent a lifetime being the lowly last kid picked. But his son will make up for it. Don't get it wrong—Coach-a-Dad isn't just a sports freak. If he played fifth sax in the school band, his daughter has to play first violin with the National Symphony Orchestra. The biggest pluses about Coach-a-Dad? 1. He communicates—as in, he *screams* assignments, instructions, and formations. 2. He spends *tons* of time with his kids—unfortunately, it's only in gyms, on courts, and at fields where they develop special signals so that Coach-a-Dad's kids can ignore their *real* coaches to run plays devised by Coach-a-Dad. Coach-a-Dad sees school as a building where his offspring can participate in the games and performances he's prepared his kids for. The notion of classroom education is of little consequence to him. High school is little more than a springboard to college, which sets the stage for the Olympics, and then, the pros. Coach-a-Dad exists as a legend in *his* own mind and sadly, seemingly needs his kids to be everything he never was . . . a talented, popular, professional star. The payoff for Coach-a-Dad when his kid hits it big? That one shining moment when the family is gathered around the TV and the camera spots the kid on the sideline, and he or she yells out, *"Hi, mom!"*

20

Being alone is never cool at a time like this. I'd rather have someone bugging me about something that I'd rather not be bugged about than to deal with what I'm facing.

The buzzer on the microwave is telling me the nachos and cheese I just picked up from 7-Eleven are ready. Since I barely ate at Jerry's, my stomach is calling for food. I read an article earlier about black males in prison. Besides bringing on thoughts of Donnie, it smacked me back to reality.

The statistics are horrifying: 12 percent of brothers between the ages of 20 and 34 are locked up. Conversely, just 1.6 percent of white guys in the same age group are doing time. Kelly beat into my head that there are more brothers doing the jail thing than there are doing the college thing. She spoke of slim prospects and even slimmer pickings. That's how Alan got her attention. He was nice. He was articulate. And he could go on a date without having to check in with a parole officer, home detention monitor, or a halfway house receptionist.

Donnie represents that dark side that Kelly warned against. On any given day in any given year since we've graduated from high school, Donnie has been arrested, rearrested, locked up, locked down, released, paroled, detained, questioned, fingerprinted, or advised of his rights. He's had lawyers, advocates, social workers, pastors, preachers, and even a rabbi intervene on his behalf. He's been through 17 rehabs, six "self-esteem" camps, and served on two chain gangs when he was caught with weed at an NCAA Final Four in New Orleans. To Kelly, Donnie and a growing group like him have ceased to be dating and marital prospects.

They weren't the type of guys you took home to your bedroom and you absolutely didn't take them home to your parents. You wouldn't take them to your family reunion, and since Donnie's rise in crime has been so well chronicled by the local media, he wasn't a date candidate for our tenth-, fifteenth- or twentieth-year high school reunions. He attended our last reunion himself and sadly, left the very same way.

Donnie and his crowd were interlopers of the worst sort. They skirted the laws. Bought off the cops. They were supported and wrongly enabled by people like me who bought 42-inch plasma TVs that they still haven't paid for. I never really considered the implications of my role in Donnie's vicious cycle. And he wouldn't let me.

Donnie believes there is a systemic crisis that made him who he was. He didn't have a chance to succeed because life dealt him a dirty hand. "My old man was a crook's crook," Donnie once bragged. "If a brother needed anything, a lawnmower, some fake IDs, Redskins tickets, he could nab them. So, basically, I'm just stepping into the family business. I'm living out my legacy."

The legacy Donnie's father passed on was one where he taught Donnie how to conceal, lie, and downright steal by the time he was five. At that point, he was a statistic in training.

When Donnie turned six, his dad dragged him from the manicured lawns of his safe suburban home front to the asphalt jungle of a crime-ridden D.C. At this point, he was a statistic waiting to happen.

Donnie's father taught him to stash drugs and to "beat the man" who was making a living off of beating him and other black men. Like any kid who looks up to his father, Donnie bought it hook, line, and sinker. By the time he was eight, he had a criminal arrest record, a juvenile record, a taste for beer and cheap wine, and a whopping lack of self-esteem.

"Your family has all that structure stuff going on," Donnie once told me. "Your old man eats dinner, my pop steals it. And when your dad is doing simple sh*t like washing the car, my father's stealing one."

He wished my parents were his parents. Especially since they didn't fill his head with the rewards of out-hustling street hustlers who were out-hustling everyone else in a maddening game of cat and mouse where, ultimately, nobody wins.

Donnie's father died in a prison riot. And his mother didn't care. By age 14, Donnie earned his first "adult" conviction. And then . . . he was a full-blown statistic.

To Kelly and a throng of single black women who are uncoupled and interested in love, Donnie's the one thing they can't and won't tolerate . . . he's a suspect. Like Kelly, I'm not interested in a suspect. Especially in my own family. That's why the prospect of fatherhood is so important. I don't want my son to be a statistic in training. And as a black father, *I* don't want to be another missing dad who adds to the overcrowded pool of brothers who don't know their kids, don't support them, and whose only connection to their children are paternity tests, mediation hearings, and court orders.

My kid deserves better. And he'll get it. I just hope that Dawn will play along. Since my phone is humming urgently, something tells me I'm about to find out.

"This is one of those 'I'm not coming over' calls," I said, noticing her number on the caller ID.

"I am so sorry, Shawn," she answered. "They changed my flight so I can have breakfast with Oprah and her staff tomorrow. Can you believe it?" she squealed. "Anyway, they sent me a limo and I'm throwing together some outfits, so I'll meet you at the airport."

"But I'm eating nachos," I told her.

"Bring them with you," she said, no doubt stuffing clothes into a suitcase. "Meet me at the Delta Airlines terminal and hurry up because my flight leaves in a couple of hours. And oh, yeah," she continued, "bring my earrings. I left them on the kitchen counter."

"No problem," I said, walking toward the counter.

I couldn't be more wrong.

There are two pairs of earrings on the counter. One obviously belongs to Dawn. The other belongs to the proverbial "other woman." Only they know whose is whose and that's not helping me right now. And with Dawn in a rush, and headed out of town, the last thing either of us needs is a last-minute Troi-induced trip-up.

"Are you still there?" she asked.

"Uh, yeah," I muttered. "I'm just looking at your earrings and I'm thinking, 'Why don't I just buy her some new ones for this great new opportunity?'"

"Because it's New Year's Day and Wal-Mart isn't open," she joked.

"But K-Mart is," I quickly answered.

"My flight leaves in two hours," she reminded me. "So I don't think we'll exactly have time for you to wait for a blue light special." She laughed. "These are my *good* earrings, so I'd really like to have them. I know it's just a woman thing that you wouldn't understand, but a sista needs her favorite earrings."

"Your favorite?" I asked, holding both pairs in my hands and raising and lowering them as if they were on an invisible scale.

"Yes, Shawn," she sighed. "They are my *good* earrings."

"The good ones," I said, smiling. "Got it. I'll see you in twenty minutes."

"Make it fifteen," she said, before hanging up.

I hurried to the airport, parked, and made my way to the Delta terminal. Though I was rushed, I took a moment to place Dawn's earrings in a tiny gift box that contained a heart pendant I'd bought a long time ago. I'd actually purchased the heart for Troi, and when things didn't work out with her I tried to return it to the store. But that wasn't happening. Landover Mall was shut down, a victim of the faltering economy, so the store where I picked it up was out of business and I was stuck with a useless heart.

Then I met Dawn and the heart had new meaning. I wanted her to have it because it represented my heart. I may have bought it with Troi in mind, but the reality was that she didn't have my heart and after I met Dawn, I knew she never would. When my parents were dating, my father had given my mother a heart to express his unyielding love and devotion to her. And I want to do the same for Dawn. She may be going away, but I want her to know how much she means to me. The heart, which I've placed on top of her earrings, will say to her that she has me forever.

"I'm over here," she said, waving.

"Hey, Shawn," said Christina, Dawn's assistant.

Christina came to BET by way of a summer internship and Dawn took her under her wing. She's a sharp-dressing, fun-loving hood rat with a tart tongue and loads of attitude. Christina keeps Dawn's schedule and has come to be a close ally. When Dawn's upset, Christina will order flowers and will sign the note in *my* name. And when Dawn interviewed Allen Iverson for her show, Christina made sure I was on the set. Though she's proof positive that you can take the girl out of the street, but you can't take the street out of the girl. In fact, if she and Donnie were finalists in the world championship of cursing, Christina would be a 5 to 1 favorite.

"You're going too?" I asked, smiling.

"You think I'm giving up a free ticket and some free eats in Chi-town?" she happily answered.

"So do I look ready to have breakfast with Oprah?" Dawn asked, holding her arms out.

"Who's paying?" I asked, laughing.

"Tell me you didn't forget my earrings," Dawn said.

"If I hear another word about those earrings . . ." Christina complained.

"Got 'em right here," I said, displaying a tiny red box.

"Shawn, you didn't have to," Dawn gushed.

"Yes, he did," Christina told her. "You would think these earrings had a nice butt, a bank account, and a penis on demand."

"Christina!" Dawn said, embarrassed.

"Would you get your earrings so we can get on the plane?" Christina begged.

"Where did you get these?" Dawn said, slowly opening the box.

"What do you mean?" I asked, surprised. "I got them from the counter where you left them."

"But I didn't leave them in a box," she recalled.

"That came with the heart," I replied, as she held it in her hand.

"It's beautiful," Dawn, said, excited. "But why?"

"You're going away and I know we have a situation to deal with . . ." I began.

"You can say that again," Christina interrupted.

"But I didn't want you to leave without knowing that you have my heart," I told her. "This means a lot to me," I said, reaching for her hand. "But it doesn't mean as much as you."

"That's real nice, it really is," Christina said, looking at her watch. "But did you think to buy a *chain* with it? Some herringbones, some links, a damn rope," she spat. "Or was Penney's all out?"

"I love it," Dawn whispered. "And I love you."

"I hope he got some hooks for the earrings," Christina said, slowly shaking her head.

"Shawn, where did you get these?" Dawn asked, now holding the earrings.

"No, he didn't!" Christina yelped. "Where did Donnie steal them from?" she asked, quickly pulling out her cell phone. "I have to put his number on speed dial."

"Yes, he did," Dawn said, kissing me on the cheek. "You see them right here."

"What did I do?" I asked, smiling proudly.

"You did the thoughtful thing and you knew you weren't even going to get a piece of ass because she's leaving," Christina remarked. "Normally, that means you've done something you had no business doing . . . but you did that last night," she said, recalling my on air "confession."

"Okay," I said. "But what did I do?"

"The earrings," Dawn said, holding them to her ears while looking in a brown MAC compact. "You didn't have to do this."

"Yes, I did," I answered. "You asked me to bring your good earrings off the counter, so I brought them."

"And you just happened to have them sitting on your counter?" Christina asked.

"Of course," I answered, smiling. "That's why I brought the *good* ones. The ones with the G."

"Let me get this straight," Christina said, fighting to contain her laughter. "You plucked these off your counter because you thought the Gs' stood for *good?*"

"Of course," I proudly answered.

"Well I'm glad she didn't ask for an S broach," Christina joked. "Because that would have stood for *stupid*. She should have asked for a B pin."

"Why?" I asked, confused.

"Because your ass is *busted!*" she exclaimed.

She might be right. Because Dawn just dropped her mirrored compact and it shattered against the freshly waxed tiled floor.

Normally, that means seven years of bad luck. But seeing the look on Dawn's face, I'm wondering exactly when my seven years starts.

"You got these off the counter?" Dawn asked, sounding tense.

"Yes?"

"And you thought these Gs' stood for *good?*"

"Yes?"

"They stand for Gucci, Shawn," she said, sharply.

"Or *'get,'*" Christina said, jumping in. "As in, we should *get* our asses on the plane before whatever he's got rubs off on us."

"Goodbye, Christina," Dawn said, pointing toward the boarding gates.

"I can see where G could stand for *goodbye,*" Christina remarked, walking away. "I *still* want Donnie's number," she whispered in my direction.

"What's going on, Shawn?" Dawn asked, her shoulders slumping. "Why am I holding some other woman's earrings when I'm about to leave my man to go to Chicago?" she asked.

"Because you asked me to bring your good earrings," I foolishly answered.

"These are somebody else's *very* good earrings," she said. "And what they say to me is that I'm in love with a man I can't trust."

"But—"

"But nothing. If this had to happen, I'm glad it happened now. I love you, Shawn, I really, really do. But this is just too much," she went on, her voice cracking. "I deserve better than this. And if this is how it is, I can't deal with it. It's over."

"But this isn't what it looks like," I told her.

"It never is," she said, lifting her bag to her shoulder.

"But—"

"Good luck, Shawn," she said, kissing me on the cheek and then wiping away a tear that was slowly rolling down her face.

"What do you mean, 'good luck'?" I asked, worried.

"Go and be a father," she whispered, her head hanging sadly. "And be a good one." she raised her head and forced a fractured smile. "The world doesn't need any more bad fathers." She handed me the earrings.

I already know that. But it's what she said before she turned and walked away that will eat at me forever.

"And I don't need you."

21

I am at an all-time low. I'm bottom rung on the ladder low. I'm a dragging muffler on a tricked-out L.A. low-rider low. I'm a pig's belly crawling into mud low. I'm even lower than an ant at the bottom of the lowest tunnel on an ant farm.

I'm low.

Losing the woman you love hurts. Especially when you think you haven't done anything wrong. How was I supposed to know what the G on Troi's earrings meant?

I've never seen Gucci earrings in my life. In fact, I've never seen a Gucci anything in my life. As far as I know, Gucci isn't sold at Wal-Mart, K-Mart, Target, or JC Penney. I've never seen their shoes at any of the "Foot" stores I frequent: Foot Locker, Foot Action or Athlete's Foot. They don't sell Gucci at CVS, it isn't a menu item at KFC, you can't fill up on Gucci at Gas–N–Sip, and though they sell everything in the world at my barbershop, I've never seen anything remotely close to Gucci, which leads me back to the same question. How was I supposed to know?!

"You actually gave shorty Troi's Gucci earrings?" Donnie asked, surprised.

"I didn't know they were Troi's," I said, ashamed. "I thought they were Dawn's."

"And she left," he said, sympathetically. "Just like that?"

"She's gone."

"Quit sounding like Hall and Oates," he insisted. "It ain't like she not's coming back."

"She said she didn't need me," I confessed.

"She'll need to get laid, so she'll call back," he asserted. "That playing with yourself sh*t gets old quick, so when she wants a tune-up, she'll call, you'll tap that thing right, and she'll be back on your jock like Tide in the spin cycle."

"The detergent is actually gone by the time the clothes get to the spin cycle," I told him.

"You shoulda known that G meant *Gucci* and not *Good* instead of knowing about some fricking spin cycle sh*t," he observed.

"Well I didn't, so what do I do now?" I asked, worried.

"This is one of them fine wine deals," he answered.

"I don't drink," I reminded him.

"You gonna have to let this sit," he advised. "She's gonna need a minute. She's gonna need a couple of minutes on this one. But if she loves you, she'll roll back through. And if she doesn't, f-it."

I'm not interested in "f-ing it," especially since I've already "f-d-it" up. But if I know Troi, she'll make me "f-it" up even worse. The message she left while I was at the airport all but confirms it.

"I'm staying at the Grand Hyatt on H street and we clearly

need to talk," the message started. "Despite my misgivings about you and your little girlfriend, we have a child to deal with and I need to know your intentions. They gave me suite 1221, the same one I had when I was last here. No more games, Shawn. I just want to see if we're on the same page."

The trip to the Hyatt is giving me a chance to take everything in. Why am I going? Because Troi's right, we have a child to deal with. What will happen with Dawn? Donnie's right. She needs time. And how will I deal with a child? I still don't know.

What I do know is that something just hit me. The closer I get to the Grand Hyatt, the more I realize what the real problem is. Parenthood is one thing. But being a dad when your child is coming from the wrong mom is another. Like many men, I've always had a fear of fatherhood. For some it's the tremendous responsibility that comes with rearing a child. With others, there's that gnawing concern that you'll never be that superhuman father figure that your father was with you.

Still others are forced to deal with the fear of simply being a dad and a role model, because they grew up with none. They often believe that fatherhood begins and ends with Pampers, milk, formula, and a new pair of Jordans every six months. The sadness of their existence is that many times, they honestly don't know any better. This is a group that doesn't fear child support because they have no plans of holding the type of jobs where paychecks, pay stubs, and payroll departments can affect their income. They ply their trades on the streets, and the very real fear of living one day to the next far outweighs any fear of subpoenas and paternity tests.

Fear is a commonality among prospective fathers. We don't know what to expect, and we fear it. We often don't know what's expected of us and we fear that. Though it shouldn't make a difference, we don't know how society will perceive us—as dads in training, future dads in training, or as sex-loving, irresponsible baby makers. Nonetheless, it's a fear.

But my fear is different. As I make my way into the spacious atrium of the Grand Hyatt and slowly walk toward the elevator and up the hall to Troi's suite where the whole baby-making episode happened, my fear is kicking me square in the pants.

"I see you got my message," she said, opening the huge double doors and holding her fluffy, white robe closed with her left hand.

"Look, Troi," I started. "We're going about this all wrong."

"That we are," she replied. "But I don't want to talk about this in the hall, so why don't you come on in? I just got out of the shower."

"Oh, yeah," I said, walking in. "Like I was saying—"

"Like *I* was saying, earlier, back at your place," she cut in. "This thing with your girlfriend—"

"She's gone, Troi," I said, flatly. "She went to Chicago to have breakfast with Oprah."

"Sounds like an incredible breakfast." She laughed.

"She said she didn't need me and that she can't trust me."

"So you're saying it's over?"

"*She* said that," I said, shaking my head. "That's not what I want."

"But she said it's over and then she left, right?" she asked, sounding excited.

"Yeah," I sighed. "Her flight was changed, so she's gone." I reached in my pocket. "By the way, these are yours," I said, handing over her earrings.

"You couldn't have found a box?" she asked, surprised.

"They weren't in a box when you left them on the counter," I remarked.

"I wouldn't have left these on a counter," she said, holding them far away from her body. "In fact, I wouldn't have left these anywhere, except at the store. Where did you get these, anyway? Wal-Mart? They look so . . . so cheap," she said with distaste.

If I was playing basketball, this would have been great. I just pulled off a classic double-double. One stupid mistake, topped only by one even more spectacular.

When I went home from the airport, I placed Troi's Gucci earrings—the "good" ones—back on the counter. And when I was listening to Troi's message, the only thing I could think of was Dawn. I wondered where her plane was. Wondered if she would call when she "needed a tune-up," as Donnie put it. And hoped one day, when she was done being a fine wine, that she would at least hear me out and let me explain that absolutely nothing happened between me and Troi and that she—Dawn—was and is my only true soul mate.

"They're not cheap," I asserted. "They're Dawn's."

"Well, no wonder," she chirped. "But why am I holding these? And why are you so hung up on a woman who apparently shops at a mart?"

"Because I love her and because she's special," I told her. "Part of the reason I love her is because she does shop at a mart. That's part of who we are."

"I thought you said she left."

"She did."

"Well, then that's part of who you were," she pointed out. "Our child won't be taking the Wal-Mart, Kmart tours, Shawn."

"And neither will we," I told her.

"That's a given," she fired back.

"What I'm saying is that on the way over here, I realized what the real problem is and I'm ready to deal with it."

"And what might that be?" she asked.

"The problem is you," I remarked. "You and I shouldn't be having a child because there's nothing between us."

"Your baby is between us," she reminded me, rubbing her ever-flat tummy.

"And that's it," I said. "We don't have anything. We never had anything, and the truth is that we never will."

"I'm fine with that," she casually answered. "I just think you should be a father to your baby."

"I will," I said. "I admit, it bothered me at first, but now I know what the real problem is. I don't want you to take this the wrong way, Troi, because you're a wonderful woman. But besides not wanting a kid in the first place, my dilemma is that I got the wrong woman pregnant."

"Great," she said. "I guess we're even because I clearly got knocked up by the wrong man. But what you're really saying is that your little Dawn with the Kmart earrings is the right woman?"

"She got them at Wal-Mart!"

"And that's better?" she asked. "Wait a minute, Shawn. I don't know why you're getting all bent out of shape. If Dawn was so great she wouldn't have left you here with me."

"That's exactly what Kelly said," I shared.

"And if Kelly was so great, she'd mind her own business."

"I didn't come to argue about Kelly or Dawn or anything else," I told her. "I just want you to know that I'm not happy about any of this, but I'll be there for my child."

"So are you expecting applause?" she asked. "Yeah . . . Shawn is going to be a decent father!" she said, clapping. "Let's give him a plaque for doing what's right!"

"I'm doing what's right, because it's right," I stated.

"You're doing what's right because you don't have a choice," she said, firmly. "Your little Dawn up and left, you probably had an attack of conscience, *and* you know I'm not going to take this sitting down, so what were you going to do? If you're proud because you made the right decision, don't be. Because I'm not about to let you off the hook that easy. You got me pregnant and now you want to act as if I'm the problem?"

"I'm not saying you're the problem," I admitted. "I'm just saying that parents do things together. And if I know anything, I know we're not together."

"Think of what you just said, Shawn," she quickly replied. "What we're really talking about here is being parents. It's not about me, it's not about you, and according to you it's certainly not about *us*. If you're really saying we're not going to be together, fine," she went on. "We won't. But if we're to do right by a baby who didn't ask to be here, we at least owe it to our child to work together as parents."

"Why?"

"Because I'm not doing this alone," she said, sitting on a couch. "And because I respect you and I want you to be involved."

"I will be involved."

"But these earrings won't!" she said, laughing. "So sit down and let's talk this through." She held her hand out. "What are you hoping for . . . a boy or a girl?"

"I know I'm supposed to say that I just want a healthy child but I'd rather be honest. I want a boy."

"Same here," she said.

That's a surprise. Women as beautiful as Troi usually want a girl. They want to dress her up, buy her lots of Barbie dolls, slap brightly colored ribbons in her hair, and develop her into the woman they never became. If a celebrated rapper has a baby girl, she'll settle for nothing less than having a daughter who's a 100 percent R & B singing diva. If a golden-throated R & B diva has a daughter, she's thinking opera, pop star, and nothing else. And when a well-known TV star has a little lady, she's taking her straight to every casting call she can find for any *movie* role available.

Baby girls, daughters, and the ever-present princesses are often latter-day lab projects to their doting moms. They're no different than little boys whose fathers were denied their shots at pro sports. These guys are among the most frustrated and frustrating coaches, fans, and referees, and their female counterparts are no different, except that they're cutthroat stage moms and scheming, murderous cheerleader coaches.

I don't see Troi as the murderous type, though I'm certain she'd scheme even better than an Enron accountant. But I'd pegged her for a hair brush-wielding, script-line-spewing stage mom who'd give her daughter the blues for not landing the part in a Cap'n Crunch commercial.

I'm shocked that she wants a son.

"I don't think I'd like a girl," she said, grabbing a bottle of Evian spring water. "Too much work."

"And boys aren't?" I asked. "First you have to keep them away from little girls. Then you have to keep them away from the wrong crowd. After that, you have to keep them away from drugs. Then, you're right back to square one."

"And what's that?" she asked, smiling.

"Little girls!" I said, laughing.

"Especially the little girls with better bodies and better makeup than Tyra Banks," she shot back. "But you know what's interesting about what you said?"

"Let me guess . . ." I began.

"The only thing you mentioned was what you're supposed to keep them away from," she observed. "You said nothing of what you're supposed to do *for* boys."

"You take them to games," I said. "You take them to church. Museums, plays, movies. You enliven them and enrich their lives. Basically, you have to show him that there's this whole big world out there and that there's so much more for them to do than what you've told them not to do."

"So your theory is to keep them so busy that they won't worry about little girls, drugs, and getting in trouble?" she asked.

"It's more about exposure," I answered. "I look at the kids I came up with and all they knew was that we went somewhere every summer and when we came back all we talked about was North Carolina or New York or some camp somewhere."

"And your point is?"

"If I went to Georgia every summer and came back with enough to talk about until the next summer, don't you think somebody should have figured out that I'd have had even more to talk about if I went somewhere else?" I asked. "It was about being exposed to different places, different people, different experiences. I want my child to see things I've never seen, to think about things I never thought about, and to do things I never thought I could do."

"And you were going to send him around the world in Kmart clothes?" she asked, laughing.

"Wal-Mart is actually a little better for clothes," I commented. "Just like Payless is for shoes."

"Wait a minute, Shawn," Troi said, holding her hand up in a T like she was calling a timeout. "If we're going to do this thing right, can we at least agree that our son won't have a Wal-Mart wardrobe?"

"What makes you so sure it's a son?"

"Let's just say that I know," she said, smiling. "You're going to be a daddy, Shawn Wayne. And you're about to have a son."

"Are you sure?" I asked, excited.

"The doctor is," she answered. "According to him, the only time he's been wrong was about a little boy who later had a sex change, so technically, he was right."

"I'm going to have a son?"

"You don't sound happy."

"I'm going to have a son!" I said, excited. "I never even wanted kids, but now . . . I'm having a son!" I exclaimed, pulling out my Sidekick.

"What is that?" she asked. "And what are you doing?"

"I'm two-waying Donnie," I told her. "We're having a son!"

"I didn't quite expect this," she said.

"Look at what he wrote back!" I happily requested.

" 'Don't be a sucker?' " she recited, worried.

"Not that part," I said, scrolling down. "Read this."

" 'You'se a stupid mother-f-er?' " she read.

"No," I said, again scrolling. "This."

" 'If a boy ever needed a good f★cking daddy, it would be your sorry ass . . . congrats, poppy . . . don't leave without tapping that thing . . . and yeah . . . tap it for me 2.' " she said, gazing at my Sidekick. "I can only hope that this is some kind of code."

"It's never a code with Donnie," I told her. "He's just saying it like it is."

"So is it like that?" she asked, seductively motioning me toward her.

I'm walking slowly in her direction and looking her dead in her eyes. And though it wasn't in my plans, I'm taking in every inch of her. Her beautiful, bouncy hair. Her enchanting face. Her firm and perky breasts. Her slim, not-pregnant-looking waistline. Her sexy, shapely legs. She's an absolute dream. And I can really tell because the robe she was wearing when I started in her direction has now fallen to the floor. The closer I get, the more I realize that she could get a rise out of Liberace.

But she won't get one out of me.

Troi is everything that any man would ever want at any time. But the one thing she isn't, is Dawn. And Dawn's the only woman I ever want to be with.

As Troi reached for me, I reached for the robe, and hurried to place it around her shoulders, covering up that breathtaking, awesome, incredible, unmatched, unparalleled, unbelievable, absolutely perfect body.

It's the single hardest thing I've done in the last three years.

But it's the right thing to do. Especially if I ever hope to make things right with Dawn.

"You don't want me?" she whispered.

"That's a loaded question," I said, standing away enough so she couldn't feel just how a certain part of me wanted her.

"I don't understand any of this," she said. "I thought we would argue and that we'd really have it out."

"So *that* explains the robe with no clothes on under it," I joked.

"That was my last resort," she confessed. "If all else failed, I didn't think you'd turn me down. Especially since I wanted you in the first place. But we're actually getting along and acting like we're going to be parents."

"We are," I reminded her. "And I'm having a son."

"And I'm shocked," she admitted. "This morning, you're ready to run me back out of town and you're telling me to get *un*-pregnant, And now you're sending two-ways and you're all of a sudden happy," she said. "What about this makes sense?"

"This," I said, reaching to hold her hands. "I've spent most of my life losing. I lost both of my parents, but you already knew that."

"I remember."

"I was an All-American in high school and college, but I blew my knee out and if I ever had a chance at a pro career, I lost that," I went on.

"Okay."

"You probably don't want to hear this, but if nothing changes, I've lost the only woman I've ever been in love with," I said sadly.

"We could have done without that, but I think I get the picture," she said.

"Everything and everyone who's meant anything to me, I've lost," I told her. "But I'm not losing my child. So if I'm happy, it's because I have a chance to hold on to something. Something that won't leave, something that won't give up on me because I brought the wrong earrings—"

"You did that to her too?" she asked, surprised.

"This is a new chance for me, Troi," I said, my voice lowering. "It's like getting a chance to correct everything that's ever gone wrong with my life ·And this may sound strange, but I just want to say thanks."

"I'm almost afraid to ask why."

"You've given me a new lease on life," I said. "A whole new attitude. Just yesterday, nobody could have told me that a kid wasn't an interruption. But now, I know the deal."

"The deal?"

"I know you've heard it a million times. But a child is a blessing."

"And you just came to this?" she asked.

"I'm a guy," I reminded her, smiling.

"Well, guy," she said, reaching for a hug, "as long as you're a good father, I'll be a good mother. But I'm sticking to my guns. You better not ever take my son into any Wal-Mart, any Kmart, or any Mart-Marts," she joked. "One more thing," she said, heading toward the door. "Where in the hell are my earrings? I hope she didn't keep them," she said, pulling the door open.

"What is it with women and their earrings?"

"Those weren't just any earrings, Shawn," she said, looking me in the eye. "Those were my *good* earrings."

The Seven Different Types of Dads

Abuse-a-Dad . . . a.k.a., "My Daddy Did It to Me" Dad

An abuser of substances, liquor, wives, girlfriends, and worst of all, his own kids, Abuse-a-Dad is the worst, lowest, most despicable man known to man. He will cowardly justify the worst behavior by recounting his traumatic childhood or his inability to adequately express hurt, pain, and anger. He hits, and knows he's wrong. He fondles, and feels guilty. He acknowledges his temper and shortcomings, and yet somehow always continues a veritable reign of terror. Abuse-a-Dad is a predator, a violator, and a malcontent of the worst sort. Does he need help? Absolutely. Will he get it? Rarely. His kids most often see him in the standard Abuse-a-Dad uniform—orange jailhouse jumpsuit—and speak to him via phone, either from behind bulletproof glass or on one of his many collect calls from the local lockup. He cares little for himself and even less for his kids. Abuse-a-Dad's calling cards are intimidation and fear. Sadly, the only real contribution he can ever hope to make to his kids (or to mankind, for that matter) is when Abuse-a-Dad is reduced to daddy dead.

22

"So you're happy about being a dad? That's a good thing."

"And it's a boy," I said, proudly.

"Yipee."

"I figured out of everybody, you'd be excited."

Kelly had called and practically begged me to meet her. We attended the same high school and have worked together for what seems like years. But Kelly sees herself as an entrepreneur and even before we graduated, she was always looking for the next big thing. Her latest big thing is a club she now manages, a new hot spot called Dream. D.C.'s official party-meister, Mark Barnes, owns the club, and it has come to define how nightclubs should be run. Its swank and upscale décor is perfect for D.C.'s high-spending trendsetters who favor the airy high ceilings and roomy

VIP lounges over the bump and grind of other, less spacious venues. Mark spent a load to bring the area a night spot that rivals and even exceeds most anything that New York could hope to offer, and Kelly got in on the ground floor. She urged him to spare no expense, and he didn't.

Kelly may have met Alan on a ski trip, but she sealed the deal at Dream. Sadly, though, the relationship she jumpstarted at Dream has become a nightmare for Kelly.

"Alan is cheating."

"What makes you think that, Kelly?"

"Fours," she said, worried.

"Fours?"

"I'm a size six."

"And he's a size four?"

"*She's* a size four."

"Do you know who she is?"

"Not yet."

"This has *Twilight Zone* written all over it," I remarked. "You don't know who she is but you know she's a size four?"

"You remember Gretchen?" she asked.

"Your girlfriend, the one from Toronto?"

"Big eyes, nice cheekbones, big boobs," she remarked.

"I thought they were implants," I admitted.

"She works at Victoria's Secret," she explained. "And she told me that Alan picked up three thongs last week."

"So much for Victoria and her secrets," I joked.

"The thongs were a size four," she told me.

"Maybe he's trying to tell you to lose weight?" I asked, knowing that was hardly the case.

"He didn't give the thongs to me," she said sadly.

"So maybe they were for . . . his mother?" I foolishly asked.

"His mother's a size ten," she revealed. "And the only time he buys her thongs are for Mother's Day."

"He buys his mother *thongs?* For Mother's Day?" I asked, surprised.

"That and Wonder Bras," she casually replied. "So if they're not for her and they're not for me, who are they for?"

"He probably thought they were a size six and he just picked up the wrong ones."

"He specifically asked for a size four," she said. "And he had them gift wrapped, so stop trying to cover for him. One pair even has metallic silver hearts on them. He's cheating, and he's cheating with someone who's a size four. How can he cheat with a tramp that's smaller than me?"

"Would it be better if it was a tramp who's bigger than you?" I asked, not wanting her to get upset.

"I'm going to get to the bottom of this and you're going to help me," she said.

"I'm not getting involved," I told her.

"Are you my friend, Shawn?" she asked.

"Of course."

"Then you're already involved."

"This is between you and Alan," I reminded her. "What you need to do is confront him."

"Oh. I'm going to ask a man who has clearly been dishonest to be honest and I should believe that he's being honest just because I asked him?" she said sarcastically. "I'm not going to give him the satisfaction. He'll screw up, because I'll help him screw up."

"And how do you propose to do that?" I asked, unimpressed.

"That will be the easy part. You must remember, Shawn," she went on. "He's only a man."

That he is.

But Kelly will reduce him to a bologna sandwich when she nails him. She's not the type that will just take her toys and walk away. When Kelly commits, she really commits. She jumps into the deep end without knowing how to swim. She firmly believes that right is right and that she's destined to fall for only the right men.

She seemingly forgets that every right guy she's dated has one thing in common with every other right guy. They're all the wrong guys.

There was Howard the lawyer, who was handling his own divorce. Kelly was with him every step of the way. Until he got his decree and took off with the court stenographer.

Then there was Melvin. He was an administrator in the county executive's office. Melvin was nice enough, and so were his four kids by four distinctly different women. Kelly was fine with his little battalion. But they never went out on a real date because he was paying enough child support to feed Guadalupe.

The *Washington Post* ran an article citing the fact that Melvin was over $470,000 in arrears in child support and that he hadn't paid a dime in over eight years. This infuriated Kelly because their dates usually started with saltine crackers and ended with potted meat. He cried broke, she settled for Spam, and the kids got nothing.

The kicker was Gary, a hot and handsome NBA baller who played for the New York Knicks. Gary wasn't the typical professional basketball player. He was a Duke grad who had that nauseating preppy Duke look, right down to his shiny leather loafers.

He had the classic Duke box-fade haircut. Square, Frankesteinesque shoulders. And he had no tattoos, no earrings, and of course, absolutely no facial hair. He read poetry, watched the Food Network, maintained a garden, lived for Sunday brunches, befriended figure skaters, and was an accomplished ballroom dancer.

As Donnie put it, "Gary was a chick with a jump shot."

He was five years Kelly's junior and ultimately proved to be lightyears ahead of her on the outrageous scale. When he was in town, he was all about Kelly. She traveled to see him play up and down the east coast, went with him when Nike dragged him to conduct clinics in Europe, and even did PR work for his foundation, Giving Back with Gary.

He stopped short of proposing, but he didn't have to because he planted a four-carat, flawless cut, H color solitaire on her "point of no return" finger and gave her the keys to his swank Manhattan penthouse—which she quickly redecorated in a very feminine Ann Taylor–like motif. They did interviews together, vacationed together, did a photo shoot for *Slam* magazine, and then, to everyone's shock but mine and Donnie's, he got married to a Laker girl.

Kelly never watched the Knicks play against the Lakers because the west coast games came on so late, but that didn't stop me. One night, Gary dove for a loose ball and landed in a cheerleader's lap at courtside. Shaq and Kobe laughed like they were watching a Wanda Sykes video, and the commentators joked that it was Gary's best play of the season.

Clearly, he agreed.

The camera did a close-up on Gary, and it was 100 percent clear that the scantily clad Laker girl was whispering her phone number. I called Donnie the next morning, who like me was watching *SportsCenter,* and he saw exactly what I saw. But Donnie being Donnie, he parlayed it into a financial windfall. He wrote down her number, recited it to Gary when he came back to D.C.—which practically scared him to death—called the Laker girl and all but blackmailed Gary into supplying him with tickets to every show, game, and concert at Madison Square Garden.

Donnie tried to warn Kelly, but she wasn't buying it. So when he displayed a wedding invite, Kelly went, passed on a front row seat, and promptly reinvented the term *home wrecker.*

She begged Donnie to engage a group of his sister-girls to "detain" the bride while a veiled Kelly walked down the aisle. When Gary pulled the veil aside and saw a demon-eyed Kelly, he fainted, the pastor passed out, and the organist somehow managed to bang out the first seven notes of *Taps* before he, too, took a dive. Gary eventually married his Laker girl and took his wife and his talents to the Portliner Mustard Frogs, in the Istanbul Pro Select Basketball League.

I'd lay odds that when Kelly's done with Alan, he'll wish he was working at Istanbul General Hospital.

"Why would he cheat, Shawn?" she asked, upset.

"You're not going to believe this, I know I didn't, but Dawn dropped me," I said, hoping to get her mind off her philandering boyfriend.

"I was so good to him," she insisted. "I mean, there's literally nothing I wouldn't have done for that man."

"She said she couldn't trust me because I showed up with some Gucci earrings that I thought were her good earrings, only they were Troi's good earrings, so she dumped me," I went on.

"We were such a cute couple."

"And then she jumped on a plane so she could have breakfast with Oprah tomorrow, but she doesn't know who's paying," I told her.

"And I know that he loves me," she added.

"Donnie says that if I let her sit and treat her like a fine wine, she'll call me when she wants to get laid."

"I think I know who it is," she told me. "And I'm going to do something about it."

"Donnie also said that you're a freak and that he wants you and Melba to do a butt-naked three-way at the rehab in an hour," I said believing she was ignoring me.

"I always had my suspicions," Kelly admitted. "But doing it will give me closure."

"You were suspicious about Donnie and Melba?" I asked, surprised. "And you're actually going to do it?"

"If I don't I'll always wonder," she sighed.

This is a moment of seismic proportions.

I was just kidding about Donnie. I didn't think she was his type, but Donnie's always been attracted to Kelly. Not only does Kelly already know that Donnie wants to pull her into a three-way, but she's actually going to do it? I never thought Kelly would roll like this, but this is what must happen when hell is doing that whole fury and a woman scorned thing.

"Use that thing that Donnie gave you and two-way him." Kelly said.

"Okay," I said, pulling out my Sidekick. "But I don't think this is what you really want to do," I told her.

"I'm a big girl, Shawn, and this is something that was bound to happen, so just get in touch with Donnie," she said. "Please."

"I'm not hearing this," I said, worried.

"Are you afraid that I won't be able to handle myself?"

"Did you hear what you just said?" I asked. "You're actually begging for Donnie? I won't let you do it."

"You can't stop me."

"I'm you're friend, Kelly," I reminded her. "I have to stop you. And besides, Melba might be into three-ways, but with you?" I said. "That's just too close to home."

Kelly's silence says that I struck a nerve.

But she had struck one with me as well.

And she was *really* about to strike one with Melba.

When a woman does a three-way, she wants to pick the partner. It's usually a lonely type from a bar who poses no long-term threat. She doesn't know her, so it's not like her man will try to make her a bedroom regular, and she won't be a cutie like Kelly whom she'll have to worry about later.

"*What* are you talking about, Shawn?" Kelly asked, breaking our silence.

"You said I should two-way Donnie so you, him, and Melba can do a three-way."

"What are you talking about?" she repeated.

"You just said that you had your suspicions and that doing it would give you closure," I reminded her.

"What in the hell are you talking about, Shawn Wayne?!" she exclaimed.

"You . . . Donnie . . . Melba . . . a three-way at the rehab," I quickly said. "Don't you remember? You changed your mind that fast?"

"Heaven would freeze over first," she replied.

"I always thought it was hell that was supposed to freeze over."

"In this case it's heaven, because God would strike me dead before I'd ever do a three-way," she said. "Especially with Melba."

"So you're saying you'd do one with Donnie?" I asked.

"I asked you to two-way Donnie because I need his help," she explained. "Does he still know that guys who owns the spy place on K street?"

"Yeah, he knows him," I answered. "But his wife caught him with another woman and he lost his shop."

"How does a man who owns a shop that's geared toward catching cheats get caught cheating?" she asked, surprised.

"He sells good stuff," I joked. "And his wife bought a lot of it."

"So Donnie can't help me," she surmised.

"He can't and he wouldn't," I told her. "Regular guys aren't much interested in scamming other guys. And if Alan is actually cheating, trust me. You'll nail him."

"I just hope I nail him before next month," she quickly replied.

"Why?"

"Because it's his birthday and I don't want to have to buy him a gift when I know he's cheating," she said laughing. "So what was this about Dawn?" she asked. "Are you saying she's left?"

"She rolled."

"Well, don't seem so upset," she said, sarcastically.

"I'm upset," I admitted. "But what am I supposed to do? I have a son on the way and I have to get myself in check."

"What makes you so sure that you're the father?" she asked. "I can't believe you'd just accept it like this."

"She said it's mine and I'm taking her at her word until something or someone tells me otherwise," I told her. "If you were pregnant, wouldn't you expect the same from Alan?"

"Had you asked me that earlier today, I would have said yes," she answered. "But now that I know he's cheating, I doubt that I'd even want him around."

"Maybe we just see things differently. I've never wanted kids, but now that I'm having one, I'm ready."

"That's great, Shawn. Especially when you consider how bad off so many children have it," she said. "I'd like to see you as a dad, I think you'll be great. But children need a father *and* a mother and I might be wrong, but I don't see Troi as the mommy type. She'll probably have your son getting his thighs waxed before he's five."

"That's why I'm going to be an involved father. You're right," I said, laughing. "Troi will probably have his infant photos airbrushed if I'm not careful."

"What's wrong with that?" she asked.

"That's exactly why I have to be involved."

"You're a good brother, Shawn," she said, standing up and putting on her coat. "And I don't want to see you taken advantage of. If you're ready to be a dad, I support you," she went on. "But make me a promise."

"What's that?" I asked, slipping into my jacket.

"At the rate I'm going, I'll never be a mother. And since I'm even more of an only child than you, nieces and nephews aren't in my future either," she remarked. "So I'm proposing a deal."

"Okay," I said, wondering where she's taking it.

"Given my friendship with Dawn and my complete disdain for *her*—"

"Her?"

"Troi," she answered.

"I'm listening."

"This will be a task of major proportions," she said. "But I'll make a full-fledged effort to befriend and even help Mommie Dearest through her pregnancy. I'll even throw her a baby shower right here at the club," she said, smiling.

"What am I missing here?" I asked. "*You'll* throw a shower for Troi? You'll probably charge her to get in."

"What you're missing is that I made a proposition," she reminded me. "And I'm proposing that I'll help out with Troi if you'll let me be the godmother."

"You want to be his godmother?"

"I wouldn't have it any other way," she insisted. "If Little Shawn is going to have a godmother it might as well be me. But you have to promise that Donnie won't be the godfather."

"Do you realize that everything with you always leads back to Donnie?" I asked, walking toward the door.

"Honestly Shawn, I do," she admitted, before turning out the lights and subjecting us to complete darkness. "But let's just hope that he doesn't. Now, tell me more about your sudden change of heart."

"It's a combination of things," I told her. "At first, I felt like I was being trapped. And when I thought about it, I realized that she might have trapped me, but I can't take it out on my child."

"So you're being a guilt trip daddy?" she asked.

"It's less about guilt and more about what's right," I told her. "What if my father believed my mom trapped *him* and decided *I* wasn't worthy of his love, his concern, and his support?" I asked. "What if he said, 'To hell with it, I'm not going to be responsible for this kid?'"

"Good point."

"I look at Donnie sometimes, and I wonder how he would

have turned out if his dad was really involved in his life, if he had cared about Donnie, and if he wanted to see him become a *man* as opposed to a *con man*," I said, slowly shaking my head. "It's amazing that Donnie's actually as decent as he is."

"There's something to be said for that," she admitted. "But Donnie's made his own choices. You can't exactly place bad decisions and bad habits at the feet of a bad father."

"I don't want that for my son or anybody else's son, for that matter," I remarked. "If I have an impact on my son, I want it to be because I'm being a role model, and because I'm doing something right. Fatherhood is about responsibility, and if nothing else, Kelly, I've always been responsible."

"You're probably the most responsible man I've ever known," she said, reaching to hug me. "You're certainly more responsible than my no-good father," she added.

"Ouch," I said, knowing of Kelly's disdain for her father.

"If you even *thought* that I was going to let you be like that coward who spilled his sperm in my mother, you were dead wrong," she spat out. "He left me and my mom with a stack of bills that *he* created, so that he could marry his secretary's sister."

"He didn't leave you, Kelly," I commented. "He left your mom."

"And that's better? First off, even no-good bastards like him should understand that you don't leave your wife for your secretary's *sister*," she fumed. "You leave for the *secretary*."

"Good point."

"And you absolutely don't leave your daughter whom you raised as a daddy's girl to raise your *secretary's sister's* daughters and then send them to private school, while your real daughter is struggling to vary wardrobe choices in public school. He actually believes that he'll walk me down the aisle when I get married," she told me. "But I have a trick up my sleeve."

"You have somebody else?" I asked, surprised.

"Of course not," she answered, laughing. "I just won't get married."

"And this from the woman who just preached about not laying bad decisions at the feet of a bad father?" I asked. "You can't let him screw up your life because he's screwed up."

"He's already screwed it up," she said, whipping out a black MAC makeup compact. "And I won't let you do the same to your child, because as long as I'm around, you'll be responsible."

"I'm going to do that anyway," I said, smiling. "It took me a minute to get it right, but when my son is born, his dad will definitely be doing the responsibility thing."

"I like the sound of that," she said, powdering her nose. "Since you're going to be so thoroughly responsible," she added, "can you promise not to tell Troi that I once saw her as a no-good, two-bit hussy?"

"Too late," I answered, smiling. "She already knows you can't stand her, and she probably thinks you think she's no-good too."

"Well, what about the two-bit hussy part?" she asked, laughing.

"I can't promise that," I said. "Especially since she thinks the same thing about you."

ONE MONTH LATER

I practically wore out my computer keyboard by e-mailing Dawn every day for three weeks. The first note read: how's chicago? . . . hope ur well . . . number's still the same . . . give me shout when u get a minute :——)))

That didn't work.

So I tried a more direct approach: did u get my message yesterday? . . . had u on my mind . . . hope im on urs . . . lets chat soon . . . 301.555.2182 . . . :-)

Then I decided desperate was the way to go: we need to talk 2nite . . . 8:00 . . . i'll be near the phone . . . ate some of ur beets and your chee-tos last night . . . they were great! . . . if i don't hear from u i'll try again . . . 2morrow :-(

Desperate was no better than direct. She never replied. And calling her has been a colossal waste of time.

So much has happened and I never thought I'd miss her this much, so in the last two days I've left at least 17 messages. And I know she's received them because on the fifteenth call, her voice mail said her mailbox was full and it wouldn't allow me to leave a message. I called back an hour later and the messages had been cleared, so l left messages 16 and 17. Each was more desperate than the last. I explained that the earrings were a mixup and nothing more. I told her that Troi and I had made peace and that I was about to have a son. I remarked on how much I wanted her back and how I would jump on a flight to see her to patch things up.

And most important, I told her I loved her.

Once Dawn and I fell in love, being without her is something I never planned on. If I have a say in it, we'll get back together and will never be apart again.

But Troi may have a different take on things.

"I didn't think you were coming to the game," I said, looking to see if Donnie had also arrived.

"What do you think?" Troi asked, holding up a red baby-sized University of Maryland basketball uniform.

"I think we should go to Kmart after the game," I answered.

"I'd much rather have a Nordstrom baby," she replied, smiling. "Have you ever noticed that they don't have shopping carts?"

"They have them at Kmart," I told her.

"My point exactly."

Troi and I agreed that our child was in need of a wardrobe. She insisted that we hit Montgomery Mall, because they have a nice selection of high-end stores. She likes their stylish displays, their large and roomy food court, and the fact that they offer valet parking.

I like little-to-nothing about it. Their posh high-end stores are overpriced and overrated. I've never seen an Ice Cube movie at their theatres. Their Foot Locker sucks. And there's not a shopping cart to be found.

What Troi doesn't get is that stores that don't have shopping carts don't have them because they know you'll never be able to afford to put a lot of stuff in them. You could go to Value City and buy several suits, matching shirts, socks, belts, shoes, underwear, and soap powder to keep it all clean.

That's not happening at Nordstrom or Lord and Taylor. Even on their best sale days, you're not stepping out of those stores with an entire evening's worth of clothes. You can probably get a bottle of cologne for the same price that you'd pay for an entire hookup at Value City, but at the end of the day, what do you really want?

To smell like you've been to Bloomingdale's or look like you've been to Value City?

Troi wants the Macy's smell. She wants to look and feel rich. And her bankroll will allow her to get there. But she wants the same thing for our child, and though I can afford it, I'd much rather keep the costs down for his clothes, especially since he won't wear them past a year old.

"Can we go down to Tyson's Corner mall after the game?" she asked. "I was online and saw that they have this cute little store called Bay-bee Boutique."

"They probably don't have shopping carts there either."

"I never knew you were so cheap."

"I'm an accountant," I reminded her. "I just believe we can get more bang for our buck at a place that has shopping carts."

"Shopping carts are for groceries," she surmised. "And not my child."

"We're not shopping for a child," I reminded her. "We're shopping for kids' clothes. Who wants to go broke buying clothes that will only fit approximately three months on average?"

"I'm not raising a cheap child, Shawn Wayne," she insisted. "So if that's what you're trying to do here, you might as well stop."

"A smart child is a thrifty child and thrifty children become adults who run multinational corporations," I told her. "I want Little Shawn to run something as opposed to being run."

"It's Little Shawn, is it?" she asked, surprised. "Aren't we presumptuous?"

"Do you have a better name?" I asked.

"Little Shawn is fine by me," she shared. "I'd already decided that your first son should bear your first name. This *is* your first son, isn't it?" she asked.

"My one and only," I said, gently rubbing her tummy. "My Little Shawn."

"How do you suppose Dawn feels about this?" she asked, immediately reminding me that my hand is on her stomach. "How are things going for her in Chicago, anyway?"

"I don't know."

"You don't know what?" she asked, carefully lowering herself to sit on the first row of the bleachers. "How she feels or how things are going?"

"Neither one," I confessed. "Why don't you move a few rows up so you can have a better view of the game?"

"Okay, *Big* Shawn," she said, smiling, and heading several rows up. "You're telling me that the love of your life is away in another state and you two aren't on speaking terms?"

"Truth be told, I figured we'd be back together by now," I admitted. "I'm trying to hold on because I know she loves me. And because I love her."

"So she's the one," Troi remarked.

"I think *we're* the ones for each other."

"What if I told you I'm jealous?" she asked.

"That she's away in Chicago and doesn't even know if I'm alive or that she's probably with someone else while I'm here with you?"

"She's not with anyone, Shawn," she advised. "She's not going anywhere. At least not for long."

"What are you talking about?" I asked.

"Men are issue magnets," she explained. "It can be anything. Liquor, drugs, violence, bad credit . . . brothers do have problems. Then you add in the lying, the cheating, the not-so-funny way that men try to strip you of your pride and your dignity. And you have women like me, and most likely like your little Dawn, who see a guy like you as a real catch."

"So because I'm not a cheating alcoholic, I'm desirable?"

"That and the fact that you're a thoroughly decent man," she remarked, smiling. "I've tried to find the bad in you, I wanted to put my hands on that *thing* that would let me see you as just another guy with a truckload of problems, but it's not there," she said. "You may have your issues—God knows you're the cheapest man I've ever met. But you're a special man, Shawn."

"You think I'm cheap?" I asked.

"Women don't leave guys like you, not even *cheap* ones," she said, surprising me. "You're honest, you're sensitive, reliable, and gentle and I know what Dawn's going through. She's sitting somewhere right now wondering why she's wasting her time being upset about whatever's bothering her. And at some point, she'll come to her senses and she'll call because she'll realize that guys like Shawn Wayne have exactly what matters most."

"What's that, Troi?"

"You're nice," she said, smiling. "And even women who are attracted to bad boys like nice."

"You think so?" I asked.

"I know it," she said with certainty. "She's stressing about you as much as you're worried about her. I should know. I went through it myself."

"Really," I said, surprised. "How did you handle it?"

"I called him up, told him I was pregnant, and high-tailed it to D.C. before somebody else could gobble him up," she joked. "Only I was too late. So as a matter of advice, find out what she's up to, quick. Don't be late like I was."

"Why are you saying this?"

"I might not be able to have you," she acknowledged. "But I have a vested interest. I'd do anything to make sure you're not like my dad."

"You'd never have to worry about that, Troi," I assured her.

"My father put me through hell," she reminded me, looking down. "When he wasn't cursing me out, he had his hands all over me. And when he wasn't trying to force me into bed, he slapped me around like I'd stolen something from him. I have no intention of seeing my child suffer like I did," she said forcefully. "It's just not right."

"I'm better than that, Troi." I said, reaching for her hand. "You're better than that. We'll be good parents because we care. I may have never met your dad, but I know there's no way he could have been a happy man. He managed to raise a pretty decent daughter," I joked, wanting to lighten the mood. "But you know where I stand. I'm one hundred percent ready for this whole parent thing. And like I told you before . . . I'm happy."

"I like seeing you happy," she said, looking up. "And if you being happy means you'll be a good father, everyone wins."

"Speaking of winning," I remarked, looking at my watch, "I'd better go talk to my troops."

My "troops" are a basketball team of eight year olds. I'm their coach. Donnie's our assistant coach. And Kelly is our unofficial team mom. I'd answered an ad seeking a volunteer coach after the team's original coach was fired for forcing the team to walk home after they failed to score a single point in their first three games. By the fourth game, one of the fathers took over, but he quit at halftime and they forfeited the second half. The fifth game was highlighted by a bench-clearing brawl that gave the guys a sense of team pride. They lost the game, but won the fight!

I took over at the sixth game, and their fate hasn't improved one bit. But it doesn't matter. Coaching has a special appeal to me because I think it will be good to be around kids before I become a father. As a single, childless guy, I'm rarely around kids and have no clue as to how they operate or how I'll function around them.

I want to know how kids talk and what they talk about. I need to see how they interact and how they socialize. I feel coaching somebody else's little kids will help me to understand how to communicate with my very own little kid. But most important, like many other dads whose professional sports careers passed them by, I *know* Little Shawn will be a basketball player.

Coaching will help ensure that I'll be with him every step of the way, though my team's current record might indicate otherwise. I took over a team that had lost six games and managed to "lead" them to a miserable zero victories in the four games I coached. We finished 0 and 10 and were bounced from the league when we lost our first playoff game by 38 points.

As we gathered for one last goodbye, Donnie noticed two of his one-time jail-mates who were still seated in the stands. He approached them, asked about their little brothers—whom we'd just played—and learned they were twelve years old. The next day, the league commissioner called and said we were now in the championship game because he couldn't tolerate cheating. "But with that pathetic team you have," he warned. "I wouldn't show up. We can just send you your trophies."

My dad always told me that games are won and lost on the court, so despite the fact that we're playing the Wildcats—who trampled us by 54 points during the regular season—we're playing.

The Wildcats haven't lost a game in three years and are the epitome of a focused, driven, and very talented team. My guys, on the other hand, are much less a team and more a group of individuals. None of them is especially talented or even much interested in basketball. They're here because their weekend dads or single moms have stars in their eyes. They believe that their son will be that one in a million player who defies incredibly overwhelming odds to make it to the NBA.

In these parents' minds, their kids have already bought the house, brandished the tattoos, and purchased the luxury SUVs that are part and parcel of being an NBA star. What they don't understand is that their barely eight-year-old sons will literally freeze and become Alaskan icebergs long before they'll become professional basketball players.

As far as the parents are concerned, my job is to make sure that they don't become icebergs. It's a job I've come to love. My only concern is my "staff."

Donnie has serious lapses in his language around the kids and rationalizes it by saying, "With all the sh*t they're seeing on MTV, there ain't nothing I can say that's gonna screw up their funky little heads." I keep him around because he knows the game and because he genuinely cares about the kids. He makes sure they have rides home, he counsels them on how to avoid the lure of the streets, and in a pinch, he even helps them with schoolwork and projects.

Kelly's an entirely different story. She's evaluated each kid's height to weight ratio, established daily menu options to ensure their cholesterol and blood sugar remain within the safe range, and put the entire squad on a team diet after the very first practice.

She cares, but she truly doesn't get it. We're actually playing in the Pee-Wee league championship, and instead of bringing Gatorade, Kelly brought soy milk.

"It's easier on the digestive tract and the boys shouldn't be putting so much sodium in their systems," she confided.

When she should have bought bags of chips, she showed up with tofu bars. And instead of buying hot dogs at the concession stand to celebrate making it to the championship, Kelly insisted that the boys eat—what else—couscous!

In less than a month, being a coach has already exceeded my every expectation. It's fun. It's rewarding. And though we've won exactly zero games, I feel I'm actually good at it.

It takes me back to my childhood when basketball literally dominated my life. Basketball was all I knew and my father was the ultimate coach and my biggest fan. But the last time he saw me play was when I was just ten years old. I scored 44 points while playing on a highly ranked "select" team. During the game, something came over me—the adrenaline, the roar of the crowd, I'll never know what it was—but it was so crazy that I jumped as high as I could, and I dunked.

The crowd went wild. And so did my father. He was so excited that his heart stopped. He died right there in the stands.

Despite my father's death, I went on to become a high school All American, and eventually earned a scholarship to the University of Maryland. I scored 44 points in my very first college game. Later that night, NBA scouts were calling my mom and telling her I'd be a top-five lottery pick.

Then, unexpectedly, I blew out my knee.

It took away more than my leaping and dunking ability—it robbed me of my confidence. I no longer believed I was the dominating force that the newspapers wrote about, and I transferred to tiny Elizabeth City State in North Carolina where I vowed never to play again. But the coach recognized me walking across campus, and demanded that I at least attend practice so that his team could see an All American firsthand.

I eventually joined the team and my game quickly returned to form. We played against the mighty University of North Carolina Tar Heels and their hotshot superstar, whom the world would come to love as Michael "Air" Jordan . . . *with* hair.

It was the best game of my life.

And then, with the game on the line I scored my 44th point on one of the most powerful dunks I'd ever made. The backboard shattered, glass flew everywhere, and the buzzer confirmed the unimaginable. We'd upset the number one team in the country. And my basketball future was back on track.

I immediately called my mom, as I did after each and every game of my career, but this particular evening, Donnie answered the phone. He delivered a line that haunts me every night and returns in the form of a nightmare that never seems to stop.

"Shawn," he said, sobbing. "Moms is dead."

When I made the dunk that won the game, my mom suffered the same cruel fate as my dad. She had a massive heart attack. I was without the parents who had raised me with more love and respect than any kid ever deserved. At that point, my life meant nothing. I went into full meltdown mode. I was clinically depressed.

I didn't date or even consider meeting women for ten years. And then I met Troi, who was a human bulldozer when it came to relationships. After we fizzled, I ran into Dawn, whom I'd dated in high school, and we started the best relationship I've ever known. She understood me, cared about me, and encouraged me to return to the court.

I played in a work league and in my first game back, had 42 points. On the last play, I dunked to score 44. Knowing my peculiar history, the entire gym went into a silent hush as everyone searched the stands to see who had suffered a heart attack.

But fate finally played into my hands. No one was dead!

A moment later, when the buzzer sounded, the crowd went wild. With that shot, I had come full circle and had gotten my life back. To this day I thank Dawn for forcing me back to basketball.

But right now, I'm thanking Little Shawn for putting me back in the game. I'm doing it for him so that in five years, I can do it *with* him. Watching the kids on our team, which we named Maryland Storm, has helped me to understand two important facts:

1. I can't wait for Little Shawn to be my son, and

2. I absolutely can't wait to be Little Shawn's father.

I know it goes against everything I've ever said, thought, or felt about kids, but sometimes a guy has to admit he had it all wrong. I can't say that I ever really expected that a "Little Shawn" would even be an issue at this point in my life. But now that he's on the way, my life will never be the same.

"Money, money and mo' money, you're not gonna believe who's up in this camp," Donnie said, watching our team stumble through warm-ups.

"Don't tell me Melba actually showed up," I answered. "I thought you were giving her the boot."

"How can I give her the fricking boot when I can't find her ass?" he asked, upset. "She rolled out of the rehab and she won't even holla back at me on a cell phone that *I* gave her. "So don't be asking me about no Melba. Anyway," he said, changing gears. "Check out who the f*cking wind blew in."

"Who?" I said, checking over our roster, and then searching the quickly filling stands.

"Section two, row five, seat twelve," he calmly remarked.

"What's Alan doing here?" I remarked, filling out our score-book. "He doesn't come to our games."

"Section six, row three, seat five," he commented.

"Rachel?" I asked, almost in shock. "Maybe she has a body double," I joked.

"Not with a body that tight," Donnie remarked, pulling out his Sidekick. "Where's Kelly?"

"Hold up," I said, reaching my hand out to stop him.

"Bump that," Donnie shot back. "I overheard them when they was walking in. Her little cousin runs with the Wildcats."

"That explains why *she's* here," I reasoned.

"And they're talking 'bout hooking up over near the Coke ma-chine during halftime," he quickly added, punching in Kelly's number on his speed dial.

"Just wait for a second, D," I insisted.

"Yo, Kelly," Donnie said, putting her on speakerphone.

"Why are you calling me?" she asked, taking her usual first stab at Donnie. "A little short on bail money?"

"Uh," he said, looking toward me. "Uh, Shawn said what's up with that soy sh★t?"

"He's looking for our soy milk?" she said, excited. "It's so much better than that gator juice you're forcing on them. I'm also bringing some pasta," she remarked. "Great for carb loading right before a game. Hey," she said, sounding surprised. "Alan beat me here."

"You know that he's up in here?" Donnie asked.

"Of course," she answered. "This *is* a championship and I told him that every team needs a staff physician."

"That's some of that 'he must be out of his mind your mind and even *my* mind type of sh★t,'" Donnie said before hanging up.

"What do we usually do at halftime?" I asked Donnie.

"Besides getting blown out?" he asked.

"Good point. What are we doing at halftime of this game?" I asked.

"If they haven't scored, we gonna kick their f★cking little asses," Donnie warned.

"Besides that."

"We gonna whip their momma's asses?" he asked.

"We're going to call them to the bench . . ."

"I'm feeling you."

"We're going to wait for the gym to clear . . ."

"I'm with that."

"And then," I said, reaching to slap him five. "We're taking our team on a little field trip."

"What the f★ck are you talking about?" Donnie asked. "Didn't nobody sign no permission slips."

"None needed," I said, smiling. "We're taking them right out to the hall."

"The hall?" he inquired.

"To see the Coke machine!"

"But what about Kelly's soy sh★t?"

And then it hit him.

"Damn, money," he said. "*That* Coke machine?"

"Our team is going to have a Coke . . ."

"And a motherf★cking smile!" Donnie exclaimed. "I can't believe that Dr. Do Nothing stepped up in here with the same piece of ass he was sporting at Jerry's."

"Rachel must have stuffed something up Alan's stethoscope," I joked. "But Kelly's going to *ram* something up it."

"A brother must have took his genius pill this morning," Donnie said, slapping me high five.

I hadn't. But it didn't matter.

"Listen up, fellas," I said, gathering the team in our pre-game huddle. "How many games have we won?"

"None!"

"How many have we lost?"

"All of them!" they yelled together.

"What do we have to lose?" I asked.

"Nothing!" they sang back.

Knowing we'd never won anything, they are 100 percent right.

"Let's have fun, fellas," I requested. "Just go out and make it fun."

"Can I get in the game now, coach?" asked Jerry, who has yet to even touch the ball all season.

"The game hasn't even started yet, Jerry," I reminded him.

Though I really like having Jerry around, this is one game I'd like to keep him out of. In fact, the only reason he'll get in is because of the "everybody plays" rule. This is one of the drawbacks of playing Pee Wee ball, because when you have a chance at a championship, you want to go with your best. The kids want the better players to play and it's the one time that teammates won't fret over playing time, because nothing beats winning a championship. Though the rules state that every kid has to play, if we have a shot, it won't be because of Jerry.

When our starters shocked everyone, including *themselves*, by taking the lead at the start of the game, it all but confirmed my theory. We were up five and then seven, and before I knew it, their coach was calling a time-out.

Because of their overwhelming size and talent, the Wildcats easily rolled over every opponent they faced. Being underdogs to such a quality team meant the crowd was squarely in our corner. They yelled at every good play and every shot we made, but it didn't make much of a difference because within minutes, we realized they were ten times better than we could ever hope to be. After a steal, a three-pointer, and two more steals that led to easy lay-ups, the crowd was quieted and we were down by eight.

By halftime the Wildcats were up by 12.

But Alan was about to be down by one . . . very good woman.

When the refs signaled the start of halftime, Kelly went into nutrition overload. While the kids sat sweating on the bench, she donned an apron that of course perfectly matched our red and white uniforms and paraded from one end of the bench to the other. When she was finished, each player was holding a plate of hot pasta, which she had retrieved from a crock pot that she had set up at the end of the bench.

It's probably the first time in history that a crock pot has been so close to the court, but there was a spare outlet near the scorer's table, so the scorekeepers allowed her to plug in when she promised them a plate.

"There's extras if anyone wants some," she reminded both the scorekeepers and the team.

"Do you think Allen Iverson eats this stuff when he's at his games?" one of the players asked.

"If you don't want yours, give it up," remarked Carl, a polar opposite to Jerry and easily our heaviest player.

"Let's go," I said, motioning for everyone to stand.

"What are you talking about, Coach?" Carl asked, stuffing his face. "The clock says we still have five minutes left."

"And I guess that means you have five plates left," guessed Donnie.

"Let's go, fellas," I repeated.

"Are we going to McDonald's, Coach?" one of the players asked.

"McDonald's?" Kelly asked, alarmed. "I'm thinking we'll do some nice Cornish hens over a bed of rice pilaf if we win."

"Are we there yet, Coach?" one of the kids asked as we hit the hall and made our way to the Coke machine.

We were—and then our unofficial team mom took over as only she could.

"Alan?" she said, tapping him on the back. "Is that you?"

"Kelly," he said, quickly pulling away. "I thought you were doing halftime in the gym. Did the kids enjoy their pasta?"

"Were you just hugging her?" Kelly asked, looking him dead in the eye.

"We just haven't seen each other and it was one of those . . . 'we just haven't seen each other' hugs," Rachel volunteered, feebly reaching out to embrace Kelly.

"I don't think so," Kelly spat out, moving back. "Save your hugs for Alan, sweetie, because when I'm done with him, he'll *need* them."

"Can I get in the game, Coach?" Jerry asked, tugging at my jeans.

"It's halftime, Jerry," I reminded him.

Kelly then lowered her head and slowly looked up.

"Why didn't I figure this out?" she said, shaking her head.

"Can I get some Gatorade?" Matthew, our point guard, asked. "I think I have some pasta stuck in my throat."

"Take this and like it," Kelly said, shoving a can of soy milk in his face. "So this is her," she said, giving Rachel a thorough once-over.

"Excuse me," Rachel asked, sounding worried. "I'm who?"

"Have you put on weight, Rachel?" Kelly asked. "I remember you being just a tad bit thinner. But now, I'd put you at, say . . . a size six."

"F-o-u-r," I coughed.

"Oh my God, I look like a size six?" Rachel said, worried. "I'm a four."

"You're not wearing it well," Kelly said, hurrying to remove her apron.

And then Kelly did the unthinkable, the unimaginable and the unbelievable, even for a woman as scorned and as angry as she was. She stomped toward Rachel, who tried to hide behind Alan, who was *already* trying to hide behind the Coke machine, and went right for the one piece of evidence that would nail Alan beyond repair.

"So we'll just have to see what you *are* wearing well!" she yelled, ripping away Rachel's tiny miniskirt. "Take it off, heifer!" she exclaimed.

"She *is* a size four!" yelled Carl, still stuffing his face with pasta.

"How the hell would you know?!" Donnie exclaimed. "You're a size twenty-four!"

"How did they get those silvery heart things on her drawers?" Matthew asked. "Do they come in cars?"

If they did, we weren't about to find out.

"Hey," said Paul, one of our forwards. "My mommy has some of those. Except her butt's bigger."

"Rachel does have a nice ass," Donnie whispered to me.

"So this is what you were doing . . ."

"I can explain this, Kelly," Alan, said, reaching for the skirt.

"Perhaps I should have said, 'this is *who* you were doing,'" Kelly remarked, waving the skirt from side to side to keep it from Alan's desperate hands.

"I can't believe she thought I was a size six," Rachel said, seemingly forgetting that the only things below her waist were her thong and some very sexy black pumps.

"I don't know what's worse," Kelly said. "That you blew me off for a fricking college student or that she's . . ."

"A size four?" Carl asked.

"No," Kelly shot back. "I can't believe you played me for a white girl."

"My mommy's white!" Paul happily exclaimed.

"Duh. So is your father," Matthew reminded him.

"No wonder your ass can't jump," Donnie reasoned.

I doubt that's the case. But it doesn't matter. The buzzer is sounding and halftime is already over.

"Don't call me again, Alan," Kelly warned, near tears. "And you, you no good piece of trash," Kelly said to Rachel. "You've been in my house. You've sat at my table. You—"

"Did she have your pasta, Team Mom?" Jerry asked, reaching to grab Kelly's hand. "Because if she did, it was the bestest pasta she's ever aten. We have to go on account of we need our soy milk if we're gonna win the game."

And with that, we turned away and quickly left. We couldn't have dreamed of a better way to head back to the gym. Jerry had saved Kelly from making a complete fool of herself, and he saved Alan from taking a soul-sistah beat-down.

But I doubt that he'll be able to save us from losing the championship, which doesn't surprise me, especially since he didn't even save Rachel's miniskirt. He grabbed it from Kelly's hand and tossed it in a waiting trashcan.

From the mouths of babes, I thought, smiling as the ref whistled the start of the second half. *From the mouths of babes.*

I can't wait to hear Little Shawn's first words.

I really can't wait.

23

"O h my God."

"Oh your God what?" I asked.

"A woman just walked by wearing a thong with silver hearts."

"What else is she wearing?"

"Alan," Troi answered, sounding surprised.

"I'll tell you about it as soon as the game is over," I said, looking toward Donnie. "How's my Little Shawn doing?"

"I don't mean to pry," she said, before hanging up. "But is that a Crock-Pot at the end of your bench?"

It is. But it's not as hot as our game.

Though I don't believe he realized it, Matthew hit two three-pointers. Then Carl made a lay-up. And after that, Paul shocked everyone by actually jumping to get a rebound and scoring on a put back to put us down by a bucket.

The margin stayed the same for three solid minutes as neither team scored. With a minute left, we were down 43–41 and within three points of actually winning a championship. With the excitement building, Donnie convinced me to call a timeout to set up a special play to win the game.

In an instant, our move toward a championship appeared to be derailed. Because we had stayed so close to the powerhouse Wildcats, I made a basic coaching mistake. I'd forgotten to put Jerry in the game. With the championship on the line, he was certain to remind me.

"Can I get in the game, Coach?" he asked, as we huddled.

"What if I get you one of them special-edition, silver PlayStations and hook you up with Madden?" Donnie pleaded, kneeling down to see Jerry face-to-face.

"I want to get in the game," Jerry answered, placing a bright red headband around his head. "My mom doesn't let me watch TV, so I can't even use a PlayStation."

If it gets any worse than this, I don't want to know about it. Jerry is that kid on every team that simply shouldn't be on the team. He comes to every practice, he follows instructions, and he truly wants to be a good player, but at this point, Jerry has the athletic talent and skill of an oat bran muffin.

His black, thickly framed glasses dominate his otherwise tiny and rail-thin face. Jerry is so small, we literally had to tie the back of his jersey with homeland security–style duct tape and we used the bad end of a tattered jump rope to keep his baggy gym shorts up around his chest.

He's the stereotypical little kid who is so sweet you can't help but love him. But you don't want him on your basketball team. Especially when the championship game is on the line.

I have no choice. Jerry's going into the game. But he knows the rule, and in case he forgets, I'm reminding him.

"Stand at half court and don't let the ball hit your glasses, okay?" I yelled.

As always, he's doing what he's done all season. He's standing at half court with his arms outstretched and yelling, "Am I in the game, Coach?"

He is. The only problems are that the clock is winding down, and an errant pass has put the ball in the very worst place imaginable.

Right in Jerry's hands.

The good thing is that the Wildcats seem to think we're running a trick play. While Jerry is standing looking as lost as the Dixie Chicks would be if they were on BET's hip-hop gabfest *106th and Park,* our opponents are racing toward our best player, Adam, who everyone in the gym knows will take the last shot.

Everyone that is, except me and Jerry.

Our options are limited and the clock isn't on our side, so we'll go with what we can and will win the championship . . . next year.

"Go, Jerry!" I yelled, seeing there is just ten seconds on the clock.

"The other way, fool!" Donnie yelled, noticing he's facing the wrong basket.

"We could have actually stolen a championship," I said, frustrated. "We got *this* close," I added, holding my hands near each other.

"Does anybody have any more pasta?" Carl asked, walking toward the Crock-Pot.

Jerry is standing two steps past half court. In practice he's never even taken a shot, and during our games, he's never as much as touched the ball. His entire season has been spent standing a half court away from the action. That way he couldn't make a mistake.

But as he's standing there lost, I'm facing what is easily *my* biggest coaching error. By keeping him away from making a mistake, what I'd *really* done was denied Jerry a chance to succeed. When I should have been preparing him to play, all I'd done was robbed him of a chance to make a play.

But he doesn't appear to be too bothered by it. Realizing this is his one and only chance to take a shot, he's quickly adjusting his crooked glasses and headband and is looking to me for approval. I'm responding with a confident wink and a thumbs-up and at the same time, am preparing my acceptance speech for the second place trophy.

Jerry, though, seems to have different thoughts. Surprisingly, he just winked back at me, gave *me* a thumbs-up and is now summoning all his strength, winding up his tiny arms to the middle of his back, and heaving the ball toward the basket.

The ball is flying in almost cinematic slow motion.

In an instant, I am seeing the referees raising their hands to signal a three-pointer had just been shot.

I see Donnie on his knees in full prayer position.

I see Kelly, still upset, but still trying to force our bench players to drink soy milk.

I see Carl managing to dig two forks into the mound of pasta he has just dug out of the crock pot.

I even see Paul's mother joining the entire crowd and rising to her feet. And though I probably shouldn't have noticed, I'm forced to admit that Paul is right. His mom's rear end is absolutely bigger than Rachel's, who's now standing in the doorway wrapped in Alan's pathetic white medical jacket.

And the one thing I see that no one will ever understand is myself cheering for my son. I see him looking toward the stands for my approval. I see him waving to me as the ball reaches its arc. And I see both of us seeking each other out as the crowd races toward the floor.

And we hug.

Unlike Alan's and Rachel's "We haven't seen each other" deals, it's a real hug. The kind that says, "I'm so proud of you, son," and that says, "Thanks for being there, Dad." It's the kind of hug that you never want to end. It's the embodiment of faith, concern, struggle, and overcoming odds to win.

It's the kind of hug between men, young and old, black and white, relatives and friends, that says I respect you, I appreciate you, and above all, I love you.

Little Shawn and I will no doubt share hugs like this our entire lives.

It's amazing what you can see in a flash of light. Your life, your fate, and your future can look almost crystal clear. It's moments like these when time seems to literally stop. It takes a standstill. As a quantifiable entity, time is all too often rushed and is rarely appreciated. But during events like this—where unlikely heroes are born—it occurs to us that if time slows and allows us to catch up, appreciating that one beautiful second when the stars align and our wildest dreams are met . . . we can appreciate that we're in the midst of the best times of our lives.

I'm having a moment like this right now. And I'm about to share it with Donnie, Kelly, Carl, Matthew, Jerry, Paul, and even his big-butt mother because the impossible has just happened.

Just like he did with Kelly, teeny, tiny Jerry saved the day. He nailed the shot. And we've won the game!

When I played ball, I hit dozens of shots that won games. But none is bigger and better than this. I took this coaching job to connect with a son I have yet to meet. And my faith and spirit tells me that one day, he'll understand that the trophy we're about to receive is all for him. The kids did the work and we came together when it counted, but unlike them, I know it was all done to honor Little Shawn.

Though I can't erase the thought of my son and the moments we'll share like this, I can't escape visions of my mom, my dad, and surprisingly, Dawn.

I know they would all be prouder than proud at this moment.

The ringing from my Sidekick says to me that someone else is proud too.

It's Troi.

"Shawn," she said, trying to speak over the noisy crowd. "Shawn," she repeated.

"We won!" I yelled, excited. "Did you see that little guy hit that shot! Tell me that's not going to be Little Shawn in five years!" I said proudly.

"Shawn," she repeated.

"Troi?" I asked, covering my ear to hear better.

My ears are telling me she's saying the one thing I'm not ready for. And my fear is telling me that the curse is back. With Jerry's shot, we had scored 44 points. I always believed what Donnie called The Curse of Double Fours was no more than a set of unlikely, incredible, and heart-wrenching coincidences. No more and no less. But the curse clearly doesn't see it that way. It's the one thing I can't deal with. And the one thing that will send me into an even worse tailspin than WorldCom, Enron, and Martha Stewart combined.

The crowd is more than loud, the connection is not the best, and though I don't want to, I hear Troi all too clear. She's saying one word. And it's ringing in my head like an echo deep in a cliff-laden canyon. It's horrifying how hearing just one word can slap you in the face. How it can rob you of your dreams. That one word can bring you crashing back to a reality that will forever haunt you.

She's saying it.

I'm hearing it.

And now, I've got to act on it.

"Help, Shawn," she said faintly, near collapse.

"Help."

24

Nobody needed a trip to the hospital to confirm it. The pool of blood at her feet said it all.

There were complications.

Something went terribly wrong.

No matter how they tried to massage it, it all sounded alike.

And meant the same thing.

We lost Little Shawn.

The doctors have convinced me, and more importantly her, that she will bounce back. She is still fertile. In the end, she will recover.

The only thing they missed was that *I* won't recover. Especially since it was all my fault. One hundred percent.

She'd had stomach cramps, but I attributed them to her refusal to eat, and did nothing to help her change her habits. She wanted a seat in the front row at the game, but I convinced her to sit higher in the stands so that she could get a better view of the action. Troi had begged me to take her shopping, but I had to have her at a basketball game. In a crowded, stuffy, gym, where my son lost his life.

Because of me.

I've been down before and there was always something else, or more to the point in my case, *someone* else to bring me back. When my father passed I was young. My whole life was still in front of me, and with his manhood lessons, my dad at least had started to prepare me for the real-life struggles and challenges of adolescence. But it was my mother who helped me recover from his passing.

When my mother died, I honestly believed I would never recover. I went into a depression that even Prozac and Xanax couldn't help. Because I blamed myself, for ten years, I gave up on even thinking that I was worthy of a real life. My mother was a peaceful, God-fearing woman who couldn't have harmed a fly if she tried. She transferred her strength to me. She endowed me with her courage. And she helped me to understand that I had to make God the center of my universe and that he would help me recover from anything.

She had a million Bible verses that could explain almost anything. But nothing she said could ever explain why she suddenly died and left me even more alone than I already was.

Still, Donnie and Kelly were there to help. They called even when I didn't want to talk, and when they weren't calling they were in my face. Even though I was often stuck with the bill for what *they* felt I should do, in the end their intervention worked. I bounced back, met Troi and then Dawn, and ultimately got on with my life.

My father often told me, "Whatever doesn't kill you makes you stronger." As a jock, I'd heard more than my share of coaches recite that line. My mom repeated it to me when I blew my knee out and thought my career was over. When Donnie first succumbed to drugs, even *he* said it.

I bought into it. I believed it so much so that I bought a tiny plaque from an engraving shop, which I'd placed over Little Shawn's crib in my home. I knew it was a heavy message to lay on a little kid, but over the years that simple phrase had come to mean much to me. Little Shawn was not going to have to face the losses I faced. He wouldn't have to deal with parents who died because of him, and a best friend who nearly lost his life and spirit because of drugs. He wouldn't have a friend like Kelly, who's spent her entire life trying to find the one thing she's never had in her life, true, unconditional love. He wouldn't meet Troi only to lose her when he never really had her. And he wouldn't blow it with his one real soul mate like I'd done with Dawn.

He'd surely face adversity. He'd suffer loses that would shake his faith and foundation. And like me, he'd have times when just plain giving up would appear to be the only and very best option.

But he'd always know, like my father and everyone who thought I would listen told me, and like the plaque on his wall reads, *Whatever doesn't kill you makes you stronger.*

Little Shawn would have known it. But at the moment I need it most, I don't. I've sat in his room for two days now.

While Troi was building a Nordstrom baby and Baby Phat designer wardrobe, I had taken a more practical approach. Little

Shawn was going to be my firstborn. And though he was months from coming, I wanted to be prepared. Troi blamed it on the accountant in me and warned, "He won't be here for at least four months, Shawn."

As far as I was concerned, after a lifetime of letdowns, four months may as well have been four days. So, I'd cleared out my guest bedroom and prepared the ultimate boy's nursery for the very best guest I could have ever hoped for, Little Shawn.

I went to Burlington Coat Factory and located a super-safe oak paneled crib. On one end of it I placed a tiny, padded basketball goal. And when Donnie noticed I had just one, he went ballistic and bought a matching goal for the other end.

"My little dawg needs to run whole court," he said.

"He'll be a baby," I reminded him. "He'll be *crawling* whole court," I said, and we laughed together.

Kelly was out with me the day I bought 23 different colored basketballs. We both agreed that given Michael Jordan's immense success and hot shot Lebron James' jersey number, it would be good for Little Shawn to wake up every day surrounded by 23 basketballs.

We bought soft bright blue basketballs. Plush orange, green, and gold basketballs. We located glow-in-the-dark balls, basketballs that talked, and a ball with water that had even more basketballs floating around its middle.

But the one that stood out was a velvety ball that Kelly bought. It was bright red with the University of Maryland logo sewn in. And she had it embroidered with LITTLE SHAWN—DADDY'S PRIDE.

His walls are plastered with images that any little boy would appreciate. I had an extremely rare, framed, autographed picture of the 1992 Olympic Dream Team that I won on an E-Bay auction. There are pictures of Lebron, Allen Iverson, and Tracy Mc-

Grady, plus AND I's Philip "Hot Sauce" Champion, Rafer "Skip to My Lou" Alston, and Aaron "A.O." Owens. I even located a picture of one of the greatest basketball players the world didn't get to know, the late, legendary Len Bias.

I wanted my son to be aware of the proud legacy of his people, and adorned one wall with an array of photos chronicling black males in history including Frederick Douglass, the Buffalo Soldiers, W.E.B. Dubois, Adam Clayton Powell, Langston Hughes, The Tuskegee Airmen, Ralph Ellison, James Baldwin, Malcolm, Martin, Jesse, Cornel West, Spike Lee, Denzel Washington, and political commentator Tavis Smiley.

I wanted Little Shawn to know he had a family and a unique story all his own. There's a beautiful picture of my mom sitting on his nightstand. I have pictures of me in my Pee-Wee uniforms, my AAU uniforms, my high school and college team pictures, and our team picture with the team I'd started for him, the Maryland Storm.

But the most important picture I have—the one that will forever remain cemented in my mind—is a snapshot of my father coaching me during a game when I was six years old. At that point, my father was my best friend. He was Superman, Batman, and Ultra Man in one incredible mix. He was the smartest man anywhere. The toughest man on the block. And he was even bigger and better than the President.

He was what every boy wanted for a father.

I placed our picture in a frame that I located in my mother's home when she passed. I wanted Little Shawn to see where he came from. To see that I was as loved as he would be. I wanted him to know that fatherhood is one of life's great joys. He needed to know that the highest of expectations had been set and that he, too, would have to be an involved, engaged, and supportive father to his children. I wanted Little Shawn to know that my dreams started with the simplest of desires: to one day be as noble and as thoroughly decent as my father.

More than anything, when Little Shawn was old enough to understand, I wanted him to realize that role models start at home, and that I was going to be the best role model he could possibly have.

I never wanted a son until I accepted that I had one coming. When I knew Little Shawn was on the way, when I saw him curled up in a sonogram—when I could literally see him growing in Troi's stomach—it felt like being a father was the only thing I ever wanted.

I've sat in his room since Monday and between considering my dreams for him and the wonderful life I was ready to provide him, it feels like I've cried myself to sleep and cried myself awake a million times.

They say there's no pain that's equal to losing your child. They're wrong. *Burying* your child is life's cruelest blow. On Monday, we had a funeral. Little Shawn was prematurely still-born. A grief counselor convinced Troi and then me that a service and a proper burial would help us find closure from the most lasting tragedy either of us will ever experience.

Everyone who heard about it came. And everyone was sad. There's just no nice way, no fun way, or no easy way to bury a child. Especially when it's yours. We placed our team trophy in his tiny casket. And then we buried him.

I still haven't found the closure the counselor spoke of. And I doubt that I ever will.

Little Shawn was gone before he ever got here. I never got to hold him. And never got to see what the world looked like through the eyes of a child. My child. He missed out on so much. And so too have Troi and I as his parents.

Can you even miss someone who was never really here? I do. And because his death is my fault, my life will never be the same.

The Seven Different Types of Dads

Daddy Dearest . . . a.k.a., "Dear Ole Dad"

Not always right, not always wrong, but always there with love, concern, care, support, time, and discipline, Daddy Dearest is the Dad every man wants to be. Sadly, far too many men have grown up without a Dear 'Ole Dad in their lives or within their reach. But despite the notion that the world is overpopulated with deadbeat dads, no-account dads, and men who are out of touch with all aspects of fatherhood, it's safe to say that there are good men being good dads everywhere. Daddy Dearest is the uncle who cares for your cousins, the grandfather who is the pulse of generations beneath him, and he's the man who takes care of his household and who instills a sense of purpose, achievement, family pride, and respect throughout his family and in others. Where others yell, he listens. While others run and leave their families in disarray, he stays and works through it. Daddy Dearest understands the importance of nurturing boys who will become men who understand that fatherhood is about responsibility, commitment, communication, trust, and that above all it is the joy of joys. He may be without a degree, but he's smart and appreciates the role of education in the life of his kids. He's a leader, a friend, a role model, the backbone of his family, and the world would be a much better place if every family had a Daddy Dearest.

The Aftermath

Donnie and Melba split when he caught her getting high at the rehab. She offered him one last three-way, but he turned it down. He had to. The word on the street was that she was two-timing Donnie. And Donnie wasn't having it. He'd been told that Melba had been to the county jail visiting Lester, a.k.a. Swipe, a.k.a. the guy who never collected for the TV he sold me because he was locked up for having the TV in the first place, a.k.a. the guy who was dating the cable-pulling lady—until she found out, like Donnie, that Melba and Lester were engaged in an affair.

Alan moved to Montana.

Rachel was so embarrassed by Kelly's tirade that she pulled the move of any smart-thinking, cold-blooded, super-vixen, student type. She turned against her mentor, played the role of the misled innocent, filed charges, and collected a fat settlement check for sexual harassment.

He lost his license to practice medicine.

But he does work at a Holiday Inn Express.

Kelly is still managing clubs, and has expanded her horizons. She no longer settles for just doctors, lawyers, and white-collar men with degrees even fancier than hers. She's now dating Phillip, whom she met while he was putting up drywall at a club she co-owns with the unlikeliest of silent partners . . . Donnie.

I foolishly tried to arrange an actual date between Donnie and Kelly. Despite their clear differences, I recalled that Donnie was always the first to come to Kelly's rescue when other guys screwed her over. I guessed that he secretly admired her and that he just needed a gentle push in the right direction.

I guessed wrong.

We met for an impromptu dinner at Jerry's one evening and Donnie made his stance quite clear. "I'd rather eat cold fish like that sushi sh*t before I'd date it," he remarked.

"That's because cold fish can't bite back," Kelly smoothly replied. "Would you mind passing the butter? It's the yellow thing on the white plate beside your right hand."

They traded insults and argued for over 20 minutes and then realized their true calling. Donnie and Kelly were meant to be either husband and wife or cutthroat business partners. Since marriage was a complete non option, they set up shop and now run the hottest club in town, Cheaters, named in honor of their philandering ex-mates, Alan and Melba.

Donnie was crushed by everything that happened with Melba. He believed she was special partially because she forced him to meet the exacting constraints and restrictions of his recovery. It didn't matter that Melba was pushing more dope than Superfly both in and around rehab. Donnie believed in her and thought—like many had before with him—that she would change.

She didn't. And it broke his heart. For about eight minutes.

He met one of Kelly's snooty friends, Trena. Trena shares Kelly's sense of trendy style, her "ladies first" view of the world, her nauseating diet and eating habits, and she and Kelly even share the same yoga and pilates instructor. I still maintain that Donnie's always had a thing for Kelly. He was very attracted to Kelly's spunk and independence. She was the only woman who dared to regularly stand up to him, until he met Trena.

Since they argue as much as he and Kelly used to go at it and because their arguments have already resulted in a business enterprise, Trena and Donnie understand their fate. They're engaged to be married. They may actually go through with it if they don't kill each other first.

The parents and relatives of our championship Pee-Wee basketball team, DC Storm, convinced me to coach the team through spring and summer leagues. They must have sensed that I needed something to keep in touch with the world around me, which I had quickly started to withdraw from.

People deal with death, guilt, and loss differently. Some rebound quickly, while others never rebound at all. My solution is simple. I go into a shell. I hibernate. I just plain give up. But the team wouldn't let me.

"You need to let this guilt sh★t go," Donnie advised. "Those little fools need you and you can't turn your back on 'em. You didn't do nothing wrong, Shawn. Let it go. Your son would have wanted you to be on that court."

Donnie was right, at least about not turning my back on the team. I tried to convince myself that perhaps coaching would let me escape the guilt. Sometimes it did. When the balls were bouncing, the sneakers were squeaking on the hardwood floors, and the parents were yelling at the refs and the opposing team's parents, guilt was the furthest thing from my mind. During practices and games, basketball was fun. It was the perfect escape.

It didn't hurt that with each and every game the team improved, and ultimately again defeated the Wildcats to prove the first beating was no fluke—though we all knew it really was. Jerry still stays at half court. But now it's *his* choice. He remembers the rush of hitting his championship winning first shot and is still talked about as "the little kid who knocked off the mighty Wildcats."

He's grown a half inch, and still asks the same question over and over, "Can I get in the game, Coach?" In the games since the championship, Jerry hasn't touched the ball again and has yet to make or even take another shot. Some would find fault with that, but not Jerry. As he told Paul after one game, "I've never missed a shot. Can you say the same thing?"

After the funeral, Troi packed her bags and left for Los Angeles. She didn't want to return to the life she left behind in Chicago and felt D.C. would only serve to remind her of a truth she desperately wanted to escape: that she'd lost her first child. And like me, she felt lost without having had the chance to raise him. I haven't heard from her since she left and doubt that I ever will.

I wish her only the best.

She'll be a mom to a Nordstrom baby one day, and she'll be one of the best.

I have visited Little Shawn's gravesite every other Monday since the funeral. The epitaph on his marker—Shawn Wayne, Jr., "Little Shawn," Gone But Not Forgotten—has special meaning to me. I'll never forget how happy I was when I finally accepted that I was going to be a father. I'll always remember carefully piecing together every aspect of his nursery, which still stands untouched because I literally can't bring myself to do anything with it.

I don't know if I'm sad. Can't tell if I'm depressed. And don't know when, if, or what will bring me back to the me I used to know.

I don't know if it matters because the more I think about it, the more I've come to accept that I'm not the man I used to be. But maybe I was never the man I thought I was.

Feeling as lost as I felt was easy, because it allowed me to wallow in a wake of self-pity. I've become good at putting up a strong front, because it makes everyone else feel good. They want me to recover, so I pretend that I have. They want me to smile and to be my old self, because it makes them comfortable around me, so I do. And because *they* need me to be happy almost as much as they'd like to see me happy, I put on a happy face and go about my day.

But at night, when I was alone, reality confronted me head on.

I hadn't recovered. Couldn't force myself to smile. And I wasn't happy about anything. I lost sleep every night. I was trapped in a web of shame, confusion, and unrelenting guilt.

Why did I have Troi at the game? Why would I put her in a position where she'd be on her feet? Had I been selfish? Unthinking? Irresponsible? I could duck these questions all day long, but at night, they ultimately won out.

The mere thought of the answers kept me in a daze—awake when I wanted to sleep, afraid when I needed courage. And weak when I sought out strength.

What could I have been thinking? And why did I have to lose

my son? I thought I'd never find out. Until I got a phone call just last night.

Are you trying to make my job harder?"

"No," I answered.

"Have you checked your e-mail?"

"No. I just delete everything."

"Voice mail?"

"No. I just erase the messages."

"What bill collectors are you hiding from?" she said, laughing.

"What's up, Christina?" I asked, surprised. "How's Chicago?"

"It's *Ms.* Christina," she answered. "And if your sorry ass watched the show, you'd already know that Dawn is leaving Chicago and that we're heading back to D.C. tomorrow," she said, reminding me of her front-and-center style. "And that's not all you'd know, Shawn Wayne."

"What am I missing here?" I asked.

"Do you remember how Carol Burnett used to rub her ear at the end of every show?" she asked.

"Yeah," I answered. "She had an ear rash or something, right?"

"Not," she shot back. "She was sending a message."

"About her ear rash?"

"Why does it feel that not one thing has changed with you, Shawn?" she asked, laughing.

"So much has changed, Christina," I admitted. "You just don't know."

"I don't *want* to know," she countered. "You've made my job impossible. Watch the show," she demanded.

"What are you talking about?" I asked.

"Just watch the show tonight," she said. "At least watch the end."

"Hey, Christina," I said, before hanging up. "How's Dawn?"

"Watch the show, Shawn," she said, "and listen."

"To what?" I asked.

"This," she said, hanging up and leaving me with a dial tone.

Knowing Christina, I'm certain she got a good laugh from hanging up on me.

Though I knew the show would make no mention of sports, I followed Christina's advice and tuned in. Dawn did a makeover special for three women whose husbands were overseas in the military. They did several minutes of special behind-the-scenes footage and actually piped in the husbands, who had been away from home so long they didn't even recognize their new and much improved wives.

They actually looked decent. But Dawn was radiant.

After Dawn's two-week run on *Oprah,* BET kept her in Chicago, where her show, "Dawn of a New Day," opened to strong ratings. Thanks to articles in *Ebony, Essence, JET,* and *USA Today,* Dawn had fast become a star. And she looked the part. She had a glow. Her skin was smoother than it ever was. And her hair was as long as it was bouncing with curls.

As the show geared down, Dawn thanked her guests, thanked her staff, bid farewell to Chicago, and suddenly looked squarely in the camera. She cautiously moved her hair, which had been covering her neck slightly, and revealed a tiny gold necklace. Which was attached to a beautiful puffed gold heart. It wasn't just any heart. It was the same heart I gave to Dawn before she left and we had the mix-up with the earrings. *Is this a sign?* I wondered. When she whispered, "Call," I knew that it was. Before she was off the set, her cell phone was blazing.

"Is this you?" she asked, sounding excited.

"Is this who you want it to be?" I said, immediately recalling how Dawn could make me feel alive with just a word.

"Where have you been?" she inquired. "And catch me up. How are Donnie and Kelly? Are they still at each other's throats? Has Kelly come to her senses about Alan yet?"

"You knew?" I asked, surprised.

"You *didn't?*" she fired back.

"How did you know?" I asked.

"He hit on *me,* Shawn," she admitted.

"And you didn't tell Kelly?"

"Kelly's a smart enough sister," Dawn shared. "She didn't need me to tell her a thing. And I might as well get it out of the way. How are things progressing with your new addition?"

I didn't know what to say. Though I'd suffered through Little Shawn's demise, I rarely talked about it. But Dawn could get anything out of me and she knew it. My silence meant nothing to her besides the fact that she knew she'd have to prod, which she would.

"Shawn," she said, sounding worried. "What happened, Shawn? Did something happen with the baby? Tell me what happened," she demanded.

"She lost the baby," I told her.

"Oh, my God," she said sadly. "I am so sorry, Shawn, What went wrong?"

"He was stillborn."

"He was a he?"

"Little Shawn," I whispered.

"If I know you, I'll guarantee Little Shawn had every throwback jersey you could get your hands on," she said, wanting to comfort me.

"Just Jordan's high school jersey," I confessed. "And Len Bias' too."

"I'm not buying that," she remarked. "I bet you and Donnie had him hooked up with every gadget under the sun."

"Not exactly," I answered. "But he had an awesome nursery."

"He did?" she said, surprised. "*You* put together a nursery?"

"I had to," I told her. "He was going to have the best."

"I want to see it," she said, surprising me. "I'll be home to-morrow. And, Shawn," she went on, "I hope you know that God is with you."

"I keep hearing that," I solemnly replied. "I keep hearing that."

We talked a while longer. She asked about Troi, I told her Troi was gone. And this time, for good. I asked why she hadn't re-sponded to my phone calls and e-mails. She said she wasn't ready for us to talk at the time and that she needed time to sort out her feelings, which she had done.

She asked if I still missed her, like I'd said I did in my messages. I told her more than she'll ever know. She asked if I thought we could start over. I told her I believed we never stopped.

The first thing she did when she came to the house was hug me. Then she grabbed my hand and led me to the nursery. By this time, I hadn't been in there in what felt like ages, but Dawn didn't care. She marveled at Little Shawn's crib and what she called, "His little sea of basketballs." She appreciated both the wall of fame and the wall with my family pictures. She located my mother's picture and recalled how much she admired her. And when she found the picture of my father coaching me as a child, she smiled.

"This is so you, Shawn," she whispered. "You were going to be the best father in the world. I am so proud of you," she said, looking around. "But you have to do one thing."

"What's that?" I asked, taking a seat in the rocking chair I'd bought for the room.

"Let go, Shawn. Let go," she begged. "Otherwise, you'll never get past it, and we'll never get on with our lives."

"What do you mean, our lives?" I asked, looking up.

"I love you and I always have," she said. "You know that."

"I do?"

"But before we can get anywhere, we have to address this."

"What makes you think I haven't?" I asked.

"You're still you and you're still a man," she said, smiling. "Put on your jacket and let's go."

Our drive over was silent and at best, it was the oddest feeling I've ever had. It was pretty overcast for what was masquerading as a spring day. But cloudy was perfect for what we were about to do. Especially since I was in such a haze.

"Introductions?" Dawn asked, grasping my hand.

"This is Dawn," I said, speaking to his grave marker.

"Just relax and go with it," she whispered.

"I'm so sorry this happened," I said, looking down. "I had such big plans for you. When I first heard about you, I wasn't the happiest man in the world," I confessed. "But the idea of you grew on me and before I knew it, you were the only thing I cared about."

"Almost the only thing," Dawn chimed in, squeezing my hand.

"I'm here because I want you to know that I'll never forget you and that I'll always see you as my first son," I said. "We were going to do so much together. I bought you a fishing pole, a golf club, a mini George Foreman grill—"

"A George Foreman grill?" Dawn asked.

"It had a bun warmer," I explained.

"A George Foreman grill for a baby?" she repeated.

"I know I don't know what you look like, but I know we'll find each other in heaven," I said. "And if you run into your grandparents, you should probably have on a jacket or something."

"A jacket?" Dawn said. "Why would anybody need a jacket in heaven?"

"If heaven's the opposite of hell and hell is hot, who says heaven isn't cold?"

"Keep going," Dawn urged.

"I pray for strength every night," I said, not wanting to cry. "I ask God to forgive me for putting your mother in the position I put her in. And now I want to let go because I know God will forgive me. I'm going to leave now, because . . ."

"Because?" Dawn said, jumping in.

"Because I've made my peace," I finished.

I then knelt and hugged his headstone. It was the same hug I remembered seeing in my mind when Jerry hit the shot that won the championship. It was long, it was deep, it was passionate, and the tears streaming down my face told me it was one I didn't want to end.

Dawn understood. She stood over me almost motionless. And then gently helped me to my feet.

I left a small basketball that I'd taken from his crib and looked skyward, hoping and praying that at least spiritually, we were in the same place . . . . at peace.

I still can't explain why the sun came out the moment we left the cemetery. And I don't understand why my heart, which had felt like it weighed a million pounds in my chest, suddenly felt light and full of life. What I'd wanted from the moment Troi fell in the stands was an explanation. I wanted to make sense of an act that to me would never make sense. I took responsibility for having Troi on her feet at a game and since she collapsed, the only thing that's stayed with me is an incredible sense of guilt.

Dawn convinced me of something I knew all along. If God was ready for Little Shawn, much like he was ready for my parents, there's not a thing I could have done to save him. Nothing.

There's a natural order to life, and I wasn't and never would be in a position to affect it, cheat it, or change it. She made me realize that I was fortunate to have even had the notion of Little Shawn in my life, because I was now more prepared for fatherhood than any ten men combined. And she must have believed what she said.

We've been married almost three months now. Dawn called from work last night and said she was coming home to celebrate. When she hit the door, I already knew what it was. Her show has picked up new sponsors and she's moving to mid-days, which is a good thing since it will give us more time together. But that's not the real news.

"I'm pregnant!" she screamed, excited. "Can you believe it?"

I do. And I've never been happier in my life.

Dawn has always been everything I wanted in a woman. But now she's what I want in a *wife*. I don't know if we'll have a boy or a girl. I just want whatever we have to be healthy. And as long as Dawn follows the rules, we'll be fine.

I'm still coaching my basketball team and we're the talk of the town. Dawn comes to all our games and with Kelly serves as co-team mom. Donnie's still our assistant and his new lady, Trena, is our scorekeeper. The best new aspect of the team is that Jerry isn't concerned with getting in the game and he no longer stands at mid court. I've given him a new job.

In the second half, as the score climbs, Jerry eases close to Dawn and gently grabs her hand. He pays special attention to the scoreboard and we've practiced the drill many times over. He knows what to do, as do Kelly, Donnie, Trena, and Kelly's new friend, Philip.

Dawn doesn't like it, but I've convinced her she has to humor me. If we ever get close to scoring 44 points, Jerry takes over and races her toward the door with one goal in mind. As Donnie has told him before the start of every game, "If the sh*t hits the fan, get Dawn the hell out of the gym!"

He does and so far, it's proved to be the perfect plan. Dawn is happy and healthy. The doctor says everything is as it should be. And her ultrasound confirmed what my *wife* has always wanted. We're having twins! A girl and a boy. And they won't be inter-ruptions. They'll be my children.

I've been through a lot, and will go through so much more. The plaque that still hangs in the nursery says it all, but my par-ents and everyone else said it even better.

WHATEVER DOESN'T KILL YOU MAKES YOU STRONGER. I'm very much alive and couldn't be stronger.

I remember when I first learned that Troi was pregnant. I felt like a poker player trapped at a high-stakes game without a shot at winning. I was the unluckiest man anywhere with the worst cards possible. I was devastated, disappointed, and shocked because I didn't stand a chance and because like a well-trained, indifferent, Vegas dealer, Troi had taken control of my destiny and determined my fate.

In the end, things have a funny way of working out. Fate couldn't have dealt me a better hand, especially since it's taught me the true meaning of fatherhood. It's bad ties on Father's Day, speeches that start with "When I was coming up," and late-night trips to the pharmacy to get a hot compress and a cold Popsicle. It's being the tooth fairy when you're broke and the Easter Bunny and Santa Claus when the costumes don't fit and when you absolutely don't want to.

It's listening when you'd rather speak, talking when you'd rather listen, and offering advice that you know will go unheeded. It's solving problems and not creating them, talking to teachers, counselors, and the police if need be, and bailing out kids who've violated all they've been taught and everything you believe in.

Being a dad means disciplining when you'd rather not, going to games in bad weather, and cheering that first home run and applauding at that first recital. It's going to church, playing board games, planning parties, attending weddings, working with the PTA, and coaching sports you know nothing about.

When you're a father, you'll pick your kids up when they're down, wipe away tears of defeat, and share tears of joy. You'll teach, grow, learn, and understand that being a dad doesn't necessarily mean that father knows best.

When you're not a scoundrel, an imbecile, and a Homer Simpson body double, you're a hero, a role model, and a friend.

It's being graceful as you are powerful, and as vulnerable as you are strong.

Being a dad is a job, a joy, and a responsibility.

It's many things to many people.

But above all . . .

Fatherhood is a privilege.

VAN WHITFIELD is the author of *Beeperless Remote, Something's Wrong with Your Scale,* and *Guys in Suits.* The award-winning author writes for UPN's hit sitcom *Eve* and is currently writing the authorized biography of former Washington, D.C., mayor Marion Barry. Visit him on the Web at www.vanwhitfield.com

Van Whitfield's
Dad Interrupted

BOOKCLUB BANTER

1. When Shawn learns of Troi's pregnancy, he is clearly upset. What do you feel is the key source of his concern? How does this compare with your experiences?

2. Donnie advises Shawn to keep the pregnancy a secret until it's confirmed that he's actually the father. What would you have advised him to do?

3. If your man informed you that his ex-girlfriend (as in the woman he dated *before* you) was pregnant, how would you handle it?

4. If you started dating a man, and learned that *you* were pregnant from a previous partner, how do you think your new mate would handle it? Would you leave or stay?

5. In *Beeperless Remote* and again in *Dad Interrupted*, Kelly is depicted as one of Shawn's closest friends. Are they attracted to each other? Would they survive as romantic interests?

6. When Troi gets to D.C. and arrives at Shawn's home, how could he have better handled the situation? Should he have immediately told her about Dawn?

7. When Troi informs Shawn that he is the father of her child, how should he have responded? Should he have accepted it and transitioned toward fatherhood? Should he have asked her

about her expectations? Should he have insisted on a paternity test (after the child was born) before he committed to anything?

8. One of the key themes of *Dad Interrupted* is how men can be completely shut out of any input in an unplanned pregnancy . . . Have you ever experienced this from either side? Is it fair? What's the solution?

9. Which one of the "Seven Types of Dads" most closely resembles your father or any male role model you grew up with? Which one reflects the father of your children or the father of someone close to you?

10. Which character in *Dad Interrupted* would you like to see in a sequel?

11. Who do you see playing the key characters in the film version of *Dad Interrupted*, and why?